Jackie O

the whole truth

PENGUIN BOOKS

UK | USA | Canada | Ireland | Australia
India | New Zealand | South Africa | China

Penguin Books is part of the Penguin Random House group of companies whose
addresses can be found at global.penguinrandomhouse.com

Penguin
Random House
Australia

First published by Penguin Books in 2024

Front cover photography and author photograph by Steven Chee
Front cover hair and make-up by Max May
Back cover photography by Damien Dirienzo
Cover design by Adam Laszczuk © Penguin Random House Australia Pty Ltd
Typeset in 12/17.5 pt Sabon by Midland Typesetters, Australia

Printed and bound in Australia by Griffin Press, an accredited
ISO AS/NZS 14001 Environmental Management Systems printer

 A catalogue record for this
book is available from the
NATIONAL
LIBRARY   National Library of Australia
OF AUSTRALIA

ISBN 978 1 76134 865 5

 MIX
Paper | Supporting
responsible forestry
FSC   FSC® C018684
www.fsc.org

We at Penguin Random House Australia acknowledge that Aboriginal and Torres
Strait Islander peoples are the Traditional Custodians and the first storytellers of
the lands on which we live and work. We honour Aboriginal and Torres Strait
Islander peoples' continuous connection to Country, waters, skies and communities.
We celebrate Aboriginal and Torres Strait Islander stories, traditions and living
cultures; and we pay our respects to Elders past and present.

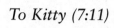

To Kitty (7:11)

Prologue

It's Friday 11 November 2022, around 10 a.m., and I'm sitting in a makeshift broadcast booth set up in the spare bedroom on the top floor of my house in Woollahra. It's not unusual for me to record from here, in this home office of sorts, with its big gleaming mirror, plush rug and a commemorative picture plaque on the wall celebrating twenty years of the juggernaut crown jewel and gift of my career, *The Kyle and Jackie O Show*.

The Covid pandemic is only just beginning to fade, and in fact I've been laid low recently by the coronavirus and a persistent lung infection that followed. I've been very sick, actually, so working remotely is the new normal. My co-host and producers are used to communicating with me through a computer and a mixing board. And a big screen, of course, so that we can see one another while we're talking and joking and laughing on air each day.

Today, however, our show is over for this week. Job done. We're almost at the end of the year, too, with three weeks to go until the summer break, but I know I won't make it that far. I'm hanging on by a thread. I've got my big headphones over my ears, and a ring light in front of my face, and I lean in to the microphone with one final thing I need to say.

I need to pre-record a message for our audience – something to be played on Monday morning, during the first show break. Listeners will hear my voice and think it's coming to them live – that I'm speaking to all of Sydney from my little patch within Sydney – but in reality I'll already be half a world away. I need to leave this town, immediately, for reasons that will soon become clear, but I also need to get out of here without anyone noticing, hence the cloak-and-dagger public message.

I'd like to think I'm a good speaker on air. I've been doing this for more than a quarter of a century. But I'm nervous about this pre-record, and I think that's because I'm not going to be telling the whole truth to our listeners. I'm going to have to leave something out. Something important. It's a lie by omission – not a blatant fabrication. I will not do the latter, so I'll have to walk a delicate line, and the anxiety shows in my cracking voice and halting delivery.

'I do want to tell you something, guys,' I say into the microphone. 'I am, look, you know – I've been not very well.

I think ever since I had Covid, I've just been struggling with this fatigue. Ever since I picked up that virus a couple of weeks ago, I've been to the doctor several times, and he said because I've been pushing myself every day, after the show all I've been doing is sleeping, and I'm not getting better.'

'I feel like it's got worse,' says my co-host and friend, Kyle Sandilands. 'I feel like I can hear it's got worse. You can't even laugh!'

'I just have to take some time off,' I say. 'So, I'm ending the show today. As in now. But you know how much this show means to me. You know how I push through anything. I would not be doing this if I didn't absolutely have to.'

'Can I just ask a question?' adds Kyle, dancing his standard daily line between blunt and brilliant, puerile and perceptive. 'Are you slowly dying? Do you have cancer? Do you have an ingrown toenail?'

'I rarely take doctor's advice,' I note. 'I'm usually, like, "Nah, it'll be fine." But not this time. At least I'll be all better and back with you all soon. It's just for a couple of weeks.'

'Have you taken a lover?' jokes Kyle, trying again to lighten the heavy moment. 'Because this is the sort of shit I do. It's very disappointing, but I totally get it.'

I start coughing then, as if on cue, and I struggle to stop. It's been this way for a while.

'See,' says Kyle, 'the poor kid can't even start laughing without a coughing fit!'

The cough is a great cover story for my hiatus, actually, because it's totally authentic. But regularly hacking up a lung is not the real reason I'm taking a break. Far from it.

'I'll miss you guys,' I say. 'I love you. And I will get well, thank you.'

'Next time someone offers to rub Vicks into your chest early in the piece, how about you don't be such a little princess about it,' adds Kyle, with that trademark smirk. 'Listen, we *love* you,' he continues. 'Come home as soon as you feel rested. And I'll be just sort of controlling this plane as it falls out of the sky, engine dropping off here, wing dropping off there.'

'Okay, I'll let you go,' I say. 'See ya! Bye! I'm out!'

With the pre-recording complete, the whole team wishes me well. I'm sure they're curious about my temporary leave of absence – because none of them really knows why I'm stepping back – but it has to be this way. I say goodbye and wave, leave the Zoom meeting, log off and go downstairs for a cigarette. I feel as if I can finally breathe again. With that last box ticked, there's only one thing left to do today – get on a plane to Los Angeles, undetected by anyone.

It'll take some doing. I start by packing my bags. My best friend and manager, Gemma O'Neill, is with me – she's been with me all week, staying by my side, walking me through this entire episode. She tells me I won't need any fancy dresses where I'm going, which I could have guessed. Instead I pack comfy clothes – tracksuits and

T-shirts and big cosy hoodies. I pack twenty packets of cigarettes, because I think I'll need them to pass the time.

We go for a walk along the cliffs near Clovelly and have lunch at a little cafe – Sea Salt – and it's then that I get a little teary, not because I don't want to go on this journey, but because I don't know what's going to happen there. I don't have the faintest idea what it will be like, and that scares the shit out of me. But I shower and change, and soon I'm ready to leave for the airport, to catch this night flight across the Pacific Ocean.

Gemma is nervous about us being spotted and wants me wearing my baggiest, most oversized clothes as well as my reading glasses. I put on a Covid mask, too – which is no longer necessary but is thankfully still acceptable – plus a baseball cap, and my disguise is complete. One woman at the terminal seems to be sussing me out – *Is that her, or not?* – but I keep my head down and eyes forward.

'Don't let one person recognise you,' Gemma warns me. 'Not one.' Because if even a single soul sees me and this little escape to LA gets into general circulation, the media will want to know why, and I don't need them asking questions. Not about this.

We check in for our flight at the last minute and tuck ourselves away in a corner of the flight lounge. Gemma goes to the buffet to get me coffee or food or champagne, so I don't have to come face to face with anyone else. 'You stay here,' she says. 'Don't move.'

We board at the last possible moment, and I end up with an aisle seat. Every time someone walks past to go to the toilet I face the other way, because the aisles are filled with Aussies. I watch *Top Gun: Maverick*, which I've seen before and loved. I watch *Elvis*, which I've also already seen and loved, but I fast forward to my favourite scenes and songs. Finally I sleep, heavy and hard, and wake up in the City of Angels, La-La Land, Tinseltown. But I'm not here for the glamour.

We arrive late in the evening, get through passport control, grab our bags and clear customs. We pick up our rental car and set a course for Palm Springs. We're headed to a little hotel there for two nights, but that's not my final destination. After our weekend in the Sonoran Desert, Gemma will be heading home, but I won't be going with her. I'm going on alone.

When she checks out, I'll be checking in – to the Betty Ford Center in Rancho Mirage. I'll be spending twenty-eight days on its famous twenty-acre campus. I've voluntarily enrolled in a Twelve-Step program there, to treat the substance dependence and drug addiction I've been able to keep secret for three long and painful years.

Ready as I'll ever be, we get into our rental car, exit the airport and head east into the night. I look out into the deep darkness of the desert and cry just a little, utterly unsure of what's to come.

One

I've never loved that bit in biographies where the author tells the tale of their childhood, but if you want to understand what comes later, it does make sense to hear what came before, so here goes.

I was born in 1975 on the Gold Coast and grew up in a place called Isle of Capri, which is kind of fancy, in a house on the canal. The house is still standing today – single-level blond brick, very retro, with a pool and a carport and a lawn, like something you would see in a postcard for that perfect picture of Gold Coast suburbia. I never understood it, but living on the canal was a status symbol back then, this baller thing, and maybe still is – as if you've somehow made it if you're on the water, even when that water is a little stagnant and brown, and sometimes so narrow it's like you're staring straight into someone's backyard across this little dribble of a stream. You can't swim in there, so without a boat, what's the use? Ha ha.

My parents weren't well off, but they saved hard to afford that house. They had met in Port Moresby when my mum, Julie, was doing secretarial work for the Royal Military College, Duntroon, and my dad, Anthony (but everyone calls him Tony) had a desk job in the accounting department of the Army. They met the very day Mum landed in Papua New Guinea. Only two days later, he asked her out on a date. They hit it off straightaway and he proposed the next year. They were married and found their way to Queensland, or so the story goes.

Memories are grey whispers at times, but in my mind, when we lived in Capri at least, my dad was a milkman – delivering dairy daily, or rather nightly, in darkness, dropping off full glass bottles sealed with blue foil caps and picking them up, empty, later – while studying on the side to become a builder. He grew up in Tasmania on a dairy farm in Devonport. The farm is still in the family. He's always had and still has a wry sense of humour. No fan of political correctness, he says everything the way he sees it, calling a spade a spade. (He's a lot like Kyle in that respect – inappropriate and unapologetic. It's funny how often in life you're drawn to people who remind you of your parents.) Dad's very Australian, very dry. Always blunt but warm, too. I never really found Dad funny, but everyone else did.

He had a temper that would sometimes flare up – never violent or physical, just swearing in the moment, and then it was over, like a flash flood, as if some valve had been released. I remember watching him once from inside that blond brick house while he was outside, fixing the pool filter. Something got to him and he let loose on this inanimate object, his eyes fixed on the filter as if it had done him wrong somehow: 'You fucking fuck, *FUCK!*' That was definitely funny, especially later that day when Mum took me shopping. She always dressed me in pretty dresses when we went to the shops. On this day, we were on the escalators, and I remember there was a little old lady travelling on the escalator going in the opposite direction, and I repeated what Dad had said to the pool filter – 'You fucking fuck, *FUCK!*' This little old lady heard this sweet little white-haired girl in a dress – I was only five – blurting out a string of obscenities. I'll never forget the look on her face. I was copying Dad, and I guess in some ways I still am. I'm exactly like him when I'm angry – I'll rage for barely a minute, and then I'm over it and happy, and I expect everyone else to be, too. The eye of the storm passes swiftly, leaving a rainbow in its wake.

I honestly don't get angry a lot, though. It's quite rare for me. I spoke to my therapist about this recently. Why don't I get angry? Why don't I have that emotion readily at hand – or at least a true outburst for expressing annoyance? That's probably from Mum, because Mum's the opposite. She's the internaliser who defaults to silent treatment for hours on end. When I was a kid, if I was naughty or not nice or spoke up or pushed back in any way, I would get that silence. I guess I learnt to suppress any rage, because it only brought silence in response.

Mum grew up in Brisbane. Her dad was very strict, and a little scary. He used to have all these shotguns along the wall. I remember that room, and all those barrels. Mum's older sister Jessie was the beautiful, charismatic eldest sibling of Mum and my aunty Margaret, and when Jessie was twenty-one she fell in love with and married a very handsome, six-foot-four American soldier. Years later, she was devastated to learn he had been cheating on her, and when he left her, she was so heartbroken that she lay on the bed with a gun in her hand and shot herself in the heart. Mum would have been twenty-eight at the time, and she talks about it when asked. What happened to Jessie isn't swept under the rug. All the girls in the family are fascinated by this missing person in our lives. We've seen the photos of a happy, carefree, gorgeous young woman – a magnet for men, by all accounts – and I think we put her on a pedestal. My grandfather, though, was never the same after her death. He often sat in his rocking chair, staring into the distance while listening to her favourite songs on the record player, with tears in his eyes. He never hid the fact that Jessie was his favourite, and Mum's family believe her death led him to his own early grave.

Mum and Dad moved to the Gold Coast when they were in their twenties, seeking a different space and pace – that nicer life, that sunny life. They had my brother, Scott, three years before me. Scott is the kind of brother all little sisters wish they could have. There isn't a bad bone in his body, and I don't recall him ever teasing or being mean to me. But he and I were never that close. He had his guy friends and was always off with them. Even in our street he was off with the neighbours, doing his own thing, not really including his little sister in his games. That made sense. The factions in our house were based on gender – Scott was a bit closer to Dad and I was always closer to Mum. But we would hang out as a family and watch TV together every night – sitting on the floor, glued to *Happy Days* at tea time, with steak and three veg in front of us. That song is ingrained in my head now, as if it's the theme song for our family.

Even though Dad was mostly out working and providing for us, I remember that he was the driver of my favourite day of the week – Sunday, when he took the family to Grundy's Entertainment Centre, which was opened by the late entrepreneur and media mogul Reg Grundy in 1981, right on the waterfront. The top floor was a giant food court, and we could walk around the space and choose our dinner – fish and chips, McDonald's, whatever – although we mostly went for Chinese. The whole family was obsessed with honey king prawns. Then we would hit the Timezone arcade to play arcade games and eat ice cream.

We went on family picnics, too, and while Scott and Dad went off fishing, Mum and me would sit on a blanket together, talking. She taught me about periods on one of those picnics. Mum and I were extremely close like that.

It felt as though she was there for me every day, taking me shopping, baking me treats and watching the dance performances I'd do for her in the living room. She was basically my best friend.

She was also very protective of me. *Don't ride too fast. Don't go near the edge. Don't go in the waves.* She had lost her firstborn child two weeks after birth, to cot death, and so she wrapped me in cottonwool. My aunt and cousins used to come and visit, renting an apartment on the Gold Coast with ocean views, and I would be allowed on the balcony but never, ever near the railing. Mum's terrified of heights, and she once had a dream that I fell out a window. That dream scarred her, and she was just too afraid that I would topple over and fall. It was all her own fears projected onto me, of course, but to this day I hate big waves, because I was raised to be terrified of them. Everyone gets dunked into the foam at some point, and most people jump right back into the surf, but I never did. I'd come up for air thinking, *Mum was right, that was terrifying, I almost died, I'm never doing that again.* I'm better about that kind of thing now. I'll go diving without fear of sharks, I'll go abseiling down the side of a building. It just took time.

In spite of this, she was also a mum who I really could tell anything and everything, and I still do. No topic is off limits. We have two-hour chats almost every single day. Mum never – ever – runs out of questions about my life. I'll say, 'I've gotta go,' but there's always 'One more thing!' – which actually means ten more things. There was always that open line of communication between us. Even as a teenager I don't think I ever hid anything from her. I've never kept her in the dark or shut her out in any way. Not until recently, anyway.

What else? My bedroom was always pink. A desk and a dollhouse. And usually a bedside table with a doily on it and an old-fashioned lamp, maybe a Royal Doulton figurine of a ballet dancer, because Mum signed me up for ballet at five. I was obsessed with *Grease*, and so I would spend all day in my room in my own little world, dressing up as Sandy. That imaginative play was all I ever needed. I didn't need the company of others. I loved to dream alone. I loved to fantasise. I loved to be creative. My bedroom was my sanctuary.

I would pretend to be a schoolteacher one week, standing at a chalkboard giving lessons. The next week I would pretend to be a bank teller, endorsing cheques for imaginary customers and saying, 'Next! Can I help you?' The week after that I would pretend to be famous, signing autographs and posing for photos and waving to fans. I didn't know that one day I'd be doing exactly that, and that there are days now when I walk from Bondi to Bronte and get stopped and asked for a selfie. People always say to me, 'I'm so sorry – you must hate this,' but truly I don't mind. I think it's lovely! I enjoy meeting people. It doesn't feel bizarre, either. Fame happened quite gradually for me. It snuck up. It's not like being a con-testant on *MAFS* or *The Bachelor*. I have no idea what it's like to go to sleep anonymous one night and wake up famous the next day. For most people in the public eye, notoriety is drip fed.

My daughter helps me understand it, though. She's an observant child and says I have no idea what happens when I walk through a shopping centre. 'You don't see it,' she says, 'but as you pass people, they turn and go "Is that her? *It is!* That's Jackie O!"'

I don't see what she sees, but I know exactly what she means. A long time ago, I was in the Queen Victoria Building in Sydney and I passed by the actor Tony Martin from *E Street*, back when it was one of the biggest soaps on TV, and I remember that as he moved through the crowd, there was this trail of whispers and glances and people mouthing 'Oh my god!' behind him. Everyone in front of him was acting completely cool, but there was this wake of commotion behind his back. I've never thought to turn around quickly to see who's watching me as I move through the world. Maybe I should. Might be fun.

Mum was a homebody, but Dad was a man who kept busy, kept moving and loved living in the world. He liked games. He liked golf. He liked footy. And he liked to gamble. That's why we left Capri. The way the story was told to me, he placed a bet, lost the bet, and we lost the house. As a kid I got the cinematic impression that our house *was* the wager, but the reality was nothing so dramatic. In actual fact, Dad was doing some bookmaking but had been losing at a steady flow, until we lost the house and packed up and moved to a two-bedroom rental unit, which was fine. You don't care too much about something such as that when you're five years old.

I don't know where I sit on that spectrum between Mum and Dad – between seeking sanctuary and stimulation, risk and reward. Maybe I'm both. I love swimming – there's no more peaceful place for me than being alone with my thoughts under clear salt water – and I love hiking, and meditating, and journalling, too. I also love lounging at home in trackie pants and a hoodie, talking on the phone. I'm more than happy to stay that little girl in her bedroom, thinking and creating, scheming and dreaming.

But if I had to lean one way, living my life out or in, I would probably be the person who says yes – to an opportunity, to an experience, to something different. I can't be quiet for long. I love to socialise too much – at dinners and parties and events. I love live music most of all – I'm at my happiest when I'm singing along and dancing with a crowd. Yeah, I want to live life to the fullest and pack it all in. I'll sleep when I'm dead!

I went to St Vincent's Catholic, a small co-ed primary school situated on the Gold Coast Highway. A tiny, one-foot-high fence was all that separated us from four lanes of traffic. That was Queensland in the 1980s for you. On my first day of school, I didn't know anyone. I didn't go to kindergarten, so there was no coming through with a ready-made cohort of friends. We were all waiting for the teacher to arrive, milling about and talking, and I remember that for some reason I had this queue of boys in front of me, lining up to kiss me. And I *let* them all kiss me – what a ho! So, I was really popular in Year One and everyone liked me, but on the first day of Year Two, it was the opposite. I think I had lost a front tooth, and that was all it took: We don't like you – you're not pretty anymore. It's a thread throughout my life – a belief that I didn't always recognise was deep-seated within me – that what you look like determines your value and how people will treat you. I remember that feeling of going from such happiness and popularity to rejection and loneliness. When the whole room says something to you *about* you, it stays with you, and within you.

My family all went to church every Sunday. We were Catholic, and when I was young I really took to the faith. I always had a Bible by my bed and rosary beads, too. I did the 'Our Father' and prayed to God before going to sleep each night. I'm agnostic today, but I also believe my religious upbringing set a firm ground for my moral compass. Every time I sinned, I would be off to the confession box, and I really did sin once. I was in Year Two, and desperately wanted to buy an ice block from the tuckshop. I'd often spend lunchtime inside the church, saying a little prayer or looking up at the stained-glass windows, and then one day I noticed a bunch of 20-cent coins in the donation box. It was all too easy to take one and buy myself that ice block. The guilt was heavy, but so was the temptation, so I did it again, just once more. After that,

I was tortured by remorse and shame. I couldn't bring myself to confess – I honestly couldn't imagine receiving forgiveness and absolution for doing something so wicked. Two weeks later it became too much to carry. We were having fish and chips for Sunday dinner, and I burst into tears and told Mum what I had done. She could see how distraught I was, and didn't scold or punish me, but urged me to confess in church. I remember how the priest didn't wear a look of disgust or even disappointment – he actually seemed quite amused. As he told me to say ten 'Hail Marys', a smile even crossed his face.

But overall, my social status at school went in waves. I think everyone experiences some level of ostracisation and embarrassment at school. I was teased for being too skinny. I was all skin and bone and teeth and ears, and it earned me a nickname: 'rat girl'. That feeling of being talked about or laughed at was horrible. But it wasn't a torturous time for me. Teachers really liked me, but my report cards always said the same thing: *She could be a great student, but she talks too much.* They didn't beat around the bush with euphemisms like 'gregarious' or 'high spirited', either – I was a chatterbox, plain and simple. I wasn't without company or friends. I was good at English and drama and humanities, but maths did not compute – to this day, I still count with my fingers. I had dreams. I wanted my own hairdressing salon. I even planned out the uniforms – red overalls with nothing else underneath, and just sequined love hearts over the boobs, like giant nipple pasties. I wanted to be an air hostess at some point, too. I guess I wanted positions reliant on beauty, where you get to talk and interact and meet new people. I never wanted to be a doctor or a lawyer or anything so serious.

For high school, I went to Star of the Sea College for girls in Southport. It was run by nuns, and I didn't love that experience. It was incredibly bitchy. My best friend, Lisa, was the target of awful bullying. She was beautiful and friendly, so I think it was based on jealousy. The popular girls decided to take her down a peg, and they were relentless. Every time we walked past they would get in her face and start barking. The comments were incessant, and a pack mentality took hold. We started to hide to avoid having to deal with them. Parents came in to complain, and the teachers gave a lip-service response – 'Be nice, girls' – but nothing really helped. Eventually the bitches got sick of it, but that lasted all of Year Nine. There's something about that age where the herd looks for an individual to attack, and you just hope and pray it won't be you.

Year Ten wasn't as bad. It was all about boys. Our brother school was Aquinas College, and we would meet up for a social – a dance – but we had no exposure to the other sex, so we were utterly boy crazy. You basically knew you liked boys, but you were also scared of boys, because you didn't know what they wanted – or maybe you kinda *did*, but you didn't know anything about how any of that worked, because there was no internet, and no one told you about sex either. Confusion and hormones and rushes of blood reigned supreme. I was clueless. Does anyone remember Peter Andre? He was at one of the schools up the road, and my friend Lisa and I were obsessed with him and his best friend, Christian Fry. We were actually using Peter to get to Christian, and we would hang out with them on the street, or at this abandoned mansion on the canal in Benowa. Two girls and two boys, not knowing what was what, and nothing happening.

All I wanted to do at that age was go to the beach and socialise, but that first meant getting out of ballet. It had become my bubble – a beautiful little prison. Dancing might have been my dream at seven, but it wasn't anymore. I was so sick of it but Mum didn't want me to quit – she had invested so much time and energy in my dancing, and she cracked it when I tried to stop. One day at a private lesson, I hatched a plan. When you're preparing to dance, you have to put your feet in resin so they don't slip and slide everywhere during a pirouette. I decided to put extra resin on, so that when I went to do a full spin, my foot would grip the floor and stick. Then I could pretend my knee had been wrenched out of alignment. I enacted my plan and fell to the floor, wailing with such histrionics – I honestly can't imagine how bad my acting looked. The physiotherapist saw straight through my scheme, of course, and he must have told Mum that there was nothing wrong with me. She would have been disappointed, but she also knew I *really* didn't want to do ballet if I'd go to such lengths to avoid it. I was finally allowed to quit and chase my real dream.

I'd seen a McDonald's commercial that year with Daryl Braithwaite playing his song 'One Summer', and there was this blond kid skateboarding down what looked like the Surfers Paradise promenade, and I remember thinking, *I want to be there, and I want to meet a guy like that.* So, one day, Mum dropped me off at the beach to explore. I was fourteen, and was left alone to wander around and meet other kids. Soon I was at Surfers every weekend, hanging out with fourteen- and fifteen-year-old boys and girls from other schools. We would loiter at a place we just called 'the tree'. It's still there: a big spiky palm tree opposite the Maccas on Cavill Avenue.

Mum allowed me so much freedom, and I think in hindsight she did that because she could see something was starting to bubble in me – this need for independence – and she figured that granting me a taste of that would keep me close. If she let me have my freedom, the theory might have gone, then I would come back to her at the end of the day and tell her everything. The alternative was me sneaking out and then hiding everything, and that was her worst nightmare. Still, she probably gave me too much leg-rope. It became a year of rapidly escalating firsts.

The first boy I ever kissed was named Matthew, and he was tall, skinny and tanned, with floppy white-blond hair. I had kissed my hand and my pillow for years beforehand, practising, but Matthew was just the worst kisser – so sloppy, with his tongue all over my face. The pillow would have been better!

I had my first cigarette, and picked up the habit immediately. Holiday packs of fifty were the cheapest, but a year later I had a cold and switched to Alpines – menthol – and have been a menthol smoker ever since. I didn't drink a lot, but I had my first West Coast Cooler around then. I went to my first nightclub – Beach Road – and almost came unstuck when the local newspaper did a puff piece on our school and ran a photo of me with the caption: 'Jackie Last, 14 years old.' The head doorman had seen it and tried to turn me away for being underage. 'If you give me a kiss,' he said, 'I'll let you in.' Imagine being a grown man – a bouncer – and trying your luck with a fourteen-year-old girl. I said no and started to walk away, and he let me in anyway. The Gold Coast is a little crazy and loose like that. Long before Schoolies week grew into what it is now, it was always an anything-goes place, and I was in an anything-goes phase. I lost my virginity that year, too.

Nathan Dean was the hot boy in our circle. He worked at Brothers Neilsen – a surf clothing store, the equivalent of being a teenage retail king at General Pants Co. today. Nathan was fifteen and he was the shit. All the girls liked him, and that's my type, my whole defectiveness: I don't feel as if I'm good enough, but if I can get the guy everyone else wants, *that* will make me good enough. This has been my pattern in life, and not a good one; one that – up until recently – came to control my life. I've always spent far too long feeling as if there's something wrong with me, as if I'm not enough.

How did I get Nathan? Back then, you told your friends to tell a guy that you liked him, and if he liked you back, he'd tell them, and then you just got together. In a time without dating apps, you made do in a way that meant you wouldn't have to face any rejection in person. We probably saw each other for three or four hangouts before we did it. My friends had all had sex already, and I felt this very real, unspoken but implied pressure to fit in. I didn't really want to do it – I don't think any fourteen-year-old really wants to have sex – but I did it to keep up with everyone else.

We picked our place for the act – across the road from Fisherman's Wharf, in a park that led to the beach. A million pine cones fall there, and we had no blanket, but it didn't matter. I just lost my virginity right there on the grass, with pine cones sticking into my back. It wasn't terrible either, just underwhelming. It was what it was. I got Nathan, but I should never have gone after the popular guy, because he moved on to someone else not long after. And he did it to me again years later. I can laugh about it now because we spoke to him on air – our producers tracked down Nathan Dean. He was nice, working on charter yachts. He seems to be doing well these days.

What a year. I went from being completely sheltered in my girls' school ballet bubble, a thirteen-year-old whose best friend was her Mum, with occasional playdates spent listening to music in my pink bedroom with porcelain dolls and a goldfish and posters of dogs, to a fourteen-year-old experiencing smoking, drinking, dancing, kissing, flirting and having sex in the space of twelve months.

As for school, at this time I was just showing up and ticking the box. I didn't wag because I was terrified of getting caught, but life for me was all about the beach. They eventually called Mum into the school, near the end of Year Ten, and she was told by the principal that I hadn't improved. *Jackie doesn't listen. Jackie can't focus. Jackie isn't interested. She's not going to do well in Years Eleven and Twelve – it's really not worth you paying those fees.*

I was moved to a co-ed school, Trinity College, in Ashmore, and they made me repeat Year Ten, but the same thing happened. I was actually worse there, because now I was distracted by boys at school. I got detentions for talking in class, too. I had to come in once on a Saturday morning for a day-long detention with a mate. We were made to cut the grass on the school oval . . . with a pair of scissors. It's amazing what they could get away with back then. I probably cut the tiniest patch of grass, because I couldn't stop talking the whole time. I really did end up in the right profession!

I pulled out of school after repeating Year Ten, and I didn't care at all. My parents accepted the outcome, too. My brother was doing well academically, and I remember Dad saying – aloud, within my earshot – 'Scott's going to be the success of the family anyway – we don't hold much hope for Jackie.' He didn't hold anything in. I do wonder sometimes if parents unintentionally set a path for their kids with those sorts of throwaway lines. Children listen to their mums and dads so closely, hearing every word. It's too easy to treat those words as your destiny and resign yourself to those expectations. *You say that's my path?'* I thought to myself. *Okay then, fine, I'll be average.*

I went to Gold Coast TAFE to study a secretarial and shorthand course. I was seventeen and had decided on a new dream – I would work on reception at one of the big hotels on the Gold Coast. The Marriott had just opened, and it was the absolute pinnacle and crown jewel. It didn't just have a pool but a sandy lagoon with an artificial reef. The lobby was all polished stone, with huge cane ceiling fans that did nothing but swish back and forth like pretty wooden palm fronds on a sea breeze.

I loved TAFE. I'd always watched *Beverly Hills, 90210* and adored the idea of kids driving to school, wearing casual clothes, and some sense that class itself was optional. In TAFE you were treated like an adult, and because of that I did well. When I first enrolled they told me I should opt for a different course that didn't involve shorthand, as my English grades weren't up to scratch and I was warned that it would be a struggle for me. I was adamant about wanting to do it, and I ended up being the top of my class. It was the first time I ever loved learning. I could drive to school in my white Toyota shitbox, wearing what I wanted, and do well, acing tests and recording the quickest shorthand time. It felt as if TAFE was something of my own doing – that, when given the chance to make choices for myself, I was making the right ones.

I'd outgrown the kids at the tree. And my boyfriend of two years, too. We had all seen this mysterious guy driving up and down the Esplanade in his matt black Kombi van. He had long dark hair and was constantly cruising the strip. We became obsessed with him, to the point that we used to just stand there, waiting on the footpath for him to come past. He knew we were doing it, too, because he wore this smirk on his face. Other times we'd scream at him as if he was a rock star. I met him in the club one night, and he was so cool that you really couldn't tell if he was interested in your or not, whereas I was the opposite – such a co-dependent people pleaser, and so desperate to get to know him that when he mentioned his house was a mess, I told him, 'I love doing dishes!' and offered to come over and clean up for him. Worse than that, I actually did go over the very next day and washed his dishes for him. I'm still mortified.

David Piper – that was his effortlessly cool name – lived in a unit in Broadbeach, and I came to learn why he was rolling the roads so frequently. He wasn't prowling for girls or anything so nefarious – he was a drug dealer. Well, he was the local weed dealer, supplementing his Centre-link cheque with a little hydroponic grow operation out of his bedroom closet. Common sense might send you the obvious warning, 'Don't date the drug dealer', but he was so lovely that I overlooked it. We started seeing each other, pashed, and he was kind and loyal and not what you might imagine.

David was just the sweetest guy. I remember that he had a waterbed, which seemed cool to me at first, but it wasn't as glamorous as I thought. It was difficult to have sex in, and whenever you rolled over during the night, you would hear this gurgle and slosh. It used to leak a little, so you'd often wake up damp. David was good to me, so we lived in one another's pockets for a couple of years, but I eventually outgrew him, lost interest and broke it off. I was a woman now, and I wanted to enter the workforce.

As soon as I came out of TAFE, I began door-knocking at every major hotel, with a perky smile and a crisp copy of my resume. When no one got back to me, I started canvassing the next rung of hotel chains. When that failed, I visited every skyscraper and apartment block with a reception desk, from Mermaid Beach to Main Beach. It took weeks to visit every one of them, but I was determined. Then I started popping in to any business that might need phones answered, and found a job in a tiny print company, taking calls and making photocopies. I worked for another company that sold motivational speeches on VHS tapes. I stumbled into real estate by chance, walking in the door of the big Ray White branch on Orchid Avenue just when they needed someone to fill in for two weeks. The fortnight passed and they kept me on.

Everything changed for me at that real estate agency. It was owned by three brothers, all good looking and with beautiful wives, and it was surrounded by restaurants and bars and lights and life. I was single and so was Natasha, the girl I'd filled in for, who became my great friend. We were adults, happy to be surrounded by that buzz of commerce and lifestyle. I was still obsessed with supermodels and glitz and beauty, and 1970s fashion was making a comeback, so it was all cork shoes and flares and halter-neck tops and big hair. Everything in my life back then felt sociable and aspirational. I felt as if I was at the centre of something. I wasn't the one navigating the high-flying property market – I was writing up contracts, following a template, and completing other secretarial work – but I was adjacent to the agents themselves. And they dressed well, had fancy cars and charisma and charm, and could talk and wheel and deal. Real estate is such a showy industry, and I liked that. I didn't have any desire for the flashy material things they were after – *Look at my watch, Look at my suit, Look at this amazing penthouse I'm selling you* – but I did want a buzzy and exciting life.

And I met my first husband there, sort of. I was working away one scorching hot afternoon and listening to the radio to pass the time. 'Ugly Phil' O'Neil was the star night-time announcer for Sea FM – the funniest thing on radio – and he was working a double shift, filling in for someone who couldn't cope during the day because the air conditioning was out. I idly called in to the station, trying to get free

Guns N' Roses tickets for their gig in Sydney, and Phil answered. For some reason he talked to me at length, chatting me up on the phone for fifteen minutes, and he gave me the tickets, too. When I came into the studio the next day to pick them up from reception, he came out to meet me in person. We clicked and couldn't stop chatting. It felt as if it was meant to be. He asked me out on a date right there and then, and we hit it off immediately.

There was definitely an element of my old self-destructive predilection here – Phil was older, twenty-nine, and was a big name, in this case famous, and he had chosen me, so that made me feel worthy – but we also had very real chemistry and attraction. And he was exciting to be around. It was as if he was taking my hand and leading the way: *Come on this adventure with me.* The coolest place I'd ever been was a nightclub called Cocktails & Dreams in Surfers Paradise, but now I was tagging along as he made appearances at nightclubs in Coolangatta or was invited to the corporate areas for the Indy 300 motor race. We were always doing something different.

He lived in a place in Main Beach that felt like a motel, with two weird flatmates. One was a stoner guy who would sit there blazed out of his gourd, like something out of a movie – like the pasty housemate in *Notting Hill* who walks around Hugh Grant's home in his dirty Y-fronts. I remember there was no food in the house one day, and he came out of his room with a pair of edible undies, which he sat on the couch and ate. My mum came over once, and when no one answered she put her face up to the screen door to see inside, and that flatmate was right there in the living room, pants down, wanking. He was that kind of guy.

Then there was the stripper they lived with, Christie. We went out one night to a club, and we came home and were having sex, and Christie decided she wanted to join us – and that was my first threesome. The idea of a threesome had honestly never occurred to me before. I'd never even considered it, because it just didn't sound like me. But I've always been bad with speaking up about my boundaries, and in this case I thought it better to just go along with it than make things uncomfortable for everyone. I had no idea what to do, though, and she was this cute nineteen-year-old with a dark bob and an amazing body, but she was only into women, and so she was only interested in me. Phil was really excited, but Christie kept slapping him away. She did her thing and then left. I didn't exactly love the experience, but it was an experience nonetheless.

There really was always something new and interesting going on once Phil came into my life. And that was just the beginning, of course. The relationship had escalated quickly. We were committed to each other. So much so that soon we were embarking on a new adventure, following his dreams of radio all the way to Canberra. We were packing up and leaving the Gold Coast together, for good.

Two

It was a lonely existence in Canberra. We had left a high-rise apartment in Queensland – bathed in sunshine and overlooking the water – for the cold anonymity of winter in the national capital, which was crisp and biting and unrelenting. We found an apartment in Belconnen. There wasn't much appeal in the architecture: it was cold and grim and full of concrete.

I got a job with a temp company, doing short placement work based on my secretarial skills. It felt as if it was dark every morning, but light enough to see my breath and the constant layer of ice on my windscreen. I'd grab the plastic cover of one of my cassette singles and use it to scrape the frost from the glass, then follow a confusing street directory to one new workplace after another, and another. I'd work at a law firm one week, a car dealership the next, and a computer repair company the week after. No one wants to teach you anything, or get to know you at all, when you're only there for a few days, so you get given all the shit jobs and you make a lot of coffees. At the computer company, I actually spilt one of those coffees on the keyboard I was using, and they made such a stink over it, as if damaging a minor part of a computer – *at a computer repair company* – was going to cost them a thousand bucks. I think they even complained to the temp agency, probably trying to get a partial refund or freebie.

Phil and I made our own fun at home. We were great at finding laughter and joy in any little thing. We were positive people, in a new place, doing new things. But we also scarcely knew anyone, and my isolation didn't help. I was suffering badly from a kind of nagging anxiety. Actually, it was much more than that, and it was something I'd brought with me from the Gold Coast, following something that happened a year prior when I took an acid trip with David Piper. I didn't feel much at the time in the way of hallucinations – although the kettle did turn into a watch for a second – but I smoked some weed immediately afterwards, some really strong buds, and together they had a perverse effect. I remember going to sleep in David's bedroom and this funny feeling came over my body, as if I was suddenly lying in cold water. I ran out to him in a panic, not remotely understanding what was going on, and I was getting more and more worked up by the minute, white as a ghost and utterly unable to regulate myself. My blood sugar had gone extremely low and I was 'greening out'. A sugary drink fixed that, but the next day I woke up and immediately felt that panic again. I thought I might be one of those people who takes a trip and their mind is never the same. I started wondering if I was just convincing myself I was going crazy. Could you do that to yourself? I couldn't get the idea out of my mind. And I couldn't stop wondering *when* the idea would leave my mind.

It kept happening to me, off and on, for the next year, with increasing frequency. I could scarcely be alone. It wasn't exactly what anxiety looked like in the movies – heart palpitations, doubled over and hyperventilating into a paper bag, thinking you're going to die – but there was a definite, inescapable and overriding sense of not being able to think about anything except butterflies and dread and fear deep in the pit of my stomach. It was a constant underlying battle between me and my brain, and it hurt my heart. I'd have a bad thought then tell myself, *Don't keep thinking that*, but the more I thought about it the more upset I'd become. I felt as if I had triggered something with that trip, and it was going to make me feel like this forever, and also make me crazy. It was a form of slow torture – an undercurrent of alarm and unease.

One night I was driving somewhere and I got lost in a place where there were no streetlights, and there was no sat nav to save me, no Google Maps on my phone. I burst into hysterical tears on the side of the road, somehow found my way out of there, and went straight to a doctor and told him everything.

'Oh, love,' he said sympathetically. 'All you're having is panic attacks. Take these, and it'll stop them.'

I have no idea what he gave me that night – they could have been a placebo – but I instantly felt better. Maybe it was just hearing the term 'panic attack' that helped – knowing that it had a name, and was something normal, everyday, almost garden variety. Before the doctor spelt it out for me with such casual relief, I thought I was on the verge of hearing voices and experiencing some sort of psychotic break. I think I took one of those pills, calmed down, and I never took them again – nor did I ever feel those panic attacks again.

Looking back, I'm actually lucky that bad experience happened to me, in a way. I was never a drug-taker outside of that one acid trip and some pot – I've never tried any other illegal drugs – and that one bad experience only solidified my reluctance to dabble in the party scene. I can't imagine what might have happened to me if I'd had a great time instead. A fun, passing high might have nudged me into a more typical twenty-something-year-old's experimentation with drugs. Given my addictive gene, and the industry in which I work, where you're constantly exposed to all of the above, I probably would have wandered down a different, darker path. Instead, I was just a kid keeping her eyes forward, hoping to survive and then thrive.

Phil and I used to make trips to Sydney to get out of Canberra just for the weekend, which was always a treat. I remember we visited one of his friends who worked at Triple M in Sydney, and the studio overlooked all of the city, and I remember thinking, *Wow, what an amazing place to work*, even though I had no broadcast dreams of my own at that point. I only wanted then what was best for Phil. He was working long, hard nights in the studio, which meant that I spent most of my time in the apartment all alone. But when he got home he was always present. I loved Phil, and was happy and excited for him, and he was energetic and funny to be around. He was quirky. He had this naked mannequin in the apartment, for no reason at all. When the Sunday newspaper in Canberra came with a free commemorative coin one day, we developed a running joke where we would hide the coin in unexpected places for one another. He would drop it into my coffee cup while I wasn't looking, and I'd go into his work and hide it in his desk. Eventually Phil proposed to me, in the bedroom of that apartment, and when he opened the ring box the coin was all that was inside. He didn't even have a ring ready. That was our stupid humour and our bond – all childlike enthusiasm and fun.

The idea of marriage didn't seem solemn in the slightest. I was nineteen and in love, and to me it felt so casual – 'Oh, excellent – marriage is just something else fun for us to do!' None of the thoughts that *should* have entered my mind ever did, such as *Is the ten-year age difference an* issue? or *Is this the right relationship for me?* or *Do I even know who I am yet?* My family in Tasmania, on my dad's side, were really opposed to the idea, so much so that they said they wouldn't be at the wedding if I went through with it because I was making a huge mistake. I remember thinking how wrong they were – but they were right, and they stuck to their word and didn't come to the ceremony. In fact, I was estranged from that part of my family for the duration of my marriage.

Maybe I was too flippant about it all, but I also like to think of that character trait in a positive light. Yes, I do tend to get carried away in life – I allow myself to get swept up in things too easily, too swiftly, with too little thought for the consequences. I've always been a dreamer – a hopeless romantic at heart. But I don't always *want* to be a rational being. What fun is there in that? What do you learn if you make no mistakes? How timid do you become if you never take any risks? What kind of life do you lead if you don't take a leap of faith or folly now and then? Acting on a whim might lead you to make some missteps here and there, but it also helps you take the biggest leaps of your life.

We were only in Canberra for six months before we took our next big leap. We moved to Adelaide, where Phil would be part of the team changing an old FM station into the South Australian version of Triple M, and I could plan our wedding – although it's a stretch to say that much actual planning was involved. I got my dress made by a local seamstress, having shown her a picture of a Chanel dress and assuming she could make the exact same thing on a budget. I wanted a white version of this stunning black number modelled in a magazine by Christy Turlington, and while I remember seeing my dress and thinking, 'This looks *nothing* like what I wanted,' it was eventually patched into something half decent. We got married in the Botanic Gardens of Sydney, among people enjoying their weekend walks or family picnics. Our 'reception' was at the restaurant right there in the gardens, too – nothing upmarket, with no set menu and no special roped-off section, just a big table booked and paid for by Mum and Dad.

I did grow up imagining my wedding when I was little, seeing myself as the bride in white, but it wasn't the dominating thought or fascination for me that it was for some girls. Being the princess who marries Prince Charming was never my fantasy, so there was no call for disappointment or regret over my humble public park nuptials with a few family members and friends. It was a lovely day to celebrate, with no thoughts of how it could have been bigger or better or more. We had no hens' night or bucks' night either, but we did have a honeymoon.

We went to New York, Los Angeles and Las Vegas. I fell in love with Manhattan. I was immediately struck by that clichéd sense of being right inside the beating heart of the world. You strut down the sidewalk in New York and can't help but see a landmark from a movie or a TV show or a novel or a song. You look up and there's some gargantuan famous bridge or building looming above you, and you look down to see yellow cabs rolling along these wide, busy avenues. That city is everything you expect and more.

And then we were in Radelaide – or, rather, North Radelaide, in a townhouse on Pennington Terrace overlooking the park and the city, and because it was the 1990s it was also super cheap, maybe $180 a week. I was temping again to make a little money, but one night Phil called – the girl who worked on the phones had been fired – so he asked me to come in and help answer calls. This girl had actually left her diary behind one day, and in an appalling privacy breach, station staff had read it, including one entry in which she talked about how much she hated working there, and which people she hated. That kind of unethical sacking would never get through an HR department today, but her end in radio was my unexpected beginning.

Phil kept asking me to fill in, and then I had to do some on-air shout-outs – hellos to the callers – and he suggested I stay on and work there. It was odd, as I had no real interest in radio – quite the opposite. I remember when we were in Canberra, Phil used to call me and *beg* me to call in to the show when the switchboard was blank – 'Just say this, and ask that!' – and I used to *hate* it so much. My exposure to radio beyond my DJ husband wasn't positive. But reading out a few names at the end of a show was simple enough. And the station was launching, which was exciting in itself – the shows were new, the hosts and producers were new.

It was just fun to hang around the station, because there were all these gatherings and all this grand ambition.

Eventually, one of the Triple M consultants came to town and heard me doing my little shout-outs, and he must have heard me saying something off the cuff that he enjoyed, because he said, 'That girl's really funny – you need to put her on, and give her her own segment.' I have no idea what he heard that night, but he pushed hard to get me on air. It was a real sliding doors moment.

Until then, I wasn't even really getting paid for my work at Triple M; I was just helping my husband. But I could see now that I wanted something more, with responsibility and compensation. I went in to see the boss, who said the most they could pay me was $10,000 a year, which was ridiculous even three decades ago, but I agreed anyway, and was soon answering phones and doing my little shout-outs and a little more here and there, and I loved being a part of Phil's work, too. I felt as if I was really along for the ride now, invested in the outcome and doing everything I could behind the scenes to ensure that he would win the ratings.

A good example? East 17 might seem like a flash-in-the-pan act deserving of a 'Where are they now?' TV special today, but in 1994 they were one of the biggest boy bands on the planet, and when they came to town to play the Adelaide Entertainment Centre, they stopped by our studio first. We were located in a two-storey office building, with glass fishbowl studios that meant people could watch you from the street, and when the band came in to chat the footpaths and roads were teeming with teen-agers. It was absolute pandemonium.

I remember the guys left behind a water bottle, and we said, 'Why don't we give this away? The audience will love it!' And so we did a competition where we asked people to send in a 'message in a bottle', and the most creative message would win the bottle that had touched the lips of a popstar. A day later I came in to our cavernous ground floor reception area, and it was just *buried* in bottles that people had dropped off to us. You could not move. In that moment, something about the reach and power of radio became clear to me, and harnessing that became our goal and our way. We were broadcasting to kids, and we would do whatever we could to take advantage of anything and everything that was hot right now.

There was one other thing about that day. My brief on-air role had earned me a nickname by then – 'Jackie the Phone Tart', which I kind of hated – and when East 17 came in and the streets were swollen with teenage girls who loved them, who weren't much younger than me, and they could see me there in the studio with the band, the only girl, the only young person with access, talking and laughing, you could see this hatred in their eyes: *Look at Jackie the Phone Tart – I bet she's a slut*. And as Phil skyrocketed in the ratings, exceeding all expectations, we began to get recognised a bit, and I began to sense a little bit of that very specific and sexist distaste some people have for famous women enjoying their life and career. Phil was about to be poached and brought to Melbourne to host the *Hot 30* at Fox FM, and I remember I asked right then if I could change my name when we moved to Victoria. Thank god I did, because that first nickname might otherwise have stuck. Instead, I got a new name. Being married to 'Phil O'Neil' would make me 'Jackie O'Neil' (even though no one knew we were married – more on that later!), so the nickname was obvious: I became Jackie O.

—

In Melbourne, I kept doing everything I could to see the show succeed. We lived in the Como building in South Yarra for a year, and I immediately jumped into work by joining the Black Thunder crew. Remember those? It was a fleet of sleek black SUVs, covered in the Fox FM logo and driven out to all parts of the city by its 'pilots', to meet people and give away free merchandise. There was a genuine sense of excitement when people heard a Black Thunder was going to be in their area. Most stations had something similar eventually – with names such as Street Team, Hit Squad, Road Runners and Rock Patrols – but Fox did it best. I would head out to schools, mostly, to hand out cold cans of Coke and bags of salty Samboy chips – and by the time each visit was done, several dozen more kids would know that Ugly Phil was going to be on the radio tonight, playing the best tunes in town.

I went out to one school with a pilot named Troy, and it was a rough campus, way out of the city somewhere. They were waiting for us. Before I knew it – before I could open the door and start handing out freebies – the kids surrounded the car and started rocking it back and forth. There was no teacher to stop them, and we began to feel as if we were stuck in a cop car during a riot. Eventually the principal came out and broke it up, and we got out of the Thunder, gave the kids all our soft drinks and snacks and magazines, and left. Job done. It was a strange business model, but we would sometimes have celebrities or musicians come along for the ride, and sometimes we would do a part of the show from wherever we went. People got excited by different things in those days, and it became the promotional backbone of the network.

I catered to the needs of our audience in other ways, too. My 'O News' segment was incredibly important to me, and gossip was such a big thing back then, but the internet was really only in its infancy, so the way you got a steady stream of gossip was through magazines. I used to go to the newsagency and buy every celebrity and gossip magazine I could find, from *Woman's Day* to *Smash Hits*. Beyond that, there was a trade publication that came through every day on the fax machine – Rock Net, direct from New York – which was almost useless. Its focus was people our audience didn't give a shit about, such as Neil Young, and you would have to read through sixty pages to find one nugget that might be of interest to the teenagers of Melbourne. But I did it, because I wanted to super-service all our listeners.

I'd also come up with the idea of a printed gossip newsletter, and I created a subscriber mailing list for it. I'd ask every single caller who rang through to the station if they wanted a free weekly gossip newsletter, and then write down their address in my little database. Then all I had to do was write, edit and produce a magazine – with no formal training! I'd sketch out my glorified pamphlet, full of funny news items and gossipy tidbits and celebrity photos, and then I'd photocopy it by hand, sometimes until 4 a.m., and mail them out.

It was all worth it – the newsletter and database, the Thunders and stunts – because I wanted Phil to be number one so badly. We loved being the underdog, the hunter, not the hunted, and we were obsessed with *our* show, so that's what our relationship became – work, work, work. We were side by side, hustling hard together, and it made our marriage strong. We were somewhere new, but we were together. We weren't ships in the night anymore – we were partners. We'd finish work and drive to a Blockbuster store, rent a few movies and stay up until sunrise. We loved what we were doing, and we were living in one another's pockets.

Waiting for the radio ratings when you're on the kind of charge we were on was exhilarating. I remember the survey panels would come through on a fax machine, but because we were working nights we would hear the news second-hand through a phone call from someone at the station the next morning. And we kept doing well, always growing, always climbing, until we were dominating. We were number one. Number one! I never had any nerves about a drop or dip either. For many people, fear of failure is their default motivation in life – it's what drives them, and it serves them well. I don't live that way. I've always leant more towards hope, even confidence. I've always believed.

I did have one bad experience, though. I was on air a little more in Melbourne, and that came with a tiny, growing profile. And then one day we were asked to host an event at a mall – Chadstone Shopping Centre, in fact, which was and still is the biggest mall in the southern hemisphere – because Boyz II Men had come to town. Forget fucking East 17 – these were the guys from Motownphilly, the balladeers behind 'End of the Road' and 'I'll Make Love to You' – and we were being asked to introduce them for an appearance in suburbia, and, damn, suburbia was ready and waiting.

The appearance was on the nightly news later, because the crowd was so big as to be almost dangerous, a crush of kids threatening to accidentally spill over the food court balcony. I remember one of our Thunder pilots, Reggie, was filling in and warming up the crowd, but the band was running incredibly late and at some point he just ran out of material, and decided to introduce me and Phil. But the way Reggie began his wind-up, it sounded as if the band had arrived.

'And now it's time, everybody!' he said. 'Are you excited? Because it's my pleasure to welcome to the stage . . . Jackie O and . . .'

And he never even got to Phil's name, because twenty thousand teenagers were booing me, but I was already out there on the stage, a proverbial deer in headlights. I was handed the microphone in a state of total shock. My body went cold. I probably smiled and said whatever I needed to say – 'Sorry, folks, they won't be long' – before leaving immediately. I'm not joking when I say I was scarred by that experience. I don't think I'd ever been on stage before, other than a ballet recital in primary school or a Rock Eisteddfod in high school, and after that I never wanted to set foot on stage again. Honestly, I think I've only just overcome that moment now, more than thirty years later.

We were in Melbourne for three years, all told, and only moved to Sydney when we went national. We were told we had to go north – the national production team were in Sydney – but we were gutted by that. We had finally been somewhere long enough to gather a great group of friends. We had a cute cottage beach house in St Kilda, and we loved that grimy, village vibe, with our time marked by raucous dinner parties and long walks down the Esplanade or in the Botanical Gardens. Sydney was an exciting prospect, but I felt genuinely uprooted, too. That move was the very definition of bittersweet.

Three

I'd been to the offices of 2Day FM before, when going up north to do interviews with talent. But it felt different to arrive there for work. The studio was in Bondi Junction, on the twenty-fourth floor, with views overlooking Sydney Harbour. It felt like the pinnacle of radio in Australia. The famous New Year's Eve fireworks display centred on the Sydney Harbour Bridge? 2Day FM sponsored the event, and played the soundtrack. If a major musical performer was coming to the city, it was always 2Day FM presenting the concert. Something about the place felt bigger than Ben Hur – as if there was nowhere better to be. They owned this town.

But it was a tough move. Melbourne had finally felt like home. When we moved away for this new setting, it was to an established station – neither a startup, nor a refresh – where firmly entrenched people already had their circles of friends, and it felt quite cliquey. Phil and I had each other, though, I suppose, and we had the work, too. We were just as desperate to ensure our success continued – maybe more so. It was easy to dream big there.

Sydney has this physical ability to inspire awe in you. Paddington was the peaking suburb at the time. The markets were there, and people would go to Oxford Street to party and shop and eat. I remember thinking we would get a terrace house there, until I realised how expensive it was and that there was no chance. Instead we moved to a place called Ultimo, which we thought looked great because it was close to the city and a good location, but it wasn't quite like being among the bustling streets of Paddington, like I'd dreamt. There is a definite reckoning between what you think your glamorous life in the Harbour City will be, and what it actually is sometimes. Most of that comes down to the rent, which we found was astronomical compared to Adelaide and Melbourne. Sydney glitters, but parts of it can feel out of reach sometimes, too.

We got the job there, incidentally, not just because we were number one, but because of something that had been done by the previous host, David Rymer. The education department had released their stats listing who topped the HSC results that year, and David decided to call that girl, to prank her – 'There's been a mistake, sorry, you're not the top' – and the teenager was rightfully upset and broke down in tears, and there was so much ensuing backlash that David got fired. This is the nature of radio. The medium is a magnet for scandal, with the potential to end relationships and careers – at worst, even lives. I don't think it hurt David too much, however. He was given a sort of soft landing – you might even call it a lateral promotion – going off air but getting a content director job with Southern Cross Austereo (SCA). Maybe that's just what happens, at least when you're a bloke. Or maybe he didn't really deserve the sack. Either way, his 'firing' was the reason for our abrupt hiring.

It took us a while to find our feet, but eventually we settled in well. We got a white Pomeranian, Buddy, our beautiful little yapper. But if I'm honest, I was beginning to question our marriage. The truth of it is that we had become almost like brother-and-sister co-workers. We were close, but the element of passion or attraction or friction was missing, and it had been for a while. I was eighteen when we met, and now I was twenty-four. Perhaps this was the reason people had warned me about the age difference between us. It wasn't so much that the gap itself was a chasm; it was that I'd met Phil when he was twenty-nine, when he already knew exactly who he was, but when I was still a child, with so much growing left to do. After the handful of years we'd been together, I was no longer that kid. I was shifting and changing and maturing, and it gave us a certain instability as a couple. And when the physical side of the relationship isn't up and running to compensate for your doubts, the gut feeling that something really isn't right between you just niggles and niggles until it's all too much to ignore.

Also, the public had no idea we were a couple. No one knew we were married, and we had to keep that hidden. We were the hosts of the *Hot 30*, broadcasting live to cynical teenagers – we couldn't do that as an old married couple, let alone a bickering pair. So we kept our relationship a complete secret.

I remember once when Phil was taking an overseas trip for work to interview a celebrity, one of the record company executives who was hosting him called me to line up the details of the trip as if I were his assistant. Specifically, he wanted to know whether Phil would like any cocaine during his trip, and what kind of hookers he preferred. I had to inform this gentleman that I was actually Phil's wife. The silence on the other end of the line was deafening. But that was how secret our relationship had become. Our coupledom remained unknown even within the most well-informed sections of the media, hanging there like some unanswered question. Even around the office there were people who wondered, *Are they or aren't they together?* In hindsight, maybe that goes to show just how little we behaved like a married couple.

We went on some of those overseas trips together, too, joining Molly Meldrum in New York to interview Puff Daddy. It was always fun travelling with Molly, especially to Manhattan. He would take me out to all the best gay clubs to dance and laugh, and somehow we would always wind up in the apartment of some Calvin Klein model. I remember arriving at Bad Boy Records and waiting three hours for Sean 'Puffy' Combs (as he was then known) to arrive. The man whose label represented the Notorious B.I.G. was notorious himself for running late, but I watched as Molly eventually did a wonderful interview. I was up next, and Diddy quickly excused himself – 'Do you mind if I use the bathroom before we start?' – then headed off down the corridor. After fifteen minutes I started to wonder if he was doing cocaine with his crew, or if he just needed more fibre in his diet. It was then that one of his cronies informed me he had walked straight out the door, ghosting me before 'ghosting' was even a word. I flew back to Sydney empty handed.

One day I got a call from a producer who wanted to talk to me about a TV show – *Popstars* – that he was interested in me being a judge on. I was shown all this footage of auditions from the show in New Zealand and asked to react, and was too naive to realise I was being auditioned myself. I must have done all right, though, as they gave me the job, which was basically a few weeks of travelling the country acting as a judge, and then you're done. They didn't pay me anything for that, either. Like I said, I was naive. I was so naive that when the producer handed out little envelopes at a bar one night with our $40 per diem for expenses, I not only didn't know what a 'per diem' was, but I literally stood up and gave him a hug because I was so over the moon to get this pocket change.

I tell you this about *Popstars* not to show how green I was, but mainly because of how that time away from Phil made me feel. It was the first time I'd been away from him for more than a day, and I felt stronger, not weaker. I noticed I wasn't missing Phil as much as I thought I would. We had lived and breathed one another, twenty-four hours a day, seven days a week, for more than five years, but surprisingly, I was enjoying my independence for the first time.

Things began to deteriorate between us somewhat, cracks starting to show in different ways, including little cracks on air. I remember one day the topic turned to something sexual, and there was an obviously crude double entendre at play, and he turned to me and said, 'Oh yeah, you'd like that, wouldn't you, Jackie,' and I shot back coolly, 'Fuck you,' which was followed by silence. There was no censor at the time. We never swore either, knowing you could – theoretically – get fired for something such as that. Kyle remembers this moment vividly from his point of view as a listener, because it was so unusual.

It wasn't long after that when Phil was offered a job in the UK. His dream was broadcasting in Britain, anyway. We went on a holiday there once and he begged a station for a shift – midnight to dawn, on Capital FM London – just to experience it. He wanted a big city, and Australia was provincial. We talked about how great we were as a team, but how it didn't feel the way it should as a couple, and so we decided to accept the reality that our marriage had run its course. We agreed to keep working together – and living together, but separately – until Phil could finalise his plans to move to England. It was my plan to stay on.

There was no dramatic moment where he stood in the doorway and I walked past with my bags, head held high, or in a teary tirade. It was just two people moving apart gradually. Not quite the positive experience people talk about today with 'conscious uncoupling', but our divorce was more amicable than upsetting. There was no squabbling about money or property – we just went our separate ways.

I moved near Kings Cross, to stay with Mandy, who was a friend of a producer who I worked with at the station. Mandy was ten years older than me and a huge stoner. We barely saw each other, but it was interesting nonetheless. She was psychic, and I'm a firm believer in the mystic realm. She was also just a truly random entity. I remember coming home one night from the *Hot 30*, opening the door to my bedroom and seeing that there was a naked man under my covers. Mandy had brought some guy home and he'd decided he wasn't going to share her bed, so he crashed in mine instead. Things like that just happened around Mandy!

My old best mate Natasha, from the Ray White real estate agency on the Gold Coast, had also moved to Sydney, and we became joined at the hip, going out all the time. We were obsessed with imagining our future and having our tarot cards read and, mostly, finding love – finding somebody, anybody – and we were erratic because of that. I had a rebound relationship with a mechanic – Dali – a

Czechoslovakian guy who was very nonchalant about me, but with whom I was besotted. The less interested he was in me, the more obsessed I was with him. We went out on his dad's yacht on the harbour one night, and we went skinny dipping and slept on the boat. When I woke up in the morning, Dali had got out of bed, got into bed with my best friend and had tried to crack onto her. Natasha was horrified and told me later that day, but I stayed with Dali for another six weeks. This was my old pattern again – a man who was not returning my love and affection must be one worth having, right? What is it they say; 'Treat 'em mean, keep 'em keen'? I hate that phrase, especially if and when it fits.

If any of this sounds a little desperate or pathetic, I should make it clear that things were also happening for me in a big way – the world was opening up at my feet. There was a long lag between filming and screening, but *Popstars* had finally come out, and it was a ratings juggernaut. I don't think the producers really knew or suspected what it would become. I was twenty-four, single, in the bright lights of a big city. People recognised me and wanted to do articles on me, and fashion magazines wanted to do photo shoots with me, and I was going out to nightclubs and all the velvet ropes and back rooms welcomed me inside. I got invitations to events and openings and parties where you'd stroll into the VIP room and go, 'Wow, that's Nick Giannopoulos' (who, by the way, I pashed one night). So, my career was amazing and exciting, but all of this was a distraction, because what I really wanted and craved was to find love.

I also remember not feeling too happy in that world, or at least uneasy. It was so foreign. I was invited to events at the homes of millionaires and billionaires. *Vogue Australia* would be hosting an event at a mansion on the water, only the elite were invited, and I'd be dressed by designers and could pick any frock or jewellery I wanted, and although everything around me was glamorous and fabulous, somehow it felt superficial and unfulfilling. There were some 'pinch me' moments that I'll never forget, though. I was having dinner at a restaurant off the back of Oxford Street, called Chicane, when Baz Luhrmann came up to me and said what a big fan he was – of me! – and how obsessed he was with the show. *You're fucking joking!* I thought. *Like, Baz Luhrmann knows who I am?* And yet, Baz Luhrmann, a man whose films have been nominated for a combined twenty Academy Awards, was not the most important man in that restaurant that night, because I was on a date with the man who would become my second husband.

Natasha and I laugh about how desperate we were for a man at that time. Shortly before that dinner at Chicane it had been Valentine's Day, and I was still heartbroken that the mechanic didn't share my affections. Natasha was in a similar state, teary and depressed. She lived in a fifteenth-floor apartment around the corner from me, and was praying that this boyfriend who didn't like her would think of her on Valentine's Day. In her despairing delusion, she saw a courier van pull up with a big bunch of red roses and screamed out the window down to street level, 'Excuse me! Are they for my unit?' When the courier shook his head, apologetically, she saw what she had become – a girl with dewy eyes and mascara streaming down her cheeks, begging a stranger for someone else's flowers – and understood how low things had got for us. So we went out, figuring screw it, let's have some fun.

We went to the Blue Room on Oxford Street, and a young British bloke approached us. 'Excuse me, my friend wanted to buy you this drink.' I remember seeing that friend from across the room and immediately clocking him as gorgeous. Five minutes later, Lee Henderson came over to say hello, we got talking, and we didn't stop the whole night. We went to the club next door, Goodbar, and stayed until it closed. We were still in the corner talking when they shut up shop and started sweeping around us, until the owner came out to let us know we'd have to leave at some point. It was like something out of a movie or a book.

I had actually just read the bestseller *Men Are From Mars, Women Are From Venus* – the buzzy book at the time – and it had explicitly said not to even *kiss* a man on the first date – keep them waiting as long as possible. That sounded like good advice. I'd slept with the mechanic on the first night, and I looked back on that as a mistake. I didn't want to play this one the wrong way, so I said goodnight to Lee, kissed him on the cheek and he took my number. We went out on that date to Chicane – a dimly lit romantic restaurant – after the show one night. I remember I was all dressed up in this camel-coloured mid-length skirt and this tight, long-sleeved black top, with boots and my little Oroton bag. I didn't let him kiss me that night, either. I really made the poor guy wait.

And he was a gentleman about that – about everything. Lee said and did all the right things. He was a walking encyclopaedia. I don't know how he retained the information he did – on literally everything and anything – but he would never have to Google the answer. Sometimes I regretted asking him a question because the answers were always so deep and incisive, but *long* – as if there was this wealth of knowledge he just had to share with someone. He was such a reader and a thinker – an impressive man – and he treated me so well.

He was quick witted and playful, too. When he asked me out to do something or go somewhere, he would always call it a 'playdate', and they felt that way. We would walk in the park holding hands, or go to the museum to absorb some art. We loved going to the markets and buying fresh produce to cook dinner at home together. You could have taken him on *MasterChef* – he instinctively knew how to assemble whatever eight random ingredients you had into a gourmet meal. He knew what went with what, and used to cook a fish and potato gratin dish that was divine. I remember looking over at him on one of those shopping expeditions, at Paddy's Markets in Chinatown one day, and Lee was wearing this khaki T-shirt and jeans, and he picked up a bunch of basil and smelt it. He seemed to be breathing it in. We had only been dating three weeks, but there was something about this guy – something considerate and cultured and caring that made me look at him in a new way. *I don't know what it is about him*, I thought, *but I think I'm in love. I want to marry that guy.*

We were young – mid-twenties, without any responsibilities – going out to bars and restaurants in Kings Cross. We would go to Iguana Bar after the clubs closed for early-morning potato wedges with sour cream and sweet chilli sauce. I was so enamoured that for the first month we were together I would wake up before he did and tiptoe into the bathroom to secretly put on make-up and then come back to bed, so he would wake up and see me looking effortlessly beautiful. I would pretend to sleep, because I'm a really ugly sleeper. I sleep with my mouth open, and I snore, but I wanted him to see me as a quiet, angelic sleeping beauty.

We loved to be affectionate, lying in one another's arms. We would go on road trips listening to his music – The Verve and Travis and Manic Street Preachers – and we would drive anywhere. We would drive three hours south to look at properties we couldn't afford to buy, just because we liked to be in each other's company. He was doing restaurant reviews at the time, and we would go out and eat like kings and queens for free. We went to the Hunter Valley for wine tastings. We went to the Blue Mountains to snuggle up in a cottage with an open fireplace and board games. We went to Berry and Palm Beach, exploring and laughing and living in our own little bubble.

How in love was I with Lee? When I had been dating him for around a year, I went to Australian Fashion Week for work and went to all the shows, and I remember being at an exclusive afterparty. Chris Hemsworth had just split up with his girlfriend, and we got to talking and really hit it off. We were getting on so well and having such a great chat. The Mighty Thor himself was single, and he was right in front of me, looking incredible and laughing at my jokes and speaking thoughtfully, and the entire time I was thinking, *God, I wish Lee was here.*

Someone had told me that if I wanted a man, I needed to write a wish list – a manifestation of what and who you want your guy to be. I knew right away. Intelligent, and funny. Tall, with dark hair. Loyal, and with a kind heart. Lee was exactly what I'd asked for, but I was also a bit intimidated by him. I'd just started learning French at the time – after someone gave me one of those cassette tapes that existed in the days before Duolingo – and I'd only got the basics down. Lee sounded so posh, and he was so British, and I tried to impress him by saying I spoke French. He didn't catch me out in that white lie, but I look back now and realise what a mistake that was – to be anything other than myself from the very beginning, to pretend to be someone else from the start. Those kinds of things, even on a small scale, set you up on a shaky foundation.

I learnt that Lee was from Brackley, a town around an hour outside of Oxford. He was working class, neither well-to-do nor poor. He was raised by his mum, and when he went to university he became friends with a lot of rich kids and upper-class cultural types. Lee was always very good at integrating into any group – a chameleon who could match his surroundings. I don't say that to make him sound like the protagonist in *Saltburn* or *The Talented Mr Ripley* – what I actually mean is that he was always great at making those around him feel comfortable. He knew how to put himself together, too.

He was always well dressed, and even did a little modelling work on the side. He spoke well, had high emotional intelligence and was also such a curious person, which I loved. He had travelled the world, spending months in India before coming to Australia and working as a journalist. He was open minded and accepting. He had done a story in which he'd immersed himself in Indigenous culture in Western Australia, and did freelance work for a gay newspaper in Sydney. We actually met when his visa was about to run out, with six months left to travel here, so we moved quickly, from zero to hundred – another typical Jackie life pattern! But when you're moving that fast, you often don't notice the things you're flying past.

I should have seen the tiny red flags early on, but we were living and loving at breakneck speed and so I just didn't, because my entire goal was to make him happy. Lee was judgemental, for instance, in small but immediate ways. I remember I wanted to get a new car, and I specifically wanted a white BMW, not because I thought it was a status symbol or anything like that, but because I had seen a photo of Elle Macpherson in a white BMW once, and she looked amazing. Lee said he would literally leave me if I bought anything as tacky as a white BMW, so I ended up with a black Ford Focus hatchback.

Lee never seemed to be threatened by my career. He was so utterly supportive. The only time I can remember when any jealousy reared its head was one day when Robbie Williams came into the studio for an interview and was flirting with me, and Lee was listening at home. He had an issue with that, and we had it out, but he checked himself quickly. That was one of the great things about Lee – he wanted me to do well. He helped me with business negotiations. He was great with advice. He seemed like someone who could do anything he wanted. He has a near-photographic memory, but he never quite had any direction for channelling that energy and intellect, or seemingly any desire to find his true north, either. And I probably enabled that.

He applied for a job with the local newspaper, the *Wentworth Courier*, who could sponsor him to stay in Australia, and he got it, working as a writer for the real estate sheet everyone in Sydney's Eastern Suburbs used to pore over whether they needed a new place to live or not. Within a couple of years we would be able to make sure he could stay in Australia with a de facto spouse visa, but he didn't really know where he sat with his career, and I desperately wanted him to be content. Lee's hobby was photography, and I encouraged him to change careers, as he certainly had the eye for that job – and so he left journalism and started fashion photography. I thought he would be happy, but he wasn't. The creative side of the work nurtured him but the industry itself was too cut-throat and superficial. Everyone had to be sucked up to. It wasn't for him, and it made him miserable.

We had moved in together quickly, renting a beautiful place in the Eastern Suburbs. I'd got a pay rise and was able to afford a nicer area, and then we moved and we bought. Our first property was an art deco apartment in Elizabeth Bay, ninety-nine square metres, run-down but with good bones. When we renovated that home I sensed his unhappiness, and put it down to his job. There's often an aimlessness to people in their twenties – not everyone stumbles luckily into their long-term career path the way I did – and it can be stressful.

We were in love, but I was still coming home to our apartment, sensing in him some unspoken unhappiness or doubt, and I was bereft of ideas. I'm a happy person by nature. I have an overflowing wellspring of love for life – I really believe life is for living – and that's not always helpful. Honestly, I didn't know how to react – what to say, or what to do – or whether it was even up to me at all.

Four

I was obviously very distracted – very quickly – by my love for Lee, which wasn't ideal, because there was another pivotal relationship in my life that began and ran in parallel, at work.

With Phil gone from the *Hot 30* chair, we needed a replacement, but no one seemed to work as well. Phil had been brilliant at his job. He was quick witted and popular, and knew the format and the culture. We trialled various people. There was Jason 'Jabba' Davis from cable TV's Channel V – a grungy host who knew his music. There was Jason 'Soleman' Sole, who had been the late-night host when we were in Adelaide, who was slick and knew the music but didn't have the humour. We talked about Dylan Lewis, who'd had a long and varied career in TV and radio, but just wasn't the right fit.

No one was really cutting it, so the temporary slot remained. This was a problem for the boss who ran the network. Jeff Allis was good looking, charismatic, funny, fair and *utterly* terrifying. He was obsessed with this book *Thick Face, Black Heart: The warrior philosophy for conquering the challenges of business and life*, and was ruled by its combative ideas. An example? He had a samurai sword in his office, and every time he would fire someone, they would walk out of the room and then he would chop that blade down on the edge of his desk – with an almighty swing – each mark representing another person he had fired.

Jeff had decided he was done with the trials and was flying someone down from Brisbane to do two nights on air. This guy apparently knew radio, was funny, and was favoured. I was summoned to the office to say hello to this boy from Brissie, and that's how I met Kyle Sandilands. He didn't look like much. He was a real country boy – everything on him was R. M. Williams – and I could tell he was really nervous and overwhelmed. Our program director made the introductions – 'This is Kyle, this is Jackie, you'll be on air tonight, best of luck to you' – and that was it.

Little did I know I had just been introduced to the man who would forever change my life and become one of my most trusted friends. His sheer brilliance and our divine chemistry together were about to make history by one day becoming Australia's most successful radio show. I would spend the next twenty-four years (and counting) of my life with this wonderful man, and if you'd told me that in that moment, I sure as hell wouldn't have believed it. Instead I just walked away wondering who the hell he was, before meeting him again when we sat in the booth together that night.

It did not go well. I immediately found that voice of his grating – he had a far higher-pitched chipmunk delivery then – and he seemed too desperate to please. In the opener of the show I remember him trying to warm up the audience – 'I've just been told there's a message from the bosses: Do anything you want, just don't say fuck' – and I'm surprised I didn't roll my eyes. *How lame*, I thought. *Who* is *this guy they've partnered me with?*

We had an interview that night with Posh Spice. This was early in 2000 and the Spice Girls were massive, meaning the interview was hugely important. Victoria Beckham joined us by phone, as planned, and Kyle accidentally hung up on her. She called back, and he accidentally hung up on her again. She did not call a third time. He got all the names of the pop bands wrong or pronounced them incorrectly. And the *Hot 30* was all about *knowing* – these kids see through you if you're pretending in any way, and he was pretending completely, because he was coming from a Triple M station in Queensland. He was used to playing Barnsey and Farnsey and The Screaming Jets and Paul Kelly, so he just wasn't familiar with pop music. I remember calling the boss after the show: 'That was a *disaster*, this is *not* going to work, it just isn't . . .'

I don't know what happened in the space of twenty-four hours – whether Kyle stayed up all night studying, or he got some much-needed sleep, or he needed that one calamitous night to blow out the cobwebs and make all his mistakes – but on the second night he was a different person. He came on air and nailed everything – every – single – thing – and was just so good. We kept going with him for a few more nights, and he kept improving, and he got the job. And he's kept it ever since.

Honestly, I wasn't paying that much attention in the early stages, because I was still falling in love with Lee at the time. Radio was my lowest priority, but it was Kyle's top priority – this was his dream. As I learnt his story, I understood why.

Kyle grew up in Wynnum, a rough area of Brisbane. He was raised in a very abusive household, his mum being a victim of domestic violence from his dad. He was a loose kid, too. He held a party one night when he was fifteen – a huge, Corey Worthington–style rager – and was kicked out of home for a year. His aunty took him in and set him (somewhat) straight: 'You need to get your life together,' she said, 'and you can live with me while you do it.' She had seen an ad for Black Thunder pilots, and he went in and applied, and lied, saying he had experience, and after that he was a hustler for hire in radio, working in Townsville or Cairns or anywhere else you could imagine, doing promotions and on-air work, little jobs that kept him near the microphone.

He eventually hosted a morning show in Brisbane with another girl, and they had shared dreams of hosting a big show together and making it in Sydney. Kyle used to look to Ugly Phil and Jackie O as the dream. He thought it was amazing that I was on *Popstars*. He was wide-eyed and a little intimidated, but more than ready to seize his big break, while I was happy to finish a shift, go home immediately to Lee, bask in his love, and come in late the next day, because I didn't care about the job at all. There was honestly no connection whatsoever between me and Kyle in that first year, because I made no effort to connect. I was being selfish.

Then we went away together to Spain, for the MTV Europe Music Awards, to interview everyone on the red carpet. We were in Barcelona, put up in the shittiest hotel you've ever seen, overlooking a courtyard slum piled with old, soiled mattresses. Whitney Houston's dancers were staying on our floor, and had their doors open and music playing on their ghetto-blaster radio so they could practise at all hours. I didn't speak any Spanish, and Kyle was the same – but he also didn't have any idea what to do. And the red carpet is brutal – it's every man for himself. You have to hustle, big time, because you're one of many media people trying to speak to all the same stars.

Here's how it works. American media seem to get their own corral, and the celebrities are mostly happy to speak to them. And then we always get lumped in with the foreign media section. You've basically got to beg these famous people to talk to you, and so you smile, and you yell out, 'We're from Australia!' because that always seems to help, possibly because there's no language barrier and less of a cultural leap, meaning musicians and actors from the US and UK can acquit their duty to do international interviews by chatting to a bubby, English-speaking host.

I had a guy from MTV Russia right next to me, with this huge camera, and then James Bond himself, Pierce Brosnan, came towards me. I knew he would be great from his smile, and then the Russian dude stood right in front of me, and I saw red. I'm not a confrontational person, but I have massive balls when I'm working the red carpet. All I remember is yanking his camera cord and pulling it out in the middle of the interview – he looked at me with a death stare, but I didn't care – then I pushed him aside and began interviewing 007. Because if you're not aggressive out there, you come home with nothing. Kyle was terrified of me.

We ended up getting really great stuff, and despite being in an exotic location surrounded by the most famous entertainers on earth, I stayed for maybe ten minutes of the awards show and then left, heading right back to the hotel. But for Kyle, this was a new world. He stuck around for it all, and for the P. Diddy afterparty. He was with his best friend, Ryan Wellington, the executive producer of the show.

The whole team had once been aligned with Phil, of course. Phil had his diva moments and tantrums, but he was generally lovely to work with, and so that crew loved him. But Kyle got comfortable quickly, and very soon the entire show was his way or the highway. You could tell the old staff didn't like that, and Kyle could tell, too, so he got rid of them, one by one, and his biggest replacement appointment was Ryan. He was a mirror of Kyle, really – both tyrants, both alphas – or maybe he was a mini Jeff Allis. Jeff had his samurai sword, while Ryan used to walk around the office with an axe. Ryan and Kyle formed a strange dynamic. It was like the top dog protecting the big dog, both prowling and growling and grinning. Their energy was intense.

They fucked up in Spain, though. They caught a special MTV chartered bus to the Diddy afterparty that night, and Ryan left all our recordings on the bus. He didn't realise it until the next day, in the cab on the way to the studio to broadcast. We called every bus company in Spain but found nothing – it was all gone. But the three of us bonded over the mad, scrambling panic. We'd got a few one-on-one interviews separately, anyway, with the likes of Bon Jovi, so we made it work. And when we came back from that trip, the dynamic between us was completely different – it was close and supportive and connected. We had the same goals, and it ignited my passion for the show again. We got down to work.

Kyle and I were marching in sync, and delivering a much better show. I loved radio again, because I had a bridge with my co-host. When I look back on any moments in our career when we've been disconnected, for one reason or another, the show was never as good. You can fake it enough to get by, but not enough to make things sing. When we're aligned and having so much fun together, though, our rapport is as natural as it is unstoppable. Each of us was finally learning how the other works, and therefore what works for us. Take ribbing, for example.

Kyle put me down a bit – that's our dynamic – but he also knew precisely how far to push things. I would shoot back, because I'm no pushover, but never with malice. We basically began to read one another, anticipating responses and reactions in the madness of the minute. We were on fire.

Around two years into our journey, when I was twenty-six, we started to see the fruits of our labour. Kyle had got a great pay rise, up to $250,000 a year, while I might have been on $80,000. I went in to see the boss, Cathy O'Connor, to negotiate, and the crux of the negotiation was this: 'I'm doing the same job as Kyle,' I said. 'I deserve more than what I'm on.'

Cathy said something along the lines of, 'There's no more money. Take it or leave it – you're lucky to work here.'

Ordinarily, I wouldn't have known what to do, but by pure coincidence Nova FM had only recently reached out to me with one of those subtle approaches. *If you're ever interested in seeing something else, doing something else, doing things your own way, look us up.* It was time to reach back, so I met in secret with their station boss, Dean Buchanan, out of curiosity more than anything. I didn't really want to go it alone, as I knew Kyle and I had something special.

How do you conduct a clandestine broadcasting negotiation? Well, you rendezvous in a hotel room, arriving and departing separately so you're never seen together. For this surreptitious little summit, we met at the Novotel in Darling Harbour. I even wore sunglasses. We sat down in the luxurious lounge of a spacious suite, and he said all the right things. 'You're the talent, we don't want Kyle, just you, because this is what we think you can do for us, and this is what we're prepared to offer.'

It was around $180,000 – a cool 100 K more than I was getting – and this was to helm my very own show at night, to go up against Kyle. Nova wanted us apart – to split us up for good – and they were prepared to pay me well to get it done. I was never going to take their offer, but I was being disrespected by my current employer. I went back to Cathy and told her about the offer, and told her I would have to consider it if they weren't prepared to give me the same, and the response was instantaneous: 'No-no-no! It's fine! We'll give you the money . . .' Which was the same amount of money that Nova had offered me – $180,000 – but not equal to Kyle's $250,000 salary. I later learned that Kyle had also expressed his disappointment to Cathy that I wasn't on more money.

Nevertheless, I took it, and we ran with it, making the *Hot 30* our own. For those who aren't familiar, the show was broadcast from 7 p.m. to 10 p.m. Monday to Friday, and it really felt as though you were left to your own devices. None of the bosses seemed to be listening – seriously, because they were probably out to dinner or spending time with their partners or putting their kids to bed – so we could do almost whatever we wanted. Radio was different in the early 2000s. Artists wouldn't just phone in for an interview – they would visit the studio and hang out, meaning we were left to cause havoc in the darkness, having fun with the biggest acts in the world. We were the mice playing while the cats were away.

Pink was exactly the same as she is now – always fun and down to earth and into whatever you've got planned. She gives you everything, every time.

When Good Charlotte visited, we had our easels and blank canvases set up, because we used to encourage acts to paint us a picture while the songs played. Acts today will give you ten minutes then leave, but Good Charlotte hung out for an hour, painting portraits and shooting the shit.

Destiny's Child stopped by when they were new to the scene, and we probably weren't all that interested in them, but they were so sweet and so lovely. It has been interesting to watch Beyoncé's progression over the years through the scope of the interviews we did with her. When she first came in, it was like interviewing someone who was genuinely wide-eyed and eager and would do anything you wanted, but as time wore on, that changed. Later, when she started to become her own woman, and globally adored, we were the sweet and lovely ones and she was the one who wasn't that interested in us. That was made abundantly clear when our producer asked if we could all stand up together for a photo with the team. 'I'm not standing,' said Queen Bey. 'I don't stand.' The difference between one Beyoncé and the next was hard to reconcile, but easy to understand.

Avril Lavigne came in once at a time when she was really struggling with her fame. She was known for being quite difficult and prickly, and she clearly didn't want to be there. I asked the first question, something really innoc-uous – 'What have you been doing since you've been in Australia?' – and she turned her back on me, shrugging and saying nothing. We didn't know what to do. It was Kyle who pulled her up. 'Listen, I know you don't wanna be here, and you don't wanna do this interview, and you don't wanna do *any* interviews,' he said. 'The record company slotted you in for a fifteen-minute interview, but if you give me everything you've got for five minutes, you can go.' And that was music to her ears. She turned it on immediately.

Jack Black was a great guest. He came in and was excited by the view alone, and that we could smoke, which we were absolutely not allowed to do, but Kyle did it and I followed suit. We would get an empty one-litre plastic milk bottle, splash a bit of water inside, and then fill it with cigarette butts as we chain-smoked throughout the night. We were careful to dispose of the evidence at the end of the shift, even if that studio smelt like an airport smoking lounge.

Jack was promoting the film *School of Rock*, and we had our movie reviewer take a look. His name was James Brown, and he was just a kid at the time – an enthusiastic and clearly intelligent wannabe filmmaker who called in once and we gave him a job. James actually went on to become a very well-known producer whose film *Still Alice* received a best actress Oscar for Julianne Moore. But at the time he was just a hopeful, and unfortunately we didn't ask James exactly what he planned to say about *School of Rock* before he came into the studio. He sat down in front of Jack Black and tore his movie to shreds, and Jack was apoplectic: 'Who the fuck are you? I'm walkin' into a fuckin ambush here!' He had a joking tone, I thought, but maybe not. I look back now and can't imagine how rude that must have seemed.

That's the funny thing. I think people assume that what we do – this kind of radio that sometimes produces these moments of tension and electricity or shock and awe – are far more intentional than they are. When I say we genuinely didn't know what James Brown was going to say, we didn't. We knew he wasn't a fan of the movie, but we weren't prepared for him to nail Jack so hard on it. We were embarrassed, and mortified, because it was awkward. To this very day, guests are prepped by their PRs and agents and managers and handlers to expect that Kyle might rip them to pieces, and we scratch our heads, because we don't do that to our guests. We rely on celebrities to prop up our show. We don't want to do anything that might burn those bridges.

But I will say that when Kyle was in a bad mood and you poked the bear, he would snap. There was a time when Savage Garden were at their peak, and the record company called ahead to say that Darren Hayes was running late. 'Sorry, he's in traffic, I'm so, so, so sorry – can you guys please fill in until he gets out of the logjam?' We understand unforeseen scheduling snags, but when a guest is late, it's not ideal. We have to change things and it stops the flow of the show, because segments are placed in a given slot for a reason. It's all a carefully calibrated and choreographed dance, and when someone is half an hour late, that throws everything else off balance and impacts the next guest.

When Darren arrived, we could see him from our studio, through the airlock where the producers stand and into reception. His entourage was emerging from the elevator, and they all had McDonald's in their hands. They hadn't been stuck in traffic – they'd stopped at the Maccas drive-thru. Kyle definitely saw it, and his reaction was swift. 'Tell them to get the fuck out – they're not welcome,' he said. 'If they're going to stop at Maccas and that's why they're late, fuck off.' But that's one of the rare instances where Kyle will really butt heads with anyone. It's incredibly rare, actually, and I'm glad of that because I hate being witness to it – let alone being an accessory.

Kyle has also always loved smut and sex talk. That's where he's thrived, and what he thinks everyone else wants to listen to, so he talks about growing up and fingering girls and smelling his hand afterwards, and those kinds of things being brought up on our show just became the norm – became my norm. I could appreciate that he was entertaining, and that when he was wild and unpredictable it was enthralling for the audience, but I'm really not a crude or smutty person. My strategy for coping with this is to remind myself to be the listener in the car, instead of someone deeply attached to him. Because my reaction – as the co-worker and friend who works with him every day – is not the normal reaction of the punter with the radio on. I'm invested. In a way, I'm like a wife when their husband says something embarrassing at a party. I might cringe, but a guest at the same party might just laugh. Early on, I probably wasn't comfortable enough to counter him, so I enabled him instead, with a nervous laugh, a sheepish giggle or a shamefaced chortle. I should have been playing the straight man, but instead I probably became his laugh track.

And this is what I mean about the cats away and the mice playing. It was clear that no parents or executives were listening. It was literally just us and the kids every night. As the ratings grew more and more, Kyle pushed the boundaries more and more. He didn't plan his ideas – he just thought of them off the cuff. Kyle has one of the quickest minds of anyone I know.

He couldn't be stopped, and still can't. He didn't push boundaries to make headlines – nor did he expect to. Radio was somewhat dismissed within the media hierarchy, and because we were the kids at night, we were dismissed too, and that infuriated Kyle. It drove him mad, because he wanted to be taken seriously. He wanted breakfast radio. I couldn't see it.

'Dream on, mate,' I'd say.

'That's where we're headed,' he'd reply.

That's what I love about Kyle. He always believed in us, in our potential, and in me.

Five

Lee and I were young, we were comfortable, we were in love, and now we were on holiday in Paris – the legendary City of Light, *la ville lumière* – so why does a negative memory stand out?

We were wandering lamplit streets, looking for somewhere to have dinner, before finally popping into one of those little French cafes with an ornate art nouveau fit-out. I felt so pretty and Parisian, and I wanted to order a croissant for dinner, but Lee wouldn't let me. 'That's embarrassing – you can't order a croissant for dinner in Paris,' he said. 'They'll think you're just a bogan tourist.' We argued for what felt like forever, and we left before ordering anything. I never got my croissant.

Yet it was actually a wonderful holiday – how could you not get swept away by that place? Lee and I were smitten with one another, exploring the world together, and Paris is wall-to-wall postcard pictures, walking down the Champs-Élysées and under the Arc de Triomphe, along the Seine and past the Louvre, across the cobblestones of Montmartre, with the Eiffel Tower always looming in the distance. But there was one thing missing from the trip. I was waiting for Lee to propose, and it didn't happen.

This wasn't just a hunch of mine, either. We had picked a ring. We were walking in Double Bay one day and stepped into an antique jewellery store. I loved the romanticism of all the dainty designs, but one stood out. I loved it. It was only $800, at most.

I wanted Lee in my life, desperately. Probably because he was utterly seductive to me – so exotic and cultured, so tall, dark and handsome. I admired and respected him. He was decent, and I trusted him. We had similar values and character, with similar upbringings. We had the same interests and tastes, and we knew how to have *fun* together. I could see him making a wonderful father. I just couldn't imagine my life with anyone else. I still saw him as this unattainable man – *He's the catch of the century, I'm so lucky to have him* – because I didn't have the sense to stop and ask the right questions.

Is this guy actually right for you?

Do you really want to spend the rest of your life with him?

And if you do, why on earth aren't you being yourself around him?

I was a tragic romantic when it came to this guy. I remember wanting to do something really thoughtful for his birthday, so I went to his office after he had already gone in, and I snuck up to the receptionist. 'Listen, it's his birthday, and I've got all these individual roses with notes that I want delivered to him every hour. This is all of them – do you reckon you could pretend a courier has come each time, and call him to reception?' She loved being in cahoots on it. He thought it was very sweet, but five hours in, on his fifth trip to reception, he knew what was going on and asked for the rest all at once.

We wrote each other a letter, being honest about our love. We jotted down the things we wanted to do better for one another. It was a beautiful exchange. We knew we were headed somewhere together. We were walking on air.

He eventually organised a romantic day out for us. We caught a seaplane from outside Catalina in Rose Bay, over to the northern part of Sydney, to a restaurant at Cottage Point you can only reach by air. We sat outside, and it was the hottest day imaginable, but the water was catching the sun and there was light in my big sappy eyes, and I remember sitting down and Lee proposing, saying all the right things – such lovely, lovely things – and me bursting with happiness as I said 'Yes'.

The only black mark on that day was my stomach. I couldn't hold down any food, constantly getting up and going to the bathroom. It turns out, I was unexpectedly pregnant. It was morning sickness. But I wasn't remotely ready for motherhood. We had thrashed it out in numerous heavy conversations, and there was no dissenting view. We felt that we were not in a position to raise a child – in fact, we were nowhere near wanting to settle down in such a way. Yes, we were going to get married, but we were also young and growing and establishing ourselves, and living through that stage in life where everything is seemingly still in flux. It sounds selfish, but we wanted to experience that, and travel, and enjoy our lives. I'd finally got a good pay cheque, and the show was finding its feet. It was an incredibly tough decision, but – through tears – we made the one we felt was right. Because we weren't ready. We just weren't.

I remember being anxious walking into that family planning clinic in Woollahra. There was some comfort in the fact that everyone in that waiting room was there for the same reason, and would hopefully feel the same degree of empathy towards everyone else. I just trusted the people around me, because we were all part of the same club, bound by the same shame or fear or melancholy.

How does it work? You go into what feels like a doctor's surgery. You sit in a waiting room for ten minutes. You go into an operating room. Then they put you under. It doesn't even feel like an operation. It's all so quick, so sober, so perfunctory. You wake up, and that's emotional. I know there were tears on my face, definitely, and if I think about it deeply all these years later, even for a moment, there are tears now, too.

In some ways I feel it more now than then. I think I put on a brave face at the time, but it just has more gravity as time goes by. When you're young, you make this decision that's not exactly flippant, but definitely functional – as if an abortion was almost an inevitable alternative to the morning-after pill, or contraception. But as your emotional education continues in life, you reflect on the actions of your past differently. Or maybe when you're young you just don't want to acknowledge that you're doing something momentous.

I definitely think it's something you consider more once you have your own child, as I do now. Watching my daughter grow up, I look back and wonder, more than a little wistfully: *What did I do?* You begin to ponder what might have been. Was it a boy or a girl? What personality would they have had? How old would they be now? You try not to beat yourself up too much, but you do the maths every year. I don't know why, but I always thought it was a boy. A son. My son would be turning twenty-three this year.

None of this was enunciated when I walked out of that medical centre in Woollahra, and let me be clear on this: I didn't regret my decision. I still don't. But that doesn't mean it was easy. I left there a little shell-shocked, and the morning moved into the afternoon, which turned quietly into the night, and I took myself to bed with a cup of tea and hot water bottle. And then I woke up and brushed those feelings under the carpet right away, took a deep breath and made the decision – for self-preservation as much as anything – to look forward more than I looked back.

—

Lee and I were married in 2003, not far away from that medical centre in a beautiful big stone chapel in Woollahra. But it was an exciting day, a great day, shared with around eighty people including my entire family, even the Tasmanian contingent. For the reception, we shut down Catalina on Rose Bay. Alex Perry designed my dress. I remember I was so skinny for my wedding. I was the ambassador for Holeproof, and I had to do a lingerie photo shoot – meaning a spread in a magazine, in my underwear. I look back on photos of myself from around that time, from before I got skinny for those pictures, and I had such a beautiful figure, but for some reason I didn't think I did. You would never have caught me in a skimpy bikini in front of anyone. *Never.* I was so insecure. And so I quite literally starved myself for those photographs. I lost 7 kilos in a matter of weeks, following a simple and strict regimen of what probably counts as self-abuse. I would exercise, have a glass of wine and cigarettes, and eat nothing. Thank god I have a healthy relationship with my body now and would never behave like that. But, snap, just like that, I was down to what I thought at the time was the perfect weight. People like to say how radiant a bride looks on their wedding day – how they glow and shimmer and shine, all luminescence and light. Kyle said I looked like a chicken carcass walking down the aisle. He wasn't wrong.

It was a beautiful 27-degree day, with pelicans perched on the balcony or floating on the light breeze above. I remember we had choreographed our first dance, but as it got closer I realised I was drunk. A lack of food and raising one too many glasses during the speeches will have that effect. We had to put off cutting the cake and the dance so I could go to the bathroom for twenty minutes, to drink water and sober up!

New Idea wanted to shoot the nuptials and put us on the cover of the magazine, and in return they would pay for the wedding – all eighty grand – and we had said 'Hell yes.' Because they had an exclusive, it made all the other magazines want photos even more, meaning I had to hide in transit on the day, with an explicit warning: 'You *cannot* be photographed in your dress.' They hired men to open umbrellas all around me, and went to other great lengths to make sure that *Woman's Day* or some other publication didn't steal their money shot. It was an absolute spectacle. I would never do it that way now, but I didn't care back then. I loved my wedding day.

Once the dust settled, we had half a year of married bliss – a honeymoon period after our actual honeymoon on Hayman Island. We always had periods like that in our relationship, where we were so aligned and happy and equal, and then it would come crashing down, often slowly, and we would gradually descend into the pits and fight until one of us stormed out or stayed in a hotel room for the night. Then we would make up, and hold each other, and hope it didn't happen again, all the while knowing it almost certainly would.

To go with that emotional pain, I was also suffering serious and debilitating physical pain. This pain was a long-running ordeal, actually, which had started back in Adelaide. I woke up one morning and had no idea what was happening to me, except that I had my period and my body was in the most excruciating pain. I went to the doctor and he tried to assuage my fears. 'It was just bad period pain,' he said. 'Nothing a few Panadol and a cuppa and a hot wheat cushion won't cure.' I believed him, too, because it wasn't happening all the time.

But I was scared. This mystery pain in my uterus would only flare up every four or five months in the beginning, but it was so acute as to be alarming. It felt as if someone had a sharp knife inside me, down low, and they were twisting the blade, slicing up my sensitive centre. It would always come on around 2 a.m. and then last for the entire first day of my period, meaning I was up all night and day with undiagnosed agony.

I went from doctor to doctor, searching not so much for an explanation as a salve. My primary concern was my suffering. I didn't care if this fucking thing had a name, only if it had a cure. It had neither. I remember doing an ultrasound to see if I had an ovarian cyst, but I didn't.

'Sorry,' they said. 'We can't figure out what it is.' And if they couldn't figure it out, what chance did I have? Even at the beginning of the new millennium, the internet was a nascent research tool and a largely untapped source of information. You didn't jump on Yahoo or Ask Jeeves to search up symptoms – there was no such thing as Dr Google. There were really only doctors, and it took years before one finally gave my pain a name: endometriosis.

It was a gynaecologist at St Vincent's Hospital who gave me the news. I had a disease – common to as many as one in ten women around the world – in which a tissue similar to that found inside the uterus grows *outside* the uterus, causing pain and inflammation, and sometimes infertility. The torture I was experiencing was exactly in keeping with the condition. 'Just so you know, the pain can be pretty much the equivalent of giving birth,' said one doctor. 'So by the time you have a baby, you'll be so used to it that you'll be fine!' He said it with a smile, as if that was a silver lining – that I would be experiencing the pain of childbirth every month.

There was an operation they could do that would limit or stop the symptoms, and I had it done, but the effect was temporary. I sought medication instead, but it was hard to find anything that could numb the sensation. I remember getting prescribed a strong painkiller called tramadol – but even that barely touched the sides. By the time I was thirty, it got to the point where Lee was driving me to hospital in the middle of the night every other month so I could stay overnight on a morphine drip, because that was the only thing that could blunt the pain.

Surely there had to be an easier way, I thought. I tried different doctors to see if there were different approaches. One finally had a solution, but he was reluctant to make the suggestion. Endone, the Australian equivalent of the drug known as OxyContin in the United States, was an option. I didn't know a lot about it at the time – this was two decades ago, before it had become infamous as the pharmaceutical drug responsible for more deaths than any other. It's the same drug that led Matthew Perry down his tragic path of addiction, although my dose was not nearly as strong, thanks to Australian laws. Before I popped my first Endone, in fact, I remember doing the O News when Matthew's addiction to painkillers first came to light, and I recall saying then that I just didn't get how anyone could become addicted to painkillers. At the time, my under-standing of pain relief medication was limited – I didn't understand the scope of the different kinds of drugs or realise there was any 'high' involved. I honestly couldn't compute the idea of something as seemingly innocuous as pain relief becoming addictive.

Now here was this doctor, prescription pad in hand, stressing the absolute importance of taking only one pill, and only when necessary. 'Please don't take them unless you have to – they're highly addictive,' he cautioned. 'I'm not really even that comfortable giving them to you.' I heard him, but part of me wasn't really listening. All I took away from the consultation was the news that, finally, *this* might be the drug that was potent enough to take the pain away. *Yeah, yeah, yeah*, I thought. *I'm not gonna get addicted to Panadol!*

I waited until my next period, and only took the Endone tablet when the pain became intolerable, and it helped in a way that nothing else had. It was miraculous. The pain was still there but also strangely bearable. Stranger still, it sent me into a state of total euphoria – a sensation so enjoyable that I almost looked forward to the next month when I could experience it all over again.

I was careful to follow doctor's orders . . . until a few months later, after a particularly tense period with Lee. I decided it couldn't hurt if I took one as a way of coping with the stress and anxiety, while also escaping to a happier place. From there on, it became a slippery slope of finding any old excuse to take another 'happy pill', and before I knew it I was taking them just for fun. After about a year of this, I stopped, not for lack of wanting but rather due to a lack of accessibility. Endone was almost impossible to get – doctors rarely prescribed it in this country. Had I been able to get them, my flirtation with the drug would have escalated to an addiction then and there. Ultimately, I was incredibly lucky. I was only taking a few a day, so I was able to stop without any severe side effects.

I threw myself into my marriage, but we were still labouring, on and off. It felt fine so often, but our communication was poor – too much of the time we left too much unsaid. I wanted to fix things, but I didn't have the emotional intelligence to speak to Lee about the heart of our differences. I don't know if I lacked the courage, or the insight, or the vocabulary. All I know is we both got used to living with elephants in every room.

Instead, I tried superficial solutions. I remember on one of his birthdays, maybe in 2006, I bought him a brand-new car – a big black Ford Territory. I found a parking spot for it across the road, outside our local cafe. I said, 'Let's go for a drive' and brought him down to our regular car – the Ford Focus. We got in, then I turned to him and smiled. 'We're not actually going for a drive in this,' I said. 'I've got a surprise for you. Look over there – it's your new car.' His reaction is one I'll never forget.

'Oh my god,' Lee said. 'I think I'm going to be sick.'

I'd been so excited to present my gift to Lee that when he said that I immediately felt sick, too. My gesture had backfired so badly, and we just sat there in awkward silence. But I think I understood. I ended up taking the Territory myself, and Lee took the Focus. And that was just one of many silly sugar-rush solutions I pursued, instead of being honest and having it out and addressing the underlying issues.

Another example? We were beginning to feel trapped in our Elizabeth Bay apartment, but we couldn't afford a house in Sydney yet, so we looked at country properties, something with land – where we could go and be still together on weekends. We scoured Kangaroo Valley, two hours south of Sydney, beyond the Southern Highlands, and we found a 99-acre property with incredible views of the escarpment, and waterfalls, and greenery, and we bought a vacant block there with the idea of building our dream home. It would be the perfect project for Lee, who was passionate about architecture and design, and for a time it was exactly that. He worked hard on it, pouring himself into it every day, and we slowly built it together – this beautiful, single-level Hamptons-style home in the bush.

It took time. When we first started, all that was there was a shed – and I do mean a shed. We put a little bed in there, and we would go every weekend and sleep there while Lee built and landscaped and brought the project to life. But that bloody shed – where we slept, with no air-conditioning or warmth, with bugs and dirt and lanterns for lights – was horrible. Lee loved it there, though, and would go down during the week to mow the lawns or build a fence, or take care of the invasive fireweed that can overtake a property. We got cattle for pets – these big furry highland cows – Galloways – and we named them all. There was Tammy and Ted, Patty and Selma, and we would hang out with them and sit with them as if they were our children.

I adored them, but they also pooed everywhere, and that drew blowflies. You would open the door to the shed and be engulfed in this blazing swarm of buzzing blowies. We put up those sticky double-sided bug strips, which dangled from the rafters like party streamers, meaning we would come down to the property on a Friday and find these black ropey strands of death swaying from the ceiling, each one stickered with a few thousand deceased flies. That was just how things went. I'd get past that and go to sleep, and a huntsman would drop on my face, then I'd spend ten minutes trying to find a monstrous spider in the covers before giving up, knowing it was still creeping somewhere nearby. I tried to live with it, or love it, for Lee, but I hated it, and that's entirely on me. Again, there was no communication on my part. I would just smile and pretend, utterly unwilling to be myself.

I've been this way all my life – a people-pleaser, preferring my own discomfort to anyone else's. All I needed to do was push through that and say three simple words – 'Talk to me' – but I couldn't even do that.

Six

At least things were going well on the radio. We were no longer the kids at night, and instead, in 2004 – in the lead-up to my wedding – we were given our own program in the afternoon drive slot. This was a massive leap. It felt as though we were being given training wheels, or a taste of the big time, in case we might make decent morning radio hosts a few years down the track. *The Kyle and Jackie O Show* was born that year, and we did well. It didn't take long until we found ourselves jostling and snarling for the number one spot in every ratings survey. This sounds so privileged, but being number one was all I had really known in radio, so I clearly remember the day when we got beaten by *The Shebang*, hosted by Marty Sheargold and Fifi Box.

They were at Triple M, one level above us in the same building. It's common for one broadcast network – such as Southern Cross Austereo, for instance – to own two stations in the same market, in the same way as Gold and KIIS belong to one entity, or Nova and Smooth. But it means your opposition is often in the same space – you see them in the kitchen, or the bathroom. You have a conversation with them in the hall, or cubicle to cubicle. I do that all the time with Amanda Keller, one of our direct opponents right now. You tend not to have a *fierce* rivalry with those in the same building – it's generally friendly. But still. I remember we ran into the general manager of the station at the elevator, and he was about to say something to us, then he saw Marty and Fifi and immediately switched his focus to them – 'Hey guys!' – with pats on the back and hugs, and a complete cold shoulder for us. And I remember this sensation slowly dawning on me, *Oh, so* this *is what it's like* not *being on top*, and I felt so slighted. I didn't like it all.

But we were clearly valued, because we were in an important role. Drive is a critical program in radio – basically the second most important slot of the day after breakfast. The two programs are almost joined at the hip, the theory being that your typical listener gets out of bed, gets dressed, has brekkie, jumps into the car, (hopefully) turns their FM dial to KIIS, listens and laughs throughout their commute, then goes to work. When they knock off for the day, and they jump back into their car at 5 p.m., the dial is *still* on KIIS, so they keep right on listening all the way home, until that car rolls into the driveway.

The two time slots bookend the most pivotal part of the daily radio life cycle.

The appointment to drive felt like more than an audition, too, because there was significant upheaval at 2Day FM. Wendy Harmer – a beloved host with a long legacy – had just resigned. They brought in comedians Judith Lucy and Peter Helliar as the new breakfast hosts, but they did not do well. The numbers took a swift dive, in part because of the absence of that heritage host. It's almost a golden rule in radio – never take over from an icon, because there's only one way to go. More often than not, the audience just isn't ready for something new, so the first person to sit in the vacated chair becomes a sacrificial lamb.

It didn't help either that Judith was an acquired taste. She always had a distinct voice and style as a performer, and it wasn't resonating with Sydney. There was a huge backlash against her, ugly enough that she would one day end up doing an entire standup tour about her unsuccessful stint there, which lasted eighteen months. Later she noted that radio announcers are required to 'leave your brain and your dignity at the door'. But full credit to her for taking in her stride, and mining that experience for whatever she could. It must have been hard.

In radio, after all, your worth isn't exactly judged on what you do – on how quickly you build a house, or how many clients you sign, or how many units you ship – but on who you are. I think that's why you become so resilient, working in this field. Even on television there's a facade you're working within, created by a vast team of producers and writers, presented and edited with exactitude. On the airwaves, however, you're speaking your truth every day, often shooting from the hip, leaving little of yourself to the imagination, and if people don't like that – if people hate what you're offering, when what you're offering is *you* – your ego can take an almighty bruising.

I was really sensitive to feedback at this time. I remember once Kyle had read a story about me in the newspaper – a journalist had written a listicle about the worst music in the world, naming various bands or artists, and in his number one spot was 'Anything Jackie O listens to.' And when Kyle told me that, all I could do was be stunned that someone hated me that much. It completely threw me for a loop, ruining my night and day, and one day after that. I was devastated – by some petty piece of snark – because I used to take it all to heart. Thank god I don't do that to myself anymore. With social media being what it's become, I'd be in the foetal position daily.

There is a question around how much commentary and abuse you can consume about yourself. It's a question that used to weigh on me a lot. Now, I don't get trolled that much – but when I do, it never spoils my day anymore. If I make the mistake of reading the comments section, I've at least reached the point now where one out of every one thousand comments might spoil my day – and I can ignore the remaining nine hundred and ninety-nine. Over the years your skin just thickens and you reach a point where you don't care, because you *can't* care, because caring would be a full-time job, and a shitty one at that.

It's liberating to get where I am now, but it's a good lesson for anyone who wants to work in radio. Judith Lucy might think you need to put aside your brains and dignity – I'd say you need to put aside your beliefs and judgements of others. If you're worried about what people will say or write about you, it will alter what you do. There are too many opinions you won't voice, topics you won't explore and places you just won't go – and you'll never deliver a good show that way. You need to be okay with making the following statement: 'This segment or state-ment might make a *terrible* headline, but it's also going to make entertaining radio.'

Getting to that point doesn't come easily, though. I remember being asked to emcee a music festival in Darwin – basically asked to introduce a few bands on stage. I don't know why they chose me, but it was a paid gig. All I had to do was fly to the Northern Territory, welcome a few bands on stage, get back on a plane and fly home, and I'd be richer by $10,000. That's a lot of money when you're paying off a first mortgage, so you snap up all those things. But I slept through my alarm that day – I could have *died* of embarrassment – and by the time I got up and going I knew I wouldn't be there until late, barely in time to introduce maybe one band, and that band was Frenzal Rhomb. To be honest, I had no business being there anyway, and I wasn't the only one thinking that, because once Frenzal Rhomb got up on stage, they said to the packed festival audience: 'Why the fuck is Jackie O here?'

I mentioned that to Kyle when I got home and, bless him, he flew into a righteous anger. 'Fuck them,' he spat. 'We're gonna go on air and nail them to the fucking wall!' He leant into the microphone that afternoon and let loose – 'We're never gonna play Frenzal Rhomb on this radio station!' – which was the funniest empty threat, given we would never play that kind of music anyway. The band caught wind of it, though, and retaliated on Triple J – 'We don't wanna be on your crappy station anyway, so fuck off!' – and that made their whole audience turn against me. I got bombarded with hate mail, constantly, for weeks on end. It was the first time I'd experienced bullying on a large scale, where people turned against me en masse. As the phone calls, letters and emails kept flowing in, I found myself in this constant depressive state, as if I'd broken up with a boyfriend and couldn't get that sadness out of my mind. When the mob comes for you, it triggers all your core wounds and insecurities, and makes you feel your defectiveness. You can get on air and pretend to be happy, but it's there, hiding behind your smile.

This went on for a full month, all day, every day. And to this day I *still* get comments on my social media feed about it, with two simple words that need no explanation – 'Frenzal Rhomb'. Only this time, I have a smile on my face. In hindsight I find it amusing, and it no longer affects me.

In a way, I look back on it and I'm almost thankful that I experienced something so extreme so early in my career, because the next time something happened, I was equipped to deal with it and cope.

You have to face criticism from within, too, of course. Producers and managers and executives all have their notes and critiques, sometimes constructive but often not. After we had done drive time for a year and were primed to take over the breakfast slot, Kyle shared a doubt he had heard about me from above. We were at his house. He lived around the corner from us in Elizabeth Bay, and Lee and I would go over there every weekend, listen to music and dance and drink with Kyle and his first wife, Tamara, and we would workshop ideas for the show. The crux of the concern Kyle had heard was this: the higher-ups were worried about me going into breakfast, because they felt that I wasn't a strong enough woman. Apparently I wasn't opinionated enough. And that pissed me off. It still does.

Why should I have to be forceful and opinionated for the sake of it? And why does having an opinion mean it has to be delivered forcefully, without any wiggle room or give? I have opinions, but I deliver them in my own way. I've always stood firm on that. Topics also come up all the time where a woman – always a woman – is expected to fight the good fight, but if I don't feel strongly about a topic in the moment, I'm not going to pretend.

The same applies to Kyle's humour. Sometimes it's offensive and sometimes it's outrageous – believe me,

I get it – and I definitely step in when I feel as if he's crossed a line. But if I don't find some specific joke or stance offensive or outrageous, I'm not going to pretend that I do because of what the audience expects. Why should I fit into someone else's imaginary box? Not everyone is loud. Not everyone is opinionated. My co-host has more than enough of that for the both of us, so why can't I appeal to those people who don't feel passionately or strongly about every little thing in this world – who are maybe just a touch softer or more introverted? The world is polarised enough already; I'm not going to exhaust myself by taking some pantomime position on every culture war or outrage.

Basically, I talk for a living – on air – for between four and five hours every day, meaning roughly twenty-five hours each week. If I were to spend that entire time second-guessing myself, that's not a good place to be as a broadcaster. I know I'm not always going to get it right, or strike the right balance, but if I'm worried about that every morning then I'm not doing my job properly.

Still, the bosses got over their doubts about me and took us on, bringing us to breakfast. This was prime time, in the biggest city in Australia. And, make no mistake, we were a gamble. We still felt like kids who had been speaking only to kids, and this was a serious do-or-die moment. Kyle is the risk-taker between us, so he was more than fine with the situation, whereas I play it safe, and vividly remember thinking we should consider just staying on drive. 'We're safe here – it's not all on our shoulders,'

I reasoned. 'If we go to breakfast and fail, we're done.' You're never going to get another major job in radio if you wilt in the brightest spotlight. Did we really have to step onto the main stage so quickly?

There was never really a choice, however, because Kyle had enough faith for the two of us. There was no doubt in his mind whatsoever. He was a complete steamroller, and the shift to breakfast was probably largely his doing, through sheer persistence alone. He was the squeaky wheel who got the grease – the one who would go in to see the executives every second day – 'When are you going to put us on breakfast?' – to badger and cajole and, ultimately, convince. I don't even know if they planned our move so much as just relented to the constant harassment from Kyle. 'Oh, for fucks sake,' you could imagine them saying. 'We'll give you your chance – just leave us alone!'

We had our work cut out for us. Nova had recently launched, and they were the brand-new shiny, slick toy. Their marketing was clever and cool – never more than two ads in a row, which was so appealing to listeners – and suddenly we didn't look so hip. They had Merrick and Rosso, cool young guys who'd come from Triple J with energy and credence, and relaxed humour. They were a real threat. By contrast, we had a bit of an old-man stink about us. They were number one when we first began competing, but that was fine. We were so far down in the ratings that we felt as if we had nothing to lose. It was a free hit, and they knew it, and they hated us, too.

We did well in the ratings right away, our numbers creeping and creeping up. We were always gaining on them, closing that gap, until finally we caught them, and that caught them off guard. We felt it in person one day. As part of the job, you often interview filmmakers or actors, and you have to go see their movie in these special screening suites at the studios before you can secure the interview. They're these little theatrettes the size of a living room, and often you're sitting there watching the film with all of your competitors. On this day we went to Sony Pictures in the city, and as we arrived Merrick and Rosso were in the lift, but the doors were closing, and we put out an arm to hold them open. How symbolic. We stepped inside and we were so bubbly – 'Hey guys!' – because it was the first time we had ever met them. But they just ignored us, genuinely and completely, with total silence – a grunt of acknowledgement, at most. And it was like that every time we saw them. Now that we're all grown up, it's a very different story. We all get along these days, to the point where Rosso has filled in for Kyle when he's been sick.

Stepping into breakfast, the tone of our show shifted quickly. It was a bigger audience, and an older one, and we had to adjust accordingly. We restructured the entire format, endlessly workshopping ideas. We used to meet up at Kyle's and brainstorm together, trying to come up with new 'benchmarks' – the set furniture pieces of the show that remain unchanged each day, such as the opener or the gossip segment. Lee was actually great at these ideas.

He came up with the pop quiz, which we started then and have done for twenty years since.

We found new ways to explore all topics, going from relationships to the news to giving back to people in need. We wanted to create a roller-coaster ride. We wanted listeners to be stunned one minute, crying the next, and pissing themselves laughing at the end. That was to be our point of difference. We were a very different show to what we are now. Now, we're a lot more authentic – trusting our own voices to meander here, there and everywhere – whereas back then it was all more contrived. It wasn't fake, but we definitely did things for shock value. There were segments I'm still ashamed of now – mortified to even remember.

We did an intervention segment, for instance, which was often harmless enough – someone bringing in their co-worker to tell them they have BO – but on the day that stands out most, a school teacher wanted to do an intervention with her colleague because she knew she was an alcoholic. It's a surprise segment. The subject doesn't know what's coming, and then they're hit with it on air – confronted and outed by a loved one – before reacting in real time. We didn't identify the woman, but who knows, maybe someone could have figured it out. Either way, it's unforgivable. It was an episode I brought up much later in rehab, actually, because I'm still deeply ashamed of it. This poor woman, maybe in her mid-forties, came into the studio, live on air, and her friend said, 'I know you're an alcoholic.' And she didn't deny it – she just sat there and accepted it and looked sad.

I remember thinking at the time, *This is horrible – what the fuck are we doing?* But something strange happens when you're on air, or even when you're planning your show. Half of your brain is thinking like a normal human being – *This is fucked up* – but the other half is in entertainment mode – *We're delivering something for the audience to talk about today* – meaning you end up with this distorted and split perspective, where you can lose sight of reality itself.

We were also number one quite soon after starting, and the thing is, while it might be hard to get to number one, it feels even harder to stay there. You're so afraid of inertia that you'll do anything to maintain momentum. You're like Lady Gaga wearing a meat dress to the MTV Video Music Awards one year, then trying to top that the following year by emerging on stage at the Grammys from an egg, and before you know it you're at South by Southwest letting a performer vomit all over your body in the name of art. You get so far into your head that you're ultimately competing with your own sense of spectacle. And I think this is where we lost our way. Big time.

'Dearly Deported' is another segment I deeply regret. We had two Vietnamese sisters on the show, one who was living in Sydney, and one who was living in Vietnam. They hadn't seen one another in seven years, and the conceit was this: we would bring them both into the studio and set them up in separate glass booths with mics and head-phones, so they could see and hear one another, without touching. If they could answer three questions correctly, they got to reunite. And if they didn't, well, then one would go back to her life in suburban Sydney, and the other would be on a plane towards Ho Chi Minh City. They got the questions wrong, and were separated – crying – without so much as a hug. I *hate* that memory.

But the biggest wake-up call for us was when we put a fourteen-year-old girl on a lie detector test. The design of the segment itself wasn't too problematic. We had done 'Lie Detector' with people in relationships – popular questions included 'Do you really love me?' and 'Are you cheating on me?' – but those people absolutely knew what they were doing, so it never felt vindictive or exploitative. The problem was we weren't looking carefully enough at how wrong it could go, and our hubris caught up with us when this teenage girl was dragged into the studio by her mum. The mum told us she wanted to know if her girl was doing drugs, but on the day itself, the mum went rogue on us, instead asking if the girl had ever had sex. The girl was unimpressed, and with good reason.

'I've already told you the story about this,' she said to her mum, 'and don't look at me and smile, because it's not funny.' She paused a moment, then raised her voice: 'I got raped when I was twelve years old.'

Kyle was doing the show remotely that day, from a studio in New Zealand, and just couldn't or didn't read the room. Instead he asked a follow up question – 'Is that the only experience you've had?' – and that felt like my cue to shut the segment down, immediately. Not that it mattered. This snippet of radio became an infamous story – a saga, really – weighed in on by police and advocates and politicians, all whacking us, and fair enough. We were even briefly taken off air. Mistakes such as this will happen when you're flying down the road at speed, zigging and zagging for fun without checking your blind spots.

That said, when you're public enemy number one for breaking the rules of decency, the people who want to hurt you have no qualms about breaking the rules of engagement. We were the bad guys now, and that seemed to mean that anyone in the press could misrepresent us or take us out of context. We were fair game.

The house in Kangaroo Valley was finished by now – a little escape from Sydney, which I loved. We would be there every weekend, me inside reading a book and Lee outside working the land. He loved getting his hands dirty, even if it meant the occasional accident. One time a tractor toppled over and would have killed him had he not slipped away at the last second. Another time, during the Lie Detector fiasco, he was there and I was in Paddington, and he was cleaning up dead wood and burning off the limbs in a great big bonfire pile, but somehow Lee ended up in the middle of the pile and went up in flames. He was transported by chopper to Sydney with awful burns all over his face and arms. When I told the story of this terrible accident to Kyle on air, one news station replayed that tape, but grabbed a separate and unrelated sliver of audio of me laughing, and stitched the two together, just to drive the boot in a little more. It was the worst kind of pile-on – literal fake news – and yet I also knew we had no moral high ground to stand on to call them out.

I need to point out that every time we've created one of these media storms, it's almost never been intentional. There was always this sense from the public that we were causing a stir on purpose – 'That's exactly what they want!' – yet I can hand on my heart say that we weren't, and still aren't. The nickname 'Vile Kyle' was born anyway, and then when no scandal ever seemed big enough to cancel him, he became 'Teflon Kyle'. But there were definitely consequences. Channel 10 fired Kyle from his job as a judge on *Australian Idol*, because television is far more conservative than radio. 2Day was losing money, too, as advertisers withdrew, and the executives did not like it one bit. Contrary to the old saying, some publicity is just shit publicity.

The biggest change was the introduction of a censor, hired by the station, specifically for our show. They built her a special desk, where she could monitor what we were saying and doing in real time, to make the call on what was broadcast. We were put on a thirty-second delay, so were no longer entirely live, and whenever something defamatory or profane or controversial was said, she could beep us. It must be the toughest job imaginable – making a judgement call on every little thing Kyle says, these constant micro-decisions trying to imagine potential fallout. *Will that become a bad headline? Or a code breach? Will it cost us advertisers?* The pressure must have been immense.

They installed a traffic light in our studio. The orange light is a warning – that you're walking dangerously close to being beeped, or worse, dumped. You get used to the orange light – it would go off once every three segments, giving you a chance to walk it back or tone it down. Sometimes Kyle will see the orange again and again and plead with the control booth: 'Stop flashing the fucking light! This is fine!'

When the green light goes off, you know that whatever has been said has been beeped – effectively censored, because you've gone just that little bit too far, been a touch too lascivious, or been loose enough to drop an F-bomb.

But if the red light goes off, it means the entire previous thirty seconds of the show has been dumped, because it's beyond redemption. Listeners get a message – 'The station you've been listening to has been dumped. This means someone has said something inappropriate, and is currently getting in trouble. The broadcast will return in seconds' – after which we come back on air while an ad break is played, allowing that thirty-second delay to build once more.

It's not foolproof. There are times when the censor didn't even throw up an orange light, yet a segment or a statement became an issue in the press. We were chatting about the story of Jesus and Mary once, and Kyle made some off-the-cuff remark about Mary being out the back of the shed having sex with someone else. It wasn't flagged at all. We went on holidays, and during our break the station social media manager remembered the clip, thought it was funny, and popped it on social media. It was shared and shared again, and this comment that had already been heard by hundreds of thousands of people – sliding right on through to the keeper without complaint – found traction on a different platform and turned into a minor controversy.

Only a few weeks after the lie detector moment, things got even worse when Kyle – yet again – ventured into an area it's never wise to tread. He was joking about Magda Szubanski, who had lost 25 kilograms as spokesperson for a weight loss company. Kyle was being a smartarse, saying that she could get more dollars out of them, because there was much more fat to shed. I suggested that she might not be *able* to lose any more weight, due to her build, but Kyle was on a roll. 'That's what all fat people say,' he said. 'You put her in a concentration camp and you watch the weight fall.'

All hell broke loose, naturally. Magda is Jewish, and her family was from Poland, the location of many of the worst Nazi concentration camps, including the infamous Auschwitz. Magda's father was a Polish resistance fighter during World War II. It was stupid terrain to joke about at all, but in connection with a beloved Jewish Australian comedian, it became a firestorm. Kyle had to be educated about the history surrounding the joke, and he did so, spending time at a local Holocaust museum. He admits that he truly didn't grasp how much he could hurt people with those words, and how offensive they were.

I reached out to Magda personally, because I wanted to apologise, and she was gracious enough to take my call. She understood I hadn't done anything, but she did have a message for me: 'If you lie with dogs you'll get fleas, and that's all I want to say on the matter.' We're now friends with Magda, and she comes on the show all the time, because we've moved on and changed as people.

People often asked me whether I was getting desensitised to our shtick. Horrible experiences such as the Frenzal Rhomb attack not only give you resilience, but they help you build a wall, and detach you from your feelings.

During this period, even as these events played out, our ratings continued to grow. It was odd to be experiencing professional growth at the detriment of my own morals and values, but I did learn from this. While it would be impossible to promise to never make a mistake again when we're live on air and making split-second decisions, I will always try to own up to and learn from those mistakes.

Seven

My private life and radio life intersect often, almost daily, but rarely is that overlap as distinct or strange as it became one day when I was in my mid-thirties. We were doing a segment on air one morning where Kyle was bragging that he had 'super sperm' – a typically outlandish claim. That boast turned into a back-and-forth with Geoff Field, our newsreader at the time, who was really the first out and proud gay newsreader in the country. Somehow it turned into a competition, in which those two and Lee would all come into the office one day, go into the bathroom at work, do their business, and get their semen samples tested. Lee was referred to often enough to be a known character to our audience, but I'm still surprised he agreed to come in to, well, come.

We were perhaps more surprised by the outcome. Kyle's

sperm was fine. Geoff's was fine, too. But while Lee had a lot of swimmers, their motility – the efficiency with which they move through a woman's reproductive system – was quite low. Lee and I hadn't struggled to fall pregnant in the past – obviously, given the abortion I'd had years earlier – but at this point we had been trying to have a baby for a year, without success, before finally sensing something might be amiss. There was always a part of me that wondered if I was going to be punished because of the abortion. I had given up that offering years earlier, and it played in the back of my mind constantly. *Maybe I won't be able to have children*, I'd think. *Maybe the universe will slap me on the wrist.*

It was Lee who suggested we try in-vitro fertilisation. I'm so thankful he did. I wasn't troubled by the IVF process. It starts with having to take these daily injections, in your stomach or your leg or your bum or wherever. You slap yourself – very hard – wherever you want to put the needle, just to numb the skin in that area, then you plunge it in. I know many women struggle with that part, but I have no issue with needles at all, so it didn't bother me. I was more affected by what was inside the syringe. The hormonal jolt that entered my body was a total nightmare.

Those shots turned me into someone I'm not. I became a bona-fide hysterical person, with all of my most potent emotions heightened, who would let the slightest little thing tip me over the edge into anger. Something that might frustrate you on a normal day – which you move past and get over, treating as a mere blip on the radar – becomes a reason for your wrath and fury. There's this rage inside you that allows any benign irritation to turn into righteous indignation. I got so swept up in the slightest things. Producers I worked with still remember me as being the biggest bitch during that time!

There was a competition we ran, for instance, to be my personal assistant – I'd never had one before – with the prize being a six-month stint working for me. We ended up giving the job to this beautiful and sheltered young boy. Chris Ledlin was maybe nineteen years old, and was new to media. And he started just as I was doing these injections. I still apologise to him every time I see him, because whenever he made the tiniest mistake, I just couldn't control my emotions and frustration. I remember standing in the office one day and saying, 'What's wrong with you?! Why can't you do your job properly?!', when I would *never* normally talk to someone like that. It was almost as though I was standing outside of my body, possessed, as if I was aware of what I was doing but no longer responsible. From the outside, I must have seemed like Miranda Priestly from *The Devil Wears Prada* – an intolerant and intolerable woman. But, who knows, maybe that was the making of Chris. He went on to be incredibly successful, working for Twitter, then running social media for the news division of Nine Entertainment, before finally joining Google and YouTube. We catch up and laugh about it still, and I recently went to his wedding.

After the hormone injections, the egg retrieval comes next. They see how many healthy eggs they can harvest, and we got a lot. Lee did his donation, and from those two contributions we were able to create eleven really healthy embryos. The majority of them are still in storage, still in a freezer somewhere. I don't know what to do with them, but can't bring myself to destroy them. We did the first insemination quickly, and not long afterwards we were at home in our Paddington terrace when we got the call from the doctor to say that we had been successful. We were pregnant, and we were over the moon about it, hugging and crying and falling about on the floor with glee.

I was thirty-five at the time, so I did those early tests to see if the baby was okay, as well as a test for gender. We were given the all-clear for any abnormalities, and when we were told it was a girl, that was even more exciting. We both really wanted a girl. I'd had such a close relationship with my mum, bonding over so many interests that you can't lean on to connect with your father. That was the ideal parent–child relationship in my mind, and I wanted to mirror that with my own child. Lee had grown up around women, with just his mum and his sister in the house, and so that was his comfort and preference, too. He couldn't wait to play with his little girl. Lee is not your typical alpha male – yes, he's athletic and active and strong, but he's also a reader and a thinker – he was never going to be that guy who's desperate to get out in the backyard and kick the footy with his son. But I think we had oddly convinced ourselves that we were having a boy, so this was the best surprise. All I remember is us screaming in the car as if we'd won a million dollars.

The pregnancy felt like a new start for us. Our relationship was going through these constant highs and lows, for months at a time, but it seemed then as if we were in a really good place. The scandals with the lie detector and Magda brought us together, in a way – because Lee is always great in a crisis. It's one of his best traits. He was supportive of me to a fault, and fiercely protective, too, and gave great advice. He steadied me and centred me. He was my rock. He was on the farm a lot at the time, raising a poor baby calf that one of our cows had rejected, and the paparazzi would be down there hiding on the other side of the property line, miles away with a huge lens, trying to get images of him, so I guess we both felt like prisoners. We were in it together, the good and the bad. It might have been the worst of times at work but it was the best of times for us, and my pregnancy only boosted that.

We had a babymoon at the luxury Whitsundays resort, qualia, on Hamilton Island, and grew more and more excited for the birth. We were going through baby names. Ivy. Willow. Jessamine. Our parents were scheduling trips to visit. The only drawback was the intensity of the media interest. The scandals had ramped up the attention, and now I had a baby bump that demanded images. It got to a point where the snappers were driving so recklessly to get their shot. They would often chase us in threes, with two men in one car – one at the wheel and one with a lens – and a third man on a motorbike, there to duck and weave through traffic if it ever looked as if we were getting away. More than once, Lee had to get out of our car in traffic to tell them to fuck off and stop being so dangerous on the roads.

Later, I wondered why I cared so much about stopping them from getting the photos they wanted. It wasn't just privacy. I think I'd been stung by the tabloid media, and I guess I wanted to deny them or punish them somehow – at least make their job harder. I've learnt now that you're so much better off letting them get their shot, because they'll leave you alone once they do.

The pregnancy itself was largely smooth sailing. I know it isn't that way for everyone, but mine was mostly without drama. I had my own set of unique cravings – such as laksa for breakfast every day. There aren't many laksa places open at 6 a.m., of course, so I'd buy one in the afternoon and pop it in the fridge to reheat the next morning. Otherwise, I found myself drawn to milk: I drank around two litres of the stuff every day.

Three-quarters of the way through the pregnancy, we hit our first snag. I was told I was going to need to have a C-section, because the baby was smaller than usual. Then, towards the end, I went in for that final check-up and the doctor paused. The baby was much, much smaller than even he was expecting. He had more bad news, too, and I was so glad that my mum had come to the appointment with me. I would need to go to hospital – immediately – and be on bed rest for the foreseeable future.

'I can't do that,' I blurted out. 'I'm still on air!'

'You have to do this,' he said. 'Your mum has to go home and get all your stuff, and we're taking you to one of the rooms on the ward – right now.'

Thankfully, it was near the end of the year, so the station was able to get Sophie Monk to fill in for me for the rest of the shows, and off to hospital I went. I stayed in bed all day and night – I was only allowed to get up to go to the toilet. At first I was excited by the prospect of bingeing TV all day, but that got boring on day two, and by day three I was going out of my mind. After a week, I was at least allowed to get up and walk around.

Because I was on the maternity ward, there were classes for new mums on how to care for your baby – washing, feeding, et cetera – and those twenty-minute chats were the biggest treat. I attended the same classes every single day, listening to the same talk, learning the same lessons. I couldn't *wait* to give birth, and otherwise just lay there obsessing about that moment to come.

I got given a half-day release soon after that, and maybe a fortnight later I was allowed to go home and onto bed rest there, with no more activity permitted than a short walk per day. It had worked. On the day before Kitty came into the world, we found a little private beach near Clontarf, and we were sitting there on this gorgeous afternoon. My belly looked as if it had really popped – a beautiful basketball for a belly, finally looking as if I was actually pregnant, as I hadn't shown much for most of the pregnancy. But I also weighed less than when I had first fallen pregnant. It was a mixture of stress and an inability to eat as much as I should have. I wasn't a big eater anyway, and with four weeks of bedrest it's stunning how quickly your muscles wither.

We came home that night, and at three in the morning I felt a contraction, but suspected it was a Braxton Hicks contraction, and part of a false labour. When I called the midwife she agreed – it didn't sound like labour. But by 4.30 a.m. I was having back pain and needed to go to the toilet, and those were apparently the magic words. I needed to get to the hospital. Kitty was going to be two weeks early, so we had no hospital bag ready, but I don't remember us being in a panic or rush.

The next hurdle, if you can call it that, was delivery itself. I was as prepared as I needed to be, which is to say not at all. I'd been told throughout my pregnancy that I would need a C-section, so I hadn't focused at all on vaginal delivery. I hadn't gone to any of those classes. Hadn't practised any breathing. I knew nothing about natural birth.

The doctor assured me I would be fine, that he would give me some gas and we would breathe our way through it together. I asked for an epidural, but he checked how dilated I was and there wasn't time for one. I was going to give birth in twenty minutes. We kept moving forward, and I asked again and again – 'But what about the epidural?' – until the doctor was left with only one way of shutting me up. He grabbed a mirror and reflected an image towards me from between my legs – 'Look!' – and the baby was already crowning.

I'd never been in so much pain in my life. I crushed Lee's hand, squeezing the dear life out of it thinking, *I'm literally going to die – I don't think I can cope with this amount of pain.* What does it feel like? For those of you who haven't experienced it, it feels as if you have a bowling ball inside of you, and your intestines are tangled around it, and someone is trying to wrench that ball out of you with your guts attached, through both holes, the front and the back. It was intense. And, let me tell you, that gas does sweet fuck-all. You may as well be sucking in thin air. Thank god it was quick. Only forty-five minutes elapsed between me getting to the hospital and giving birth. I don't think I had time to adjust to any of what was happening. I wasn't present – I was in shock. But suddenly I was a mum. I knew it because of that wonderful feeling of her lying on my chest, skin on skin, the touch of love.

Kitty was so tiny. We got the smallest Bonds singlets you could find – size 00000 – and even those seemed to swim on her. But she was immediately alert and ready for the world. I remember the midwife saying that the way babies are born is indicative or predictive of their personality. And that makes perfect sense, because Kitty is the ultimate FOMO baby – one of those kids who doesn't want to miss whatever is going on. If she could have spoken inside of me, I know exactly what she would have said: *What's going on out there? Get me outta here! Let me at it! Let's get this party started!*

She was that way all through her infancy and beyond. She never wanted to lie in the pram facing the person pushing – she always wanted to look out onto the world. She was a people-watcher from the very start. Most parents get that blissful couple of months when their baby is sleeping, or dozing, and cooing and gargling. But as Kitty got to four and five months, she wouldn't even sit in a pram – she wanted to be up in the BabyBjörn so she could see what was going on – never closed off from the universe, always at the right height to eyeball everyone else.

I got mastitis early on, and after three months of breast-feeding had to switch to baby formula. But I never felt guilty about that. Whatever works for you, works for you. And Kitty thrived when she went onto formula, because I don't think she was getting enough milk from me prior. Mums tend to beat themselves up about things like that – 'mum guilt' is so wrong, but it plagues you anyway. You're so afraid of anything happening to the new life you're respon-sible for that you tend to blame yourself whenever anything goes wrong. Having a child is the greatest blessing, but it's the greatest terror, too. There are sporting coaches who like to say that they hate losing more than they love winning, and I think I understand that from the point of view of a parent. The love you have for your child is so deep and abiding and reverent, but the fear of losing it is almost stronger. That fear weighs on you, pressing down on every thought and consideration. Not a day goes by without some morbid 'what if' scenario popping into your brain, and you need to have the answer every time. You really are an adult once you have a baby to care for.

Did I feel judged? Ask any woman that question and the answer will be yes, I wager. By contrast, if a dad puts in any effort or enthusiasm at all, they get treated like the original super-parent. Walk down the street with your kid strapped to your chest, singing a little song to amuse them, and you're father of the year. But be a mum and put a foot wrong, and you'll feel the wrath from all directions. Anyway, we stayed in the Kangaroo Valley house for a lot of the first few months, because it felt secluded and secure. We had this picturesque homestead, perfect for our own little family bubble. But we came back to town often, too, and I remember being badly judged one day when we were walking down the streets of Double Bay, when Kitty was maybe three months old.

We were shopping – nanna, mum and Kitty – and Kitty began crying, needing a feed. I asked Mum if it was okay to walk with your baby while feeding, and she said that if I felt fine doing it, then that was my answer, so I did. But a photographer was there taking pictures, and because the camera sometimes lies, one of the frames made it look as if Kitty wasn't fully secure – and obviously she was very secure. You cannot imagine the scrutiny I came under. For the way I was holding my baby. Over whether I should have been feeding the baby. About why my baby didn't have socks on. (It was hot that day, that's why.)

This wasn't just feral comment sections on social media. Opinion pieces started rolling off the presses. Then Liberal politician Pru Goward had a go at me, likening the image to Michael Jackson dangling his child from a balcony. Mia Freedman wrote an opposing column about mums being judged so harshly. And then of course I had Kyle making light of it, having a go at me and taking the piss on air. All over some photo. I'm just happy we're in a different time now, even a decade on, because I really don't think that would be acceptable anymore. The morality police would never allow that kind of attack on a new mum.

I returned to work in the new year, broadcasting from Kangaroo Valley for three weeks, which was the perfect soft step back into my vocation. Lee was thriving as a stay-at-home dad, hands-on and eager, meaning we had no need for a nanny. We were soon back in Sydney but realised how unsuitable our place in Paddington had become. It had been bought on a whim, after all. We first saw it on the day it was going to auction, but no one had bid, and so we made an offer that was immediately accepted. We hadn't been thinking about children, and the layout – over several floors – made no sense with a baby. So we moved quickly, renting a new place for ourselves that was family-friendly and more suitable. Then I returned to the office, and that's when things started to go pear-shaped again for me and Lee.

Breakfast radio hours are a strange beast – only *just* manageable before you have a family. I'd wake up at 4 a.m., make a latte with full-cream milk and two sugars, wash and blow-dry my hair, do my make-up – tiptoeing throughout the entire process. I ran late every morning, making it to the studio by the skin of my teeth. And then the work begins, in which you've got to be alert, focused, ready to react to anything, bubbly when the moment demands it and serious when the content changes for a solid four hours. You don't come out the other end of that wringer on an adrenaline high, either. No, you're exhausted, and go the opposite way, longing to shut down immediately. Doing breakfast radio is like existing in a constant state of jetlag, fighting to stay awake and adjusting to the time zone everyone else is enjoying. The tiredness is always there, not just because of the interruption to normal circadian rhythms, but the daily brain drain. Most people who do it will have a nap in the afternoon to recharge their batteries, but I had no chance for any of those, because Kitty would never nap.

We had neighbours who had a daughter the same age, and she would nap for two hours every afternoon. I couldn't imagine such a sublime and regular reprieve. Kitty would go down for ten restless minutes before opening her eyes and wanting to play again. Naps were non-existent for her, and so they were non-existent for me. I also wanted to be there for all those parenting moments at night, because I was missing every morning. I wanted to be present for dinnertime and bath time, story time and bedtime. And I was, but before I knew it, it was 7.30 p.m., and I needed to wind down with a glass of wine. I'd actually never had much interest in alcohol before, but now I was looking forward to it. *When is it 7.30?* I'd think. *I need that chardonnay!*

Naturally, this sense of overwhelming exhaustion became a point of friction in my marriage to Lee. The following scenario will probably be familiar to anyone with kids, but when your energy is already low, and you're working full time, and you come home from the office, you can't help but want that moment to yourself – thirty minutes, maybe even an hour – but you end up with the opposite. Instead, you're handed your baby, and every-thing that entails. And I struggled with that. Sometimes it annoyed me that Lee wasn't struggling, at least outwardly.

Lee was an incredible dad, and still is. He was so atten-tive and so beautiful, and the bond he was building with Kitty was ironclad. He was a natural, too – he just knew what to do. He wasn't clumsy or lacking common sense. He wasn't going to fumble his way through changing nappies or be dragged kicking and screaming into doing what he needed to do. He wasn't going to complain about a 2 a.m. feeding – he was mindful of my responsibilities and manned up and did much of that, so that I could get some sleep before waking at 4 a.m. The day-to-day of managing an infant was like breathing for him, but it was also a full-time job, so he needed rest as much as I did, and we never had a great system in place.

Although Lee was a good father, he was less interested in helping or supporting me. I would return home every day to a messy home, and the burden of handling all the household chores intensified the strain on our marriage, fuelling resentment between us.

We began to squabble about who had done what, looking to balance out the domestic equation – 'I did this' versus 'Well, I did that' – with both of us thinking we had contributed more. It turned into a constant battle over who deserved more rest. Both our families had dispersed – my mum back to the Gold Coast, and Lee's mum back to Ireland – and so we had no relatives to lean on or give us a break, let alone to allow Lee and me time to connect.

If I could do this all again, or give advice to anyone about to go through it now, I would focus on the importance of protecting some small sliver of time for the parents to come together as a couple. It's too easy to lose that when you have a child. Your child is your priority, which means your partner sits in second place, and even though that's understandable – it's the way it has to be – you can also still carve out a moment for a gesture or a kind word. It might make all the difference.

I'd also emphasise the need to ask for help from people. We never got a nanny, even for a few hours. *We don't need a nanny*, we thought. *We're perfectly capable people.* But sometimes it's not about need. We were people with means – I was earning good money – so why did I deny myself that little bit of assistance, especially when I could see my relationship was floundering?

A disconnect built up in us both, and it wasn't really awful, but it wasn't really good either. He wasn't understanding me and I wasn't understanding him, and, more importantly, we weren't supporting one another. Things didn't get truly bad until later, but I think we never quite recovered from this disconnect. One last thing I did certainly didn't help.

I had given up cigarettes during the pregnancy – actually, well beforehand, when we first started trying. But I picked it up again when Kitty was a toddler, on the sly, knowing Lee would freak out if he knew. The idea was to have just one Alpine on the way to work – my little menthol treat. But the lengths I went to in order to avoid detection were ridiculous. I had cough lollies and mints, of course. But I would also wear a pair of pink plastic dish gloves, because no matter how much you wash your hands, that nicotine stink just attaches itself to those two fingers – a smell that threatens to bring your secret undone.

I wore those gloves while smoking in the car on the way home from work, but at that hour of the day I'd have to take a drag so quickly, to avoid people in other cars seeing this ridiculous woman in the fluorescent rubber gloves. A ute full of tradies pulled up at a traffic light one lunchtime and one of them wound down their window – 'Jackie O! You've gotta take my business card! I'll fix whatever you need in the studio!' – and I remember having to reach out and grab his business card. He looked at the pink dish glove, looked at me, then thankfully the light went green and I was gone.

It got to the point where the dish glove became a part of me. I got so complacent I didn't even care who saw me wearing it. I remember going to a big Channel 10 event where they were launching their slate of new shows, and

I wore my lovely little clutch bag, with my dishwashing glove inside. I went outside to smoke with Kyle and all the station bigwigs – heavy hitters such as executives Stephen Tate and David Mott – and we were in a little semicircle having a chat when I pulled out my dish glove and lit up. Kyle had to explain it to the group.

'I'm sorry, guys,' he said. 'This is Jackie. She's a lunatic.'

I couldn't get away with it forever, though, and my charade finally came undone one night. Lee had gone out with his sister to the hotel up the road for dinner. Kitty had gone to sleep and I was home alone. I knew I had a precious window of two hours up my sleeve, and I was unashamedly *thrilled* to have a couple of cigarettes and a glass of pinot grigio. But forty minutes into the pub dinner, Lee had an argument with his sister and stormed off, arriving home unexpectedly early. I heard him coming inside and quickly put the cigarette out, but it was too late – he saw straightaway. Time for a big fight. 'I can't believe you've been hiding this from me. Why would you do this?' It took days for us to recover.

And, again, it was my fear of conflict at fault, avoiding it at all costs to the detriment of my marriage. In my head I was saving the relationship by not bringing up a point of tension, but in reality I was destroying it by not being honest about my needs and wants, my foibles and faults. By not being truthful about who I was. But still, I kept on smoking. I made it clear that I wasn't quitting, at least offering that one scrap of honesty. The damage was done anyway, and I needed the nicotine!

Eight

Two thousand and ten was a big year in more ways than one. Kitty was born, yes, but it was also a year in which Kyle and I became quite disconnected.

He had got divorced from Tamara and was struggling with the separation. Tamara was a key plank in making Kyle's and my partnership happen – she created a lot of the connective tissue for us outside of work in those early years. She was a wonderful host, a beautiful girl, and when their marriage broke up, in a way our friendship disintegrated a little, too.

Kyle has been open about the fact that he partied hard and did a lot of cocaine to cope. He began mixing with new faces and friends in Kings Cross, and his world became just so radically different. He went from being this domesticated, stay-at-home married man to an unhappy guy who was doing lines and going on benders.

I think I understand the world he was living in at the time. When you separate from a partner, you tend to become really selfish in your sadness, and the only thing that's important is the next high – to save you from your new normal, which is low. This new version of him was foreign to me, but I was also foreign to him – and neither one of us was in a place to help the other. He really didn't want to know about the new life I was living, trying to start a family. 'You're a boring mum,' he would joke. 'I don't want to be around that.' We still had a friendship but we were walking in different directions. For example, I texted him on the day Kitty was born and didn't get a response, which was so unlike my usually caring friend.

This all happened gradually. It wasn't as if one day he was there and the next he wasn't. But I was sad about not spending time with him in my life. I always love it when Kyle and I are on a similar wavelength, because that feels like he's being his true self, and when he's in touch with that he's a happier person. When he's off track – even if he's enjoying his freedom, living his life to the fullest and going hard – he's much quicker to anger.

He was sick all the time, too. At least, he was always taking sick days. And there's nothing worse than when your co-host leaves you in the lurch with an hour to go before you're on air, and you have no one to fill the spot. It used to drive me up the wall. I was tearing my hair out because the sick days were once a week, then twice a week, and always requested in the same way. He would text the station – *Can't come in – got a migraine* – and then someone would call me, and if my phone was ringing that early then I'd know exactly what was about to happen.

We would ring around town, calling the usual suspects to replace him – Jules Lund, perhaps, or Osher Günsberg, maybe Andy Lee. People aren't available at the drop of a hat – because no one answers the phone at 4 a.m., and even when they do, they're coming in as a guest, so you have to drive the whole thing and hold it up. And that meant sitting opposite random people I'd never worked with before, which was tough. You often can't build enough instantaneous rapport and rhythm to carry a four-hour show. The mental exertion was draining.

I suppose you could give Kyle the benefit of the doubt and say that because he was burning the candle at both ends, he was leaving himself too weak and once in a while genuinely falling sick as a result of his lifestyle. He turned forty during this time and was clearly struggling with life. I was worried about him and his mental health, as I could sense that he was genuinely in a bad place, and I couldn't sit by as a friend and watch. One day I went over to his house and rang the doorbell, and he didn't answer. I knew he was home, but it made me realise he didn't want to accept help yet – he wasn't ready.

During this time, Kyle would often escape to Los Angeles at the drop of a hat – for the smallest reasons, like maybe because he'd lost his driver's licence – and then he would do the show from a house over there.

I remember we had a big fight once, based on something that had really triggered him during those *Hot 30* days. He was asked to fill in for Paul Holmes on the breakfast show with Wendy Harmer and Peter Moon. Paul was the anchor who did minimal announcing, and when Kyle filled in for him he reported back to me that night, off air.

'Oh god, Jackie,' he said. 'Moony's in Melbourne, Wendy's in Sydney, and they *hate* each other. Every time there's a song or an ad break, Wendy's telling me, "Turn him off!" so that Moony can't hear Wendy bitching about him.'

Something about that internal drama really stuck with Kyle. Wendy and Moony were known for their special kind of toxic chemistry, but Kyle was still incredulous that it went that far. 'I *never* want to be that,' he told me. 'I never want us to be *that*.' And he would bring that moment up from time to time. Wendy turning off Moony's microphone – so she wouldn't have to listen to her co-host – was the ultimate slight in Kyle's eyes.

All these years later, we were doing the show together, remotely, because he was in LA, and that memory came up. We were off air during an ad break, and I was trying to listen to a piece of audio I wanted to play in my upcoming O News segment. Kyle was in his house in California, talking with Ryan, and I couldn't hear my audio. I said,

'Can you just mute Kyle for a second?' but he didn't hear that. Then when Kyle went to talk to us a moment later, he could tell that he was on mute, and he made an instant assumption: 'She's bitching about me, just like Wendy about Moony.' That was it – he cracked it and he left, and went to Mel's Drive-In, the iconic Sunset Boulevard diner, to sit and fume.

Those times were incredibly volatile. I felt worried for Kyle, because I could see he was stuck in escape mode, trying to dodge an emotional pain he hadn't dealt with. I don't blame him, because I know how powerfully separation can change you, and how bad habits can take over. It's like the devil on your shoulder. It grabs hold of you and you just don't care about anything else. I've had that experience, in a different way. But I couldn't really look at it from his perspective at the time – I had my own problems. I was exhausted with a newborn, my husband wasn't attracted to me anymore, and my marriage was basically falling apart.

I talk for a living, but I was barely even talking to Mum at this stage. She was witnessing things in my marriage that she thought were bad signs. She heard comments from Lee, putting me down, and she would bring them up later, and I would get defensive – defending Lee – because I didn't want to face the truth. I had no thoughts about leaving, so I didn't want to hear any of it. It was just easier not to hear from her at all – to give her a little bit of the silent treatment she used to give me.

After Kitty was born, I put on a little weight those first eight months, but I attribute the lack of intimacy in my marriage to all of the stressors that come with newborns and a chaotic workplace. Still, as time went on, it became harder to ignore one of the primary reasons. My weight has always fluctuated a little, and whenever I added kilograms in my marriage, it was never tiptoed around. I was told. I remember getting changed in the walk-in wardrobe, standing there naked and vulnerable, and Lee walked past and I caught him looking at me in the mirror with an expression of disdain or disgust. I'll never forget that look. Sometimes he would wrap an arm around me and grab a spare tyre. 'Look at that!' he'd say as a joke, but I wondered if it really was.

It was the worst possible hang-up to target, because weight had always been an issue for me. It was all too familiar, in truth. Even as a girl, I would go to the fridge to get some ice cream and would hear my dad's voice behind me: 'Jeez, darling, that arse is getting big on you.' Mum did the same thing, perhaps more tactfully, but also more frequently.

Mum is one of my favourite people in the world, but my looks were always important to her. I've almost never had a choice but to place this skewed value on my appearance, because I'd get comments and praise when I looked good, and when I didn't get comments, I knew what it meant. I felt I was loved more when I looked good. She would see it as just wanting the best for me – because good looks do give you a leg up in life – and she probably also saw it as honesty – 'If I don't tell you, no one else will.' I recently had a conversation with her about this, and she said she never felt pretty herself, and also felt that I'd been given this gift that she hadn't had. But she leant in to this a bit too much, unaware how deeply her good intentions were being taken to heart.

I remember when I was five, with straight white hair down to my shoulders, angelic and innocent, and Mum liked to shop at a high-end clothing store for girls, meaning I was always dressed up like an immaculate porcelain doll. People would stop her at the shopping centre – 'What a beautiful young girl you have!' – and I think she liked that attention. I think she wanted me to stay that way.

I remember getting beauty products for my birthday when I was seven – moisturiser and cleansers and toners designed to make your skin look better. I remember being on a diet – fruit only for breakfast – and I still hate fruit for breakfast to this day. I've never had a clinical eating disorder, but I have always had a very unhealthy relationship with the way I view eating. I've always been on a diet. And whenever I wasn't on a diet I was binge-eating all weekend, because, well, 'I'll start on Monday' – stuck in a constant loop of making and then breaking some new rule around food. I tried the lemon detox. I tried fruit-only and soup-only. Keto and Atkins. Anything that was in *Cleo* or *Cosmo* or *Dolly*, where there was only ever one acceptable body shape. That was amplified by where

I lived. On the Gold Coast, it's all about being able to walk down the street in your bikini. I became obsessed with looks, and with supermodels.

Food was always an issue in our house when I was growing up, but whenever someone pressures me to do something, I tend to rebel and go the other way, so when Mum would say, 'You shouldn't eat bread', I wanted it even more. I'd set my alarm for 5 a.m. just so I could get up and make myself some toast. I liked it with peanut butter *and* butter (double the butter!), or butter and cinnamon sugar, always on white bread. Mum was so attuned to the sound of the toaster that I would open the grill on the oven instead, because it was silent, yet she always found out! You cannot hide anything from her. If there was even a crumb left on the bench, she would find it and connect the dots (ha ha).

Even as an adult, whenever I made a professional splash and had a photo shoot or found myself on a red carpet, the feedback was only ever tied to my skin or my hair or my dress – to what was flattering, and what fell flat. I think that's why I accepted those kinds of comments from Lee, and ended up in another relationship that placed such high value on my appearance. There was even one time when he suggested that I go to get a full body scan, because he thought I was obese. I went and got one – dutiful little Jackie going and getting a DEXA scan for body composition and bone density – to see how much excess body fat I was carrying. And I wasn't obese.

I was overweight, though. Probably just eating my feelings, and my palette wasn't discerning. The wine was becoming more and more appealing as a night-time emotional crutch – no longer one glass but two or three, or more. The tiredness meant that I wouldn't cook as much, either, and so I would go to my favourite poison – savoury foods such as hamburgers and hot chips and pizza. But I'd be just as likely to turn sweet. The night that Lee busted me smoking again, for instance, I'd just finished my 'dinner', which was a glass of champagne and a jar of Nutella.

We needed something new, and after renting in Watsons Bay for a year, we found it. We had been looking for a dream home in a family-friendly suburb, and we found it right around the corner – two streets over, in Vaucluse. It was an old, run-down house on a big block of land in a street lined with oak trees and with a little school at the end of the road. It was on the market and in incredibly rough shape, but the whole knock-down idea wasn't as popular at the time, and every open inspection day seemed to be rainy and dreary, making it less appealing to the other bidders. We got lucky.

I had always loved the house from the movie *Father of the Bride* with Steve Martin and Diane Keaton. I'd watched the movie obsessively with no real care for the plot – just for the house. That white picket fence guarding a grand two-storey home with black shutters and double hung windows, lived in by a couple with a perfect marriage and a grown-up daughter. I thought if I could build the house from that movie, maybe that could be my life, too.

Lee has an amazing eye for symmetry and scale, and all the things required to pull off a well-built and aesthetically pleasing house versus one that looks not quite there. We didn't even get an architect – Lee just drew up the plans and took it to a draftsperson, and then he became the project manager on the build. It cost next to nothing for what it was, and took only a year to construct.

And we were good again. Great again, actually. Because once more we had hope and a distraction – 'This will make us better' – with Lee occupied looking at timber samples and me picking out cushion fabrics. We moved into our forever home, and then I got a call from Kyle that changed everything.

—

We were coming to the end of our contract, and 2Day FM were really dragging the chain on negotiating. Usually, if your contract expires at the end of the year, you would expect your renegotiation to begin in May, but we got to the end of September and had still heard nothing. *What are they playing at?* we wondered. *Are they trying to act as if they don't care if we stay or go, in the hope they might re-sign us for no extra money?* Was this gamesmanship? Or were they genuinely not interested in re-signing us?

That would be strange, given we were still number one and had been for years.

Lee was pivotal here. We had been on a holiday to Fiji together that year, and he had got to know a group of people we met there, who all dealt with the stock exchange, specifically commodities in media. It was their job to find out things exactly such as whether or not *The Kyle and Jackie O Show* was being renewed, because those sorts of movements shift share prices and affect markets. It meant that Lee had this backdoor channel into the heart of our world, because one of those guys was talking directly to a C-suiter at Southern Cross Austereo, and had even point-blank asked what their plans were for us. That response, shared with Lee, was dismissive, to the effect that we would be signed again, but it might be the last time. *Maybe they're on the way out. We're thinking we can get a younger, fresher team to replace them.* That was fed back to us, and was a game changer.

It seemed ridiculous. We weren't remotely faltering in the ratings. It was partly philosophical. SCA had always said – and still say openly – that their strength is not their talent, but the team and network's heritage and loyalty. They've always believed that talent can be replaced, and, in fairness, that's been the case for them in the past. They created shows that were monstrous hits – not just us, but Hamish and Andy, too. And inside that worldview, we were indeed replaceable. The station was changing a little as well, from the managers running the shows to the music on the station itself. But we were still strong. The only competition was Nova. Mix FM was just a daggy little station, always destined to sit at the bottom. We were pissed off at the idea that we were somehow over the hill or washed up.

I remember that Kyle called me on Halloween. And we *love* Halloween. We were into our new house, which was perfect. I got all the decorations and treats, and I was so excited for it. Kitty was four and dressed up as a little witch, in her hat and cape and broom. It was late afternoon, and the kids hadn't quite arrived to trick or treat, when Kyle called.

'Darl, we're going to Mix.'

What the fuck?

Kyle had just spoken to Duncan Campbell, the content director there, and had said to him that if they were willing to rebrand the station – turning it into KIIS FM – that we would come over. They had made an agreement already, over the phone. What's more, Kyle had told SCA that he wasn't interested in returning to radio. He told them he was leaving – but without telling them he was going to the opposition.

What has he done? I thought, as my head spun. *Because whatever he's done, it's final.* I was miffed that I wasn't consulted, but I knew exactly how this would have happened. I *knew* he would have made that decision when he was stoned. He loves his weed, and I know what he's like. He hatches these harebrained schemes and enacts them immediately.

Meanwhile, Lee and I had just got a mortgage for our dream house and were at maximum debt. And it's not as if we had been left out in the cold completely by SCA – they had finally come to the party by then and made us an offer, and it was good and solid, millions of dollars of income. Now we were going to uproot everything and relaunch on Mix, a station no one listened to?

All of this was rushing through my mind as kids in costumes started knocking at the door. I was wrapping my head around the broad strokes of the biggest commercial deal of my life while handing out candy from a plastic pumpkin. I couldn't help but be mad with Kyle. *How could you have done this?* I was thinking. *This agreement is so bloody drastic. Like, what the actual fuck?*

I explained to Lee what had happened, and he wasn't angry. He was calm. He was bemused, if anything. 'Here we go again,' he said, with a smile. 'Never a dull moment.'

We would be meeting with KIIS in secret the following week, in a conference room at the Sir Stamford hotel in Circular Quay. It's a small boutique hotel that exudes historic luxury, all wood panelling and antique red-velvet chairs. In the room, there was a huge mahogany table with a few men sitting at the end of it, telling us how they were prepared to change the whole station for us – an expensive exercise – and how they saw it all working. They told us how excited they were for the opportunity to work with us, and how *crazy* it was that we weren't being valued – how they couldn't believe their luck that anyone would let us slip through their fingers. They said they didn't see it as a three-year relationship but a ten- or twenty-year bond between us. They said all the right things. Ego alone made you nod along with them. It was a risk, and we were willing to accept.

We had to tell SCA, obviously, that we were retiring from radio. We couldn't tell them we were going elsewhere, because then they would kick us off the air immediately. We didn't want to be off air for a handful of weeks, giving them a chance to embed a new show and keep our audience for themselves. They were stunned that we were retiring, but Hamish and Andy had done the same thing only recently, so it wasn't implausible.

We had to say this on air, too, which was unfortunate, because it meant lying. And then a whisper emerged in the press about us going to Mix.

Our content director at 2Day FM, Donna Puechmarin, did not gel with Kyle. She was well-meaning and lovely, but was also never quite the right fit for us, and she had only been there a few months when she came in after the show one day to confront us. 'I've heard you're going to Mix,' she said, 'and I just want to ask you, to your face, looking you in the eye, are you going to Mix?'

Kyle stared right back at her. 'Donna, I swear, on my life – and I'm looking you in the eye right now – that I will *never* be on air at Mix FM.'

That was easy enough for him to say, of course, as Mix FM would no longer exist. Donna hadn't said anything about KIIS FM, and how could she have? They were creating it for us. She smiled and replied. 'Do you know what? I believe you,' she says. 'That's all I needed to hear.'

They made such a big deal of our last day on the air. Balloons, flowers, catering, every staff member in attendance. It was epic – the biggest send-off I've seen, full of love and laughs, but I was cringing inside the entire time. Mix had told us that they couldn't wait long to make the announcement. 'We'll be listening to the show,' they said, 'and as soon as you're off air – fifteen minutes later – we will make the big announcement that *The Kyle and Jackie O Show* is coming.'

We did the last segment of the show, and everyone was cheering. There were maybe two hundred and fifty people there for that final break. We were supposed to come out and mingle and enjoy the spread – have a party with the staff to celebrate our careers coming to an end. We emerged from the studio and Kyle said he would be right back, after a quick pit stop in the bathroom. I said I need to go as well. In reality, we went downstairs for a cigarette. We hadn't expected any of this hoopla, so we hadn't planned an exit strategy.

'Okay,' Kyle said. 'I'm leaving.'

I said I couldn't. I'd feel terrible walking out of there without going back and saying something to all those people.

He looked at me in astonishment – 'Fucking good luck if you wanna do that!' – and left.

I turned to our executive producer, Simon Greally, who was coming with us to KIIS, and said I had to go up and at least say goodbye to a few people. I dashed in to say some quick farewells, but in the office I could see all these executives and directors at a central desk, putting on their headphones, listening intently to something. The Mix announcement was a full ten-minute package with music, and they were hearing it live, glancing up and around, amazed and furious, and making eye contact with me. I felt stuck to the floor, without a clue what to do. Simon said to me, 'Mate, we need to get out of here *now*!' So we spun around immediately and left, heading downstairs and then to a bar, Gazebo, for a drink.

A few people from the station came to meet us there and told us what had happened. Every poster, every scrap of signage, every promotional photo with our faces and names on it had been torn down, immediately stripped from the walls and then rubbished in a bitter fury. That was our last day at 2Day FM.

I felt guilty. I won't pretend I didn't. I was so thankful for the career I'd enjoyed there. Let's be pragmatic, though – I wasn't some charity case who was handed a career. We did well in the ratings, and they fed on that and reaped the rewards. But it was a long-standing working relationship, and it ended on a nasty note that was far from ideal. And there was blame in all corners. I didn't like the way our contract had been delayed, or how this idea that we were finished had got out into the market, behind our backs.

Why be loyal to someone who has no intention of showing you that same loyalty in kind? We were wounded by that, and were acting on that hurt.

A bit of self-preservation kicks in, too. You're a fool if you don't consider how to protect your career and give it the length and breadth it deserves. Yes, I hated the way we needed to be secretive and clandestine before our exit, but also, that's radio – it's a competitive industry. It was the right decision for that point in our lives, in refreshing ourselves somewhere else and going where we were valued more. KIIS had said they saw their partnership with us lasting a decade, maybe two decades, which probably sounded fanciful at the time. It doesn't anymore. We've already worked there for ten years, and have signed on for another ten years. It was always the right move, and in a strange way I'm thankful for Kyle and his afternoons getting stoned – it led to a bold decision that ultimately paid off.

My parents on their wedding day.

Me as a baby – with my brother being told to hold Dad's cigarette so Dad could hold me for the photo! Everything just screams 1970s in this pic.

Me at four years old.

Right: My first Holy Communion. With Dad, Mum and my brother Scott.

Bottom left: All dressed up with my ballet friends. This was around the time the 'rat girl' nickname started.

Bottom right: Ballet days.

Top: Hanging out at 'the tree' on the Gold Coast.

Middle: The tree (friends).

Left: Me at the start of the 1990s.

With my boyfriend
David Piper, and a koala.

My old friend Natasha from
the days of clubbing and
working in real estate on the
Gold Coast.

Phil and me at the airport, leaving the Gold Coast for a new radio job in Canberra.

Phil, Will Smith and me.

Interviewing James Van Der Beek at the height of the *Dawson's Creek* craze.

Phil and me in a promo shot from the year 2000. (BOB BARKER/ NEWSPIX)

The old days of radio. This would have been around 2000.

An early promo shot of
me and Kyle from the
2Day FM days.

Me and Lee when we
first met.

The dress Alex Perry designed for my wedding day.

The spectacle of my wedding, and trying to stop *Woman's Day* from getting a shot!

The lingerie campaign
I was starving myself for.

This is when I started
getting invited to fancy
parties at mansions in
Sydney, hosted by the
likes of *Vogue*, off the
back of *Popstars*.
(PATRICK RIVIERE/
GETTY IMAGES)

With Jennifer Lopez (I spent the day with her in Darling Harbour, Sydney, just as she was breaking up with P. Diddy), Justin Timberlake and Taylor Swift (in the early days of her career).

One of the many parties at Kyle's. Kyle in the middle (holding a prop gun), Kyle's then wife, Tamara, next to him, Lee sitting on the couch and Ryan 'Axe-Man' Wellington in the back in the blue T-shirt.

With Kyle on the red carpet for the MTV Australia Video Music Awards in 2006.

(KRISTIAN DOWLING/GETTY IMAGES)

Presenting an MTV Award to Good Charlotte in 2007.

Lee and me at our Kangaroo Valley property.

In the shed with one of the rejected calves that we had to hand-rear.

Pregnant with Kitty.

The day Kitty was born.

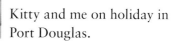

Kitty and me on holiday in
Port Douglas.

With Chris Martin from Coldplay, Lady Gaga, and receiving a pie to the face from Jason Biggs.

Renewing my vows with Lee in 2012 in a stunt for the radio show, based on the TV show *Big Fat Gypsy Weddings*, alongside Kyle, my best friends Gemma and Kim, and *Kyle and Jackie* O newsreader Emma Duxbury.

A happy family snap.

The Million Dollar Dawn Dig, and the look of shock
after winning one million dollars!

At the mic in the 2Day studio. (JOHN GRAINGER/NEWSPIX)

With Khloé Kardashian, Harry Styles and Niall Horan, and Ben Stiller.

Broadcasting our breakfast show live from the Kardashians' house.

Prime Minister Julia Gillard allowed us to do an Easter Egg Hunt with our listeners and their children at Kirribilli House.

Kitty and me goofing around as we were moving from our house in Paddington to a more sensible home in Watsons Bay.

The night everything went pear-shaped – Halloween, 2013, when Kyle told me we were moving to Mix/KIIS.

The move to a new studio and a new station – KIIS.

The photo of Kyle and me that was used to launch KIIS FM.
(TOBY BURROWS PHOTOGRAPHY)

The day we went straight to number one after debuting at KIIS.

Dua Lipa
(I have no memory
of this day!),
Justin Bieber
(and Bieber Island)
and
Shawn Mendes.

The interview between Kevin Hart and Pharrell Williams that seemed like a good idea at the time . . .

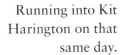

Running into Kit Harington on that same day.

Ed Sheeran surprising our listeners with a performance at their wedding.

Kitty and me, baking, at the *Father of the Bride* home.

Immediately after the announcement of my divorce, I went away with my best friends Gemma and Kim, and our kids.

The first Christmas as a separated family, at the Bondi Beach apartment. Kitty, my dad, Tony, my Mum, Julie, my brother, Scott, and his girlfriend, Natalie.

Me looking miserable on that kayak with Gemma. (JAYDEN SEYFARTH/MEDIAMODE)

Travelling incognito on the way to California and rehab.

Having my last cigarette before entering the Betty Ford Center behind me as we waited for the results of my Covid test.

My share room at the Betty Ford Center.

Enjoying life and spending time with family shortly after returning home from rehab.

Returning to work after rehab to my supportive team, who are like family to me.

Revisiting 'the tree' many years later, at the Gold Coast with Mum in 2023.

In Los Angeles with my friends Damien (bottom left), Brooklyn (top left), Daniel (middle) and Michael (top right).

With my beautiful assistant, Brittany.

Celebrating my 49th birthday with my friends Pip and Milly.

With Prime Minister Anthony Albanese at Kyle's wedding in 2023.

My first Logie Awards in more than a decade.
(DON ARNOLD/GETTY IMAGES)

The day we were pitched the new deal with KIIS, with ARN CEO Ciaran Davis and Chairman Hamish McLennan.

Interviewing Gwyneth Paltrow onstage when we flew her to Sydney for a besties speaking event.

Back in Sydney, long after rehab, and enjoying life with Gemma again. (A stark contrast to the kayak pic – ha ha!)

Kitty and me enjoying a trip together to Europe. This was taken at Cap Ferrat in the south of France.

Dancing and feeling full of joy at Jackie O bar in Mykonos.

Nine

We had all of the summer holidays to prepare for our first shift at KIIS, and we needed every minute. We were consulted on the new station logos and the colour palette, even the refurbishment of the studio. We had been in the city with 2Day FM, but now we were thirty minutes out of town in North Ryde, the middle of suburbia, with not much else around – a university, shopping centre and a few office buildings. My commute went from eleven minutes to thirty-six, which is a difference that matters when your alarm goes off at 4 a.m.! It was a complete culture shock, spending money at 2Day FM levels on this shiny new endeavour, while trying to break away from the old Mix mentality.

Launching KIIS with a blank canvas was one of the most fun times in my career, but it was also tough. We had to micromanage everything, because we no longer had our well-oiled corporate machine behind us to keep things running. We had recruited and guarded a group of gun staff over the years, for instance, but most of them couldn't come with us. They were under contract and couldn't just jump ship, which meant we were this odd mix of a few familiar faces but a lot more unfamiliar ones, which required constant coaching and rearranging. It was exciting, but terrifying.

We worked so hard in the summer of 2014, just hustling, hustling, hustling. Our show is our baby, so we protected it with every tool at our disposal, whether running the rule over production planning details or giving up personal time for that extra piece of press. That's always been there within us, and has always kept the show evolving. We've always been mindful to keep the show at a certain level, making sure it never became stale, always growing while we grew as people. Complacency was never for us.

For our first day on air – the moment of truth – they made this grandiose introduction, and it felt new and invigorating, but there were no real nerves. We simply sat in front of the microphones and quickly realised that all we were doing was plonking ourselves down in a different chair with the same goal. We felt good immediately and had complete confidence that our new home was the right one. Still, there were enough external doubters to plant just a tiny seed of worry.

Speculation was rife in the media about whether our audience would actually change stations and follow us, because that kind of loyalty was completely untested at the time. Most of the usual megaphones and mouthpieces hedged their bets, stating only the facts, not wanting to make the wrong prediction. But there were a few who said it would never work. *Sydney Morning Herald* journalist Peter FitzSimons wrote about us in his column. He said, 'I predict disaster,' citing other broadcasters who had struggled at new stations, such as Mike Carlton or Doug Mulray. 'In both cases, their otherwise devoted audiences simply didn't know where to find them on the dial and so didn't follow. It will be the same for the (ex) 2Day FM duo.' Others were more pragmatic and circumspect: Why wouldn't our audience follow us, they reasoned, when to do so asked nothing more of them than flicking a switch or pressing a button?

We were getting information fed back to us from our old masters at Southern Cross Austereo that they were confident of riding comfortably over the upheaval we had caused. They had brought in a celebrity-focused show to replace us, hosted by Mel B – Scary Spice herself – as one of four co-hosts alongside Merrick Watts, Sophie Monk and Jules Lund. Asked on *The Today Show* why they needed four hosts to replace two, Merrick replied: 'Well, to be completely fair, Kyle is the size of three.' Shots fired, Merrick doubled down and aimed a second barrel at us, going on to claim that we were sacked by SCA. Again, this is perfectly normal in the competitive world of radio. You throw a few jibes before your real jabs, almost like boxers at the weigh-in for a title fight.

All the whispers and predictions and doomsaying did have a way of insinuating itself into your brain. SCA had always spoken about the machine behind their shows trumping the talent behind their mics, and maybe that was true – they were the powerhouse, always able to attract the best producers, catching the eye of the most powerful publicists, and they were in the CBD instead of what was seen as the middle of nowhere. They had a great line-up with real glamour factor. They weren't resting on any laurels, either, instead putting a lot of money into their campaign, which almost went viral. (They used footage of the new crew dancing on the street to the Pharrell Williams song 'Happy', catching the song *just* as it was blowing up, and I remember thinking I wish we'd thought of it first.) It began to feel as if things could go either way.

Kyle wasn't helping my nerves, either. People would ask us about our expectations, and I'd give my usual measured and honest response. 'These things don't necessarily happen overnight,' I'd say. 'They can take time, and we're prepared for that.' And then Kyle would cut me off. 'No, I'm not prepared for that,' he would say. 'If we don't go number one I'll be *very* disappointed.' You hate him and you love him in those moments – hating that he sets the stakes so high, and loving him for that unwavering belief. I think it's half the reason everything falls into his lap in life. Consider the phrase 'What you put out there is what you get in return' – it's impossible to deny that kind of truism when you see Kyle in full flight.

Still, I had that many doubts that I actually called a psychic, which I hadn't done since I was twenty-four. I needed to know – I needed to prepare myself for the fall, should it be on the horizon. Miss Irene was her name, and I'd found her in the back of an issue of *Woman's Day*. She had told me a few things that were true all those years ago, so I called her again and asked what would happen.

'You're going to be number one again,' she said, 'but you're going to tie.'

'Wait,' I said. 'We're actually going *straight* to number one?'

'Yes, but with someone else.'

We started in the middle of January, and our first ratings was a half survey, assessing our initial six weeks on the job. The day the numbers arrived, I remember going into work with such nerves. I was terrified we would end up with egg on our faces. I don't think I've ever felt so much ego and pride tied up in a single moment. We finished the show, and our executive producer Simon Greally walked through the door of the studio. At first I couldn't see anything in his body language, and then I noticed the people behind him. He was like the Pied Piper, followed by our new CEO and all of our staff trailing in his wake. He wore the biggest grin on his face, and he held up his right hand with a single pointer finger raised.

'Number one?' I screamed. *'Number one!!!'*

I'd been expecting number three, hoping for number two, and instead we shot straight to the top. And sure enough, Miss Irene had been right. It was a tie – only, not with 2Day FM. 2Day had plummeted. The ratings between the two stations were literally flipped. The exact size of the audience that had been listening to us on 2Day FM was now listening to us on KIIS, and vice versa – the number of people who had previously listened to Mix was the same as the number now listening to 2Day. Our rise came at the expense of their fall, and that felt big, to know that our listeners were so loyal. They didn't come with us in dribs and drabs, but all at once. They didn't even give the opposition the courtesy of a chance. This is where our audience astounds me. We genuinely have been on a journey with them – with many of them listening to us for decades. We've grown up together and endured.

We shared the win with our stablemates, too, in Jonesy and Amanda at WSFM. It was a massive day for our new company, Australian Radio Network (or ARN), who threw us a matching massive party, shutting down the Cargo Bar in Darling Harbour. Both teams came together to enjoy the moment, with hundreds of people cracking open champagne and doing press, celebrating the removal of all that uncertainty. It was overwhelming to feel so vindicated. Elated. Triumphant. Relief is such an underrated emotion.

Being number one has its own gravitational pull, of course. We knew that much from past experience, and now we got to see it in action once more. In that first six-week stretch when we were unproven, it had been harder than ever to get big guests out to North Ryde, most of them preferring to call in for a phone interview. All of a sudden, though, they were back in the studio, hanging out with us in person.

The US comedian Kevin Hart came in to see us just as he was really taking off. We had entered a new era by then, in which you never get real time with real celebrities. If you're lucky you get ten uninterrupted minutes, maybe fifteen, but Kevin was prepared to do an entire half day with us, maybe three hours, doing whatever we wanted to do. We pitched to his people that we would take him in the back of a limousine to see all of Sydney – our own personal tour – doing segments from the stretch limo or the streets. Kyle was sick that morning. And we didn't just have Kevin that day, either – we also had to do an interview in the city with Pharrell. I had to carry the whole thing on my own, but it was lovely. I did segments with Kevin trying to guess the meaning of various Aussie slang phrases. He was amazing to work with, making it all effortless, offering so much golden content.

Rather than drive him all the way back to the station after our tour, we also had the idea that Kevin could be part of the Pharrell interview. Two superstars in one clip. We walked to the Park Hyatt to get it done, but Pharrell wasn't ready, and then he kept us waiting for so long I was starting to get embarrassed. Kevin Hart – an actor who's starred in a film that grossed $800 million, a performer who at one point was tapped to host the Academy Awards – was being forced to wait with me in a hotel corridor as if he was some pleb journalist, for ninety minutes! In the end I had to take him outside for a wander around Circular Quay – showing him the Opera House and the Harbour Bridge – anything for a moment of distraction. I stayed bubbly, but I was mortified.

We were lucky enough to run into *Game of Thrones* actor Kit Harington, who was ambling around Sydney as a tourist. That was a stroke of luck, because I'd already met him once – the day prior, in fact. Kit had come on the show, although I'd never watched an episode of *Game of Thrones*. That happens often, where people are obsessed with some pop culture touchstone of another but Kyle and I haven't cottoned on to it yet, and so we sit there thinking, *Let's get this over with*, and we stumble our way through an interview. That's what happened with Kit, who really just looked like some average British boy. ('You know nothing, Jon Snow' – more like you know nothing *of* Jon Snow!) Only later did we understand the global obsession with his show and start fangirling over the fact that he had been in our studio.

Kevin and Kit took photos together and we made it work, and had fun, but I could also see that Kevin was losing patience. His exterior was nice – all smiles – but he was (rightfully) getting pissed off, because Pharrell was *aware* that Kevin was going to do the interview with me, so in a way it felt like a power play. It looked to me like a battle between two egos, and in the end the interview probably wasn't even worth the wait. Pharrell was in serious musician mode, so it wasn't anywhere near as playful as it could have been. It was almost a mismatch. But, thankfully, Kevin has come back on the show since, and he's always been gracious and full of fondness when recalling that day.

We were always getting in scrapes of one sort or another on the show. Former rugby league footballer and commentator Braith Anasta was our sports reporter who would come on occasionally to give us some gossip, for instance, because neither of us had any interest in sports. One morning in 2016, we were talking about the Paramatta Eels captain Kieran Foran, and I barely knew who that was, so I referred to the chat screen where we can read notes and prompts from our producers. They would often leave ideas or topics or questions there for us to raise, just in case we need extra material to fill a quiet moment.

On this day, Braith brought up Kieran, and I noticed a line in the chat screen that read: *It was in the newspaper today that he had an affair.* I thought that sounded newsworthy, so I brought it up, and Braith's face just fell. He stumbled for a moment, then brushed right over it and on to the next thing. I didn't understand why until later. The item in the newspaper, it turned out, was actually an anonymous 'Guess who, don't sue' nugget, but I had named Foran and stated his alleged indiscretion verbatim, referring to rumours that questioned the paternity of his second child.

It didn't take long for this to hit the mainstream sports news. A prickly NRL reporter led a Twitter campaign against me that afternoon – 'How dare she make such an accusation on air? Kieran should sue her' – and the Eels skipper did exactly that. We were served papers over the weekend, and I then had every NRL fan trolling me for the next two weeks.

Those fans are brutal, by the way. I'd never want to be a rugby league player, or a female sports reporter for that matter, because when they pile on, they are *vicious*. By that point I'd developed enough digital protection mechanisms – the crucial stealth skills of muting and hiding and blocking – that I didn't see most of what was thrown in my direction, but at the same time, I also understood. *I get it*, I thought. *This is ugly, but I know where it's coming from.*

I was genuinely upset by what had happened. When I spoke, I honestly thought the truth of whatever had happened in Kieran's private life had already been printed and was publicly known. I wasn't swimming in the sporting news every day, so I assumed it was the running story of the day. I had no idea I was saying something that would hurt a family and throw its members into emotional turmoil. I apologised on air, profusely. I actually got choked up because I was so sorry. I didn't want to be mad at the producer who slipped that note into the chat screen – it was hard not to be angry, even though she was remorseful, too. It was one of those horrible happenings, but this is live radio, and we do sometimes make mistakes.

If anything good came out of that episode, it's that reminder of consequences. I'm careful never to do or say anything defamatory, but it was a good lesson to always be on guard. Which we mostly are, anyway. We have to go through the broadcast codes every year, and you become so well briefed about what is acceptable and what's not. The station lawyer comes in with this hefty physical document – pages upon pages of examples not just about potentially costly defamation, but also taste and decency. Not just written information, but audio examples as well. If anyone has done something that's crossed a line in the previous year, they get added to the list, and every one of your peers gets to have a listen and learn from your error of judgement. Alan Jones was always in there. Kyle is always in there. I've been used as an example, too, more than once.

I was an example that very year, in fact, cited under the taste and decency rules after I had told a story on air from when I was five years old. As any parent knows, five-year-olds are genuinely weird creatures and do bafflingly weird things, and I shared one of those moments from my childhood. I thought it was an innocent and funny story, but it was found to have crossed a line, and became a cautionary tale for every other radio host in the country to listen to and learn from.

Dear lord, this is embarrassing to retell, but it'll be over quickly, so here goes.

I was in Year One at school and sitting at my desk next to my best friend. I grabbed a peanut and put it inside my undies. After a few minutes I took it out and asked my poor unsuspecting friend if she wanted a peanut. She did, and she ate it.

Like I said, kids are deeply weird creatures. Weird enough to do stuff that – when recounted to an audience – will lead to complaints, which will get you cited by the Australian Communications and Media Authority for breaching the professional code of conduct established by the federal *Broadcasting Services Act*.

Hey, it's a living!

Ten

It was probably a long time coming, but *The Kyle and Jackie O Show* that existed at KIIS was no longer driven by stunts. Kyle will always be opinionated, and will always offend – that will never change, and in some ways we don't want it to, because we are what we are – but anything contrived or crafted just to grab attention seemed to fade away. People were no longer on the receiving end of intentional cruelty or snark, because it just wasn't sitting right with either of us anymore.

Instead, we were starting to lean more on our platform to be able to do good, giving back to people. Kids who had lost their parents in a car accident, or a mother emerging from domestic abuse who was living in her car with her daughter. Our listeners.

Once upon a time it wasn't that way. I remember one

segment we used to do where, if a woman suspected her husband was cheating or just wanted to test his faithfulness, we would call him on the phone – 'It's the florist, you've won a free bunch of flowers, who would you like to address them to?' – and see whether he wanted to send flowers to his wife or to a mistress.

There was another segment called 'Heartless Hotline', where we would feature a real sob-story on the show – someone in need of cancer treatment, for instance, or whose house had burnt down – and we would open the lines and count down the clock for sixty seconds. If no one called in to the station during that time, the person with the sad story got to keep whatever money was on offer – maybe $10,000. But if anyone called in and said, 'I want it,' then the money was taken away and given to the caller instead. I know what you're thinking, no one would be heartless enough to make that call, right? Wrong. The money was claimed by someone else *every single time*. I hated that segment, but whenever we did the spot it became the only thing anyone was talking about.

There was a similar stunt that I didn't like, which we did at KIIS FM, and did for too long. We would find someone in need of something very specific – an amputee in need of $5000 for a new prosthetic leg, for example – and our street guy, 'Intern Pete', would go out and grab a random person in the street – 'Do you want to be part of a radio contest?' – and they would come in to the studio. We would explain to them the sad story of the person in need, and tell them they had twenty-four hours to decide whether they would let the amputee have the $5000 or keep it for themselves. They almost always kept it for themselves.

Those conceits never felt nice, and they reached a tipping point for us at KIIS. We were finished now with those honeytrap situations that would bring out the worst in people. Now we didn't want to see the worst in humanity, but the best. We were growing up, and we were sick of setting people up for a fall and not really caring about the impact or real-world outcomes.

We began relying more on our personalities to carry the show, too. Kyle and I started spending more and more time talking about anything and everything, rolling around in the issues of the day, and it felt instantly more authentic and real. We realised we didn't need the gimmicks as much, and it resonated with listeners. The audience was giving us that feedback – 'I've been away two years and have just come home, and your show is so different!' – but none of the changes were conscious. We weren't even aware that we had shifted until people told us. It was just coming naturally. In essence, I think we were growing up. We were no longer kids in their twenties, who probably didn't know any better. The show of the past felt a little childish and contrived. We were pushing forty now, and ready for a different kind of conversation.

I remember one couple who couldn't afford to have a wedding, and were going to tie the knot in their backyard. We did a 'give back' segment where we paid for their wedding, but that wasn't enough – we wanted to do more. That was always the question we asked in our production meetings: 'How can we make this even bigger? Is there *anything* we're missing – any idea – no matter how high in the sky?' No one was ever discouraged from putting forward an unlikely, shoot-the-lights-out suggestion, whether it was an interview with Tay Tay in the limo on the way to her show, or filming inside Buckingham Palace while having tea with the Queen. Most of those grand schemes won't come off, but when they do, look out . . .

Anyway, this particular couple were huge fans of Ed Sheeran, and the song played for their first dance as man and wife was going to be 'Thinking Out Loud'. Ed happened to be in town at the time, which seemed like a sign, but getting him to take an hour's drive from where he was staying in the city to perform at a wedding in The Shire in Sydney's south – and then including a lot of hanging around for the right moment to spring the big surprise – was a complete long shot. But we got in touch through his record company, and he gelled with the idea, right away, because Ed Sheeran is one of the nicest and most down-to-earth stars in the world.

I've interviewed Ed a few times, but I don't remember the first time. Honestly, you never do, because they're never that big at the start. I was looking through the photo album on my phone the other day and saw an image of Dua Lipa in the studio, and I have no memory of it whatsoever. It's one of those bittersweet things about the job – you're exposed to a constant stream of talent and charisma, but mostly it's experienced in ten-minute bites, so it's all too easy to spend your days not even noticing as the superstars of the future flow on past.

Anyway, Ed was down with the idea, because he always gives his time freely, stretching the window you've been granted. He sat opposite me in the studio one day and performed an acoustic version of 'Castle on the Hill' that made me cry. He's so generous in that way. He even helped us with a prank once directed at Hughesy and Kate in the afternoon. They came into the studio early to do an interview with Ed, and we convinced Ed to be a real arsehole to them. We were literally in his ear telling him how to avoid answering any of their questions. He felt terrible doing it, and Kate eventually cracked it and said in her brilliant, humorous way, 'I thought we were coming in to interview Ed Sheeran, who's this cruel fuck you've dragged in?', because Kate Langbroek doesn't take any shit from anyone. But the point is that Ed was up for the fun, because he's generally up for anything, which in this case meant being up for driving out to a suburban wedding and hiding in a room while waiting for the big moment. The guests were shocked enough when Kyle and I walked in, but when Ed strode out into the reception with his guitar, he blew the roof off everything. And it was such a privilege to be part of that.

It's funny working with celebrities in this way. You spend these interesting times with them, but as the years go by you fangirl less and less over such moments. The celebs become like just another customer coming into the shop, another client on the end of the phone. It's business, after all, and there's always work to be done. I get far more excited over an unexpected celebrity sighting in the wild. If Beyoncé or Bill Clinton is coming in for a radio spot, I don't really care that much. But if I run into Sally Field while shoe-shopping in a Los Angeles department store, and she's sitting next to me trying on a pair of pumps, I'm so excited that I'm practically dying inside.

Getting guests isn't always simple. The tagline for our whole show when we started in radio was 'Breakfast with the Stars', so we had to deliver. *Sunrise* and *Today* didn't fight us for those same guests initially, but that changed over time, and it created this incredibly competitive situation where in our industry the publicist becomes god. You need to suck up to them, especially the American ones. Here they're not quite so precious, but in Hollywood you would swear they're running the country, probably because they often represent so many stars all at once. Piss off the wrong publicist and you suddenly don't have access to anyone on their books. It's happened to us a few times.

I remember Lea Michele from *Glee* was on the show during our 2Day FM days, and there had been all this press about how the *Glee* cast had signed on as unknowns and not got paid much, and as the show exploded they were stuck on the same crappy contract. I brought that up, and she was pissed. If I play devil's advocate and try to see it from her point of view, it could be considered rude to ask someone about their compensation, but on the other hand, this was news. And they do call it show *business*. But Michele went silent. The entire interview turned frosty. Her publicist was furious, and she blacklisted us for years.

Will Ferrell was in town once on a day when I happened to be in a bad place, unhappy or just sensitive for whatever reason. We all have bad days. We did the interview with him in the studio, and I introduced him, pronouncing his last name 'feh-rell' rather than 'feral', an innocent mistake. But when I came out of the interview, his publicist – this tall, skinny, mid-fifties guy with long, dark, slightly greying hair, who looked more like a roadie than a PR professional – was standing by the door. And he berated the shit out of me.

'Why would you call him Will Feh-rell? How unprofessional are you?'

I apologised and said I hadn't realised, but he wouldn't let up. 'He's not *Pharrell* Williams! Is this amateur hour or something?'

He kept going and I kept apologising, and he kept hammering me even as I walked off with tears welling in my eyes. Simon Greally, our executive producer, caught me as I was walking down the corridor – 'What's up, mate?' – so I told him, and then Kyle heard about it, and they were both *furious*. I didn't want to see what went down, but they went and kicked him out. Kicked them all out. And of course, then we were on another blacklist, and when you're punished, you're punished harshly and for a long time.

But those are the few – the many are wonderful. We met One Direction backstage, interviewing the boys before they were about to perform. We waited for an hour for them to arrive, which is fine, because you learn to expect it. Most stars don't have that much time for you – for anyone, really. I remember going out to have a cigarette in the loading dock, and there was Zayn Malik, chain smoking, and there were all these screaming fans at the gates, who could see him, and were begging him to come over and say hi, while he just stared straight at them – almost through them – as if he carried a deep sadness. He did not smile, did not wave, just drew on that smoke without any expression whatsoever, except maybe one of mild disdain. And then I went back inside the green room and Harry Styles was the complete opposite. 'I'm so sorry to keep you waiting. Can I make you a cup of tea? Can I get you a water? What can I get you?' He was divine – a gorgeous human.

There was also 'Bieber Island'. There's an island in Sydney Harbour, called Cockatoo Island, which we turned into a massive concert with Justin Bieber. We gave away thousands of free tickets, and had the whole morning with him. Justin is a really lovely person and is capable of turning it on when he needs to, but you can also really see how tortured he is inside. This guy struggles with fame. You can sense it some-times in celebrities, because you have this chance to observe them when no one else is watching them, and you know the ones who are okay with the attention and the ones who have demons. Justin went on stage and was great, but as we were leaving Bieber Island we got in separate boats, almost like water taxis, with outdoor bench seats at the stern. We were side by side, the radio crew in one boat, Justin in the other, and I'll never forget the sadness on his face. All of his crew were laughing and joking with one another while Justin sat on his own, with his head hanging down. He was not in a good place, and it makes sense that he's since taken a big step back from the spotlight.

It felt as if we were on the right path at work. We could all feel this natural progression. The shift in the show was entirely organic – as if we were finally being fully true to who we are. There was no interference from above, either. We had proven ourselves, and so we had complete control and free rein. There was no pressure from anyone. Any time a pitch arose that was even slightly nasty, either myself or Kyle would shoot it down and instead suggest something positive in its place. I guess we had just reached a place where we wanted to feel good about ourselves.

There were so many other great radio moments. I remember at 2Day FM, when the new Twilight movie – *Breaking Dawn Part 1* – was coming out, and they wanted to integrate a promotion into the show, so we came up with this idea for the 'Million Dollar Dawn Dig'. We don't actually have one million dollars to give away, so these kinds of stunts can only be done when an insurance company assesses the odds and backs the gamble. This seemed like a safe bet for them, so they buried two hundred and fifty little bags at Bondi Beach at 2 a.m., and then hours later one person – selected from ten thousand entrants – would have exactly sixty seconds to dig around the sand and try to find a maximum of five bags. Then they had to choose two of those bags to open, and hope that one of the two was the big winner. The odds were ridiculous. We knew it would never be won. But the idea captured a crazy amount of attention, because it had never been done.

It was a gorgeous morning on the day of the dig. We were broadcasting from Hotel Ravesis. The girl selected to dig was Isabella from Ryde – a beautiful, bubbly young schoolteacher. Kyle was in LA and didn't come back for the dig, because that's how remote the chances were of anyone winning. I remember Isabella frantically digging with her hands and a shovel. I was on the beach with her, narrating what was happening to paint the picture for listeners, and when she opened her first bag and there was the card: *WINNER*.

I don't think I've ever been more shocked in my life, or so swept away in a moment on the show. I screamed like a hysterical fool and dropped my microphone on the sand without realising, when it was my one and only job to tell listeners that she had won the million dollars. All Kyle could hear was me screaming while I hugged Isabella, having lost all sense of where I was or what I was there to do. You live by one rule in radio – 'Paint the picture, tell the audience' – and this was so unlike me. But it was the most elated I had ever felt in my entire radio career. Isabella bought a house with the money and set up a life for herself, and I love that we could do that for her. It was a privilege.

Then there was a boy called Ziad, who needed a life-saving operation to remove a brain tumour, but it would cost around $100,000 – $50,000 for the specialist hospital care itself, and another $50,000 for the expert hands of Dr Charlie Teo. (Dr Teo has since been mired in controversy, found guilty of unsatisfactory professional conduct, but at the time he was the only surgeon willing to perform the risky operation.) We knew we could give around $20,000 at most – and even getting that kind of money quickly is hard – so we decided to turn the rest over to our listeners, hoping they would make a dent in the bill. I was checking the cash counter in real time – refresh, refresh, refresh – and it surged so quickly. We got to $100,000 in less than an hour. It was incredible to watch Sydney come together to give back and save the life of a beautiful boy. We don't do this kind of thing often, because it's harder to have the same impact time after time, but we were so touched in that moment. It's one of the highlights of my career, to have felt that love on such a scale.

It was a truly joyous thing, and I recognised it for what it was, because I had frequently struggled with our show. We've been given this amazing platform, but what for, and to what end? When you use it for good like that, you have your answer. It feels so *right*. The best feedback I get from people on the street is always of the same sort: I was struggling with depression, or I'd lost my mum, or I was in hospital being treated for cancer, and you guys were the only thing that took my mind off it and made me laugh each day. It's easy to forget that there are so many people out there doing it tough, and that your little contribution matters. You're making a difference by making them laugh or making them smile, even for a few minutes – to start their day that way, with that little bit of relief and happiness.

—

Over the years since Kitty was born, Lee and I had begun to sleep in separate bedrooms. I don't think anyone remembers the exact day that happens to a couple. It's temporary and then gradual, starting because one person is extra tired, perhaps, or maybe because one person is snoring. You tell yourself it's just easier in separate beds. I'm a noisy sleeper, snoring and moving and shifting constantly, and I have to get up so early, so it made sense that we lived in different rooms for years on end – me in the master bedroom and him in the spare room – but I also felt as if I was walking on eggshells every day. We fought constantly, over the smallest things, and even our fighting styles didn't match! I would want to spew it all out at once, whereas Lee was more sullen or passive aggressive. It just became impossible not to argue, and that's exhausting. There really was no winning.

Eventually, I started facing these small thoughts in my head. They crept in during quiet moments. *Is this really how I want to live the rest of my life? I'm not sure it is.*

But when you have a child together, it's difficult to see the way out. The idea of separating seems too big a mountain to climb – far too disruptive and painful. Better to just endure, because maybe this is just the way of the world. *Am I expecting too much of life? Maybe it's not all roses.*

But I knew deep down I had lost my true self, and who I was. And in some ways that became the pivotal shifting point for me, against which I could create change. It's one thing to go up and down in your relationship, experiencing intense periods of love and laughter and sweetness, alternating with the suspicion you're being underappreciated or mistreated. You can almost live with the rhythm of those peaks and troughs – dark valleys become tolerable for a while, because you can always look forward to eventually sitting on a mountaintop in the sun. But the greater, growing doubt – the nagging concerns that wouldn't go away – was the idea that I was losing my identity. Or maybe that I had lost it already.

The thought of starting all over again and being a single forty-something woman was a concern. Your child's age is a worry, too. Is this the right time for them, the best stage, or should I wait until she leaves home? Should I sacrifice myself and stay, to ensure she's in a stable family unit? Or by staying am I ensuring she grows up in a family of dysfunction?

Ultimately, I came to the conclusion that the environment wasn't just wrong for me, but wrong for Kitty, too. Lee sometimes said things in front of Kitty that were derogatory about me, putting me down, and I said to him one day, 'When Kitty's grown up and living with her boy-friend, and you go to visit them and her boyfriend speaks to her that way you just spoke to me, would you be okay with that? I know you wouldn't. And you can't let her see that as the way she should be treated.'

But nothing really changed, and for me that was the deciding factor. He was an incredible father, but we were no longer an incredible couple, and I couldn't let her grow up thinking this was how a healthy relationship looks. It was too detrimental.

Still, we were prisoners of circumstance. We were living in my dream home – the *Father of the Bride* house – and we were in our groove with work, and our daughter was flourishing, and that keeps you in place for years. You can't help but think you need to suck it up. You hear a voice in your head saying things aren't right, and then it goes away, and it comes back again, and goes away again. The only thing that changes is the gaps between those thoughts. The frequency. They kept returning more and more quickly, until I felt as if I was living with them constantly.

It's hard to say what pushed me over the edge. I do remember watching an episode of *The Good Wife* in which one of the characters was talking to her mum in hospital about what makes a good marriage, and how you know when your marriage is over. She called it 'the garage door test'. If you come home from work and you see his car in the garage, are you immediately happy, or the opposite? That reaction would give you your answer.

It gave me mine. I'd get home each day and want the place to myself, even for an hour. I just did not want to walk into the energy I knew was waiting inside. That was it – that was my decision. And although I'm the kind of person who avoids confrontation, once I make my choice it can't be unmade.

I'd wanted marriage counselling a year prior, but Lee wasn't keen. Now, I wasn't interested in that anymore. We sat on the bed and talked about where we had gone wrong and why separating was the best option. It wasn't a tearful, flailing, dramatic discussion. It was almost a shock to both of us, and maybe a relief. We had been in the same doom loop for so long. I went to sleep and to work the next day, telling no one, ready as always to be bubbly and funny in a one-way conversation with a few hundred thousand people in Sydney, because that's the job.

We finally separated in August 2018, and the logistics were a nightmare. I moved into an apartment in Bondi Beach. I couldn't drive Kitty to school because of work, so I had to be the one who left our home. We initially told her that I was living away temporarily for work, because we didn't want to do too much all at once. Drip-feeding the change seemed like the best way into a soft landing. She enjoyed me picking her up from school and coming to my new place and playing at the beach. After six months we had a conversation with Kitty about Mummy and Daddy fighting, and living apart for a while, and she accepted that without confusion.

It was kept under wraps publicly – although Kyle and my bestie Gemma knew – meaning there wasn't any flash of media attention to navigate. Karl Stefanovic had not long before that split up with his wife Cassandra, and I witnessed what happens when the media get a whiff of something without confirmation. If they get that sniff and you're not forthcoming, it becomes a frenzy. They write whatever they can, and hound you to your door. I felt it was better that we got on the front foot, and so I made an open announcement in the show opener one day. It was still a media circus, but only for a day or so, because there was nothing else to say. *We've separated. It was amicable. We're still friends. We love our child.* You spit out that one simple truth, and everyone moves on.

Moving on is one thing, of course, but finding your own new normal takes a little longer. Or a lot longer. I've talked to friends who have been through the same thing, and we would all say to anyone who asks, it takes three years to extricate yourself from that shared existence and to get out the other side and start seeing the light as an individual. That's daunting to think about, and of course it can vary. Some splits are worse than others, depending on how toxic partners are – depending on fights over the estate – but I was lucky. Lee and I were both so motivated by making life easy for Kitty that we became perfect friends on this shared mission. But it wasn't remotely easy. It was hard, and a dangerous habit I'd formed was about to make it even harder.

Eleven

I had a modern apartment now, overlooking the ocean at Bondi Beach, directly opposite Icebergs. I was single, with a clean slate, and it felt as if anything was possible. I felt liberated in my freedom, but also dangerously untethered. I didn't have Kitty half of the time, and I was utterly lost on those days when she was away.

I had started taking painkillers again during the final years of my marriage. This was nothing like the Endone I'd taken for my endometriosis. It was Nurofen Plus, bought over the counter, and I would take a few pills at a time with a drink. I don't remember exactly when or why I started, but I knew if I wanted a release from the world when I was stressed out, or sad, I could take a couple of these codeine pills with a glass of wine and get the sense of palpable escape I needed.

It was casual at first, until it wasn't. Truth be told, while over the years when times got tough, I'd go to the chemist and grab myself some Nurofen Plus to take the edge off, now it was different.

I don't want to downplay what I was doing to myself. I described the dosage above as 'a few' – and it definitely was that to begin with – but I use that language because that's so much easier to lay out the actual truth. To experience any kind of high, I had been taking roughly ten Nurofen Plus tablets at once for years. Now that I was deeper into my addiction, I was taking that much three or four times a day.

As any parent will tell you, the initial months and even years after a divorce can be an emotionally excruciating time. Every moment apart from your child feels as if half your heart is somewhere else. Even the smallest reminders – a toy left behind, or a drawing on the fridge – can trigger waves of sadness and loss, not to mention the guilt you face from not being there for them every day, and missing important milestones. In an attempt to cope with the loneliness and guilt I was feeling, I made another bad decision. I began taking sleeping pills – Stilnox – on the days I was alone, as a way to numb the loneliness. It was a coward's way of dealing with my pain, finding comfort in what was slowly becoming an addiction.

And an addiction to prescription medication requires effort, in the form of doctor shopping, which was exhausting and embarrassing. I knew this already, because

I'd done it back when I was taking Endone. You have to find different medical centres every month, and with a new patient showing up and asking for powerful painkillers, they're immediately suspicious and full with questions. It takes hours out of your day to go to some faraway GP and lie.

I couldn't give a fake name, because I'm recognisable, but I had no idea how the internal checks and balances of the medical system worked, so I started giving a fake date of birth. I have no idea why. I did that once and the receptionist glanced up at me with a quizzical look – 'So you were born on the thirtieth of February?' – and I just said yes, before realising how ridiculous that was. I was stunned into an embarrassed silence and couldn't get out of there quickly enough.

As this unravelling came about in my life, I was hit by a stroke of good luck – or incredibly bad luck, as I see it now – when I met someone who was able to access prescription medication for me. I knew it was dodgy as hell, but I risked it anyway. At the time, the government was putting a stop to codeine being available over the counter, meaning I'd be required to have a prescription to buy Nurofen Plus, which would mean more doctor shopping. I remember the day our newsreader, Brooklyn Ross, announced the new regulations on air. Panic set in as I wondered what the hell I was going to do. Now, my problem was not only solved, but even better, I'd be able to get a stronger codeine painkiller, Panadeine Forte.

Access to Panadeine Forte meant taking fewer tablets for the same high, which was one bonus. Another was escaping the damage I'd already done with my rampant Nurofen Plus intake. I hadn't realised this when I first started swallowing them, but Nurofen Plus contains an anti-inflammatory agent which, if taken in excess, can give you stomach ulcers. It had given me an internal slow-bleeding ulcer – a constant dripping tap, leading to extremely low levels of iron in my blood, meaning I was not only experiencing severe abdominal pain from the open wound, but I was also falling asleep at the drop of a hat, once even nodding off entirely during an on-air break. When I finally had an operation to remove the problematic ulcer, my doctors were perplexed. They had no idea how I'd developed one of the biggest ulcers they had ever seen.

None of this shocked me into action, however. Instead, I started drinking more heavily, and taking more and more pills, and life became a blur. I felt numb. I didn't care about myself. I was suddenly lost. I no longer had to dance with doctors or face interrogation from chemists to get what I needed. I could basically buy whatever I needed wholesale, through my contact, and ingest it as I saw fit. If I looked hard at the empty pill packets, I could have seen that I was only one unlucky night away from death, but I didn't want to acknowledge how dangerous I was being, and I couldn't remember that much anyway, because the Stilnox would wipe my memory of entire evenings.

It creates this alternate reality for you, almost like sleep-walking, where you can carry on and function yet record none of what you've done in your internal hard drive. I'd wake up in the morning and have no recollection of what I'd done the night before. Then I'd scroll through my phone and sit there horrified by messages I had sent – flirting with guys I barely knew, or having conversations I didn't remember with my oldest friends. People began to notice that things weren't quite right with me, but most of the time there was nothing specific they could put their finger on, beyond a bit of drunken enthusiasm or frustration. I guess that's part of the insidious nature of the addiction. You feel as if you can carry it and pull it off, because for all intents and purposes, you often can. I was scattered, yes, but I was also a highly functional drug addict.

I had just been asked to join a TV show called *The Masked Singer*, where I would be judging acts alongside Dave Hughes, Dannii Minogue and Lindsay Lohan. Lindsay wasn't in the greatest of places at the time, either, but she and I got on really well. I had her back when articles began trickling out about her being late to set, or difficult, or irresponsible. I was super protective of Lindsay and would defend her to the hilt. But she was also unstable, and I probably was, too. Pairing us up was a recipe for disaster.

I remember the day when one of the singers had been revealed to be former dual-code rugby star Wendell Sailor, and he came on to the radio show to do an interview about the experience. He made an off-the-cuff joke about how we were running late for filming because of Lindsay, but he moved on to another topic quickly, so I didn't say anything to interrupt him. He was kidding anyway, and it would have stopped the flow of the show if I'd said anything, but Lindsay heard the segment and decided I hadn't defended her, and the next thing I knew I was on the end of a barrage of late-night text messages from the Hollywood actress about how I'd been a traitor and let her down.

I was drinking and taking Stilnox that night, too, so I quickly reached my own flashpoint of annoyance and sent a volley back in her direction. *What do you mean, I'm not a girls' girl?* I thought. *How* dare *she?* I took great offence and I let her have it. The feud faded quickly enough, but we were archnemeses for a few days there, all because I was doing things I would never normally do, wading into interactions and confrontations I'd usually avoid. I guess I was just hurting. Some people take their hurt and do something worthwhile; they become productive. I chose to be destructive instead.

I lashed out at people, such as my good friend Natasha from the real estate agency on the Gold Coast and later my flatmate in Elizabeth Bay when we were in our twenties. She was living in Melbourne and came over to see me one night. We had a few drinks and I thought everything was fine, but it wasn't, and she called me the next day. 'I'm really worried about you, Jackie,' she said, crying. 'You're just not yourself.'

I couldn't think of what I'd done to make her feel that way, but my behaviour must have been odd. However, rather than admit anything to her, or to myself, I hatched a much better plan: I would shut her out. That seemed easier, to simply remove a person from my life, keeping all my secrets tightly bound. Natasha had reached out to help, but I played it down, telling her I was fine.

Once the *Father of the Bride* house was finally sold, it was time for me to buy again. And after living in Bondi Beach, where any paparazzi could stand out the front and get a shot of me on my way out the door to work, I now wanted privacy. I found a house in Woollahra, a modern recent build at the top of Cooper Park, and it was a fortress. On one side the trees went miles up – it felt like being in a rainforest, completely cut off from the world – while on the other side it was like concrete ramparts with a gate. I was surprised it didn't have a moat.

Inside, this palace was cold marble and stone, with floor-to-ceiling double height windows. It was like living inside a Westfield shopping centre – chilly and soulless. It looked beautiful when you opened it up, with the birds chirping and the pool that was like something out of a Balinese retreat. It had certainly seemed that way when it was filled with eager buyers during open inspections on sunny afternoons. But by myself, at night in particular, it was hell on earth. I don't think I could ever even go back to that place to visit, because my memories of being there are so toxic. I hit my all-time low in that house.

During this time, we were still going through the restrictions of the coronavirus pandemic. It had started when I was in Bondi, and even now in 2021 it was still surging, meaning I was locked down like everyone else, isolated in my concrete tower. I tried warming up this luxe prison, bringing in an interior designer, and sageing the entire house, but nothing could salvage it. Kitty wouldn't sleep in her bedroom. She said there was something in there, and she couldn't explain it, but it wasn't good. She was terrified, and would sleep with me instead.

There were cameras throughout the house, even in her room, and one night the garage door had been left open and a leaf blew in, which set off the motion-sensor alarm. We were just about asleep when this screeching, full-volume alert went up: *'Intruder! Intruder! Intruder!'* Kitty was scarred by that moment, and from then on every night I had to check every camera around the house on my phone, in all the rooms and throughout the yard. We would check them together, and only then would she be able to fall asleep.

One night I was looking at vision of her bedroom – the one she wouldn't go inside – and I saw there was a white orb darting about all over the place, the size of the moon in a children's picture, hovering and zagging and floating, on and on. I checked everything I could the next day to try to make sense of it – maybe a spider's web had drifted in front of the lens – but nothing did. I'm not a big believer in the paranormal, but I did find it hard to shake an overwhelming sense of dread inside that building.

I lost my driver's licence for three months, on points – a few too many speeding tickets or red-light cameras – and while this was definitely inconvenient, it also made me feel as though I could take more pills and drink more alcohol, because I didn't need to preserve my clarity behind the wheel. By the time I got my licence back, I hardly needed to plan my drug use around driving, as during the two years of the pandemic I rarely left the house or needed to go in to the studio.

I would have to taper my use on days when I had Kitty, but my body was beginning to become reliant on what I was taking. I knew I couldn't take enough to get high, or even attain that warming numbness I craved, on those days, but I could never be entirely off the pills, either. Panic would set in at the thought of leaving them at home, or my supply running out. If I went several hours without them, my hands would begin to tremble and shake. I'd get chills and stomach cramps, and nausea and diarrhoea would set in far quicker than you'd imagine. If I didn't want to feel dizzy and faint, I needed something to get me through.

My life took on an added element of planning and scheming and subterfuge. I'd found that Panadeine Forte, for instance, would only give me a high if I took it during the fifteen minutes before eating a meal. I don't know why that was so, or if it was even true, but in my head it was real, so when I went out to dinner with people I had to excuse myself before our food arrived, so I could get to the bathroom and swallow six codeine tablets. You can't exactly do that at your table without being noticed, so I'd always go to the toilet, and I'd pray the bathroom had a private sink, because if it had a public sink and someone walked in on me drinking from the bathroom tap – well, what kind of feral does that?

I thought I was pulling all of this off incredibly well, by the way, but more than a few people picked up on my behaviour. 'Jackie, what are you talking about?' they would say to me. 'We had this entire conversation yesterday.' My best friend Gemma, in particular, was spotting little lapses that she couldn't explain, and was probably closer than anyone else to knowing what was going on.

I'd nod and laugh, and act as though I was having a Covid moment, but I began to realise that I had no memory whatsoever of longer and longer stretches from my nights and days. And so, for every phone call or Zoom conversation that I had while I was alone and on pills, I began writing down the contents in dot-point form, on Post-it notes, as we talked or immediately afterwards. I was like Guy Pearce in the movie *Memento*, except instead of tattooing reminders on my body, I was sketching them with a ballpoint pen and leaving them on the kitchen bench. *Talked with [such and such]. She complained about her husband. She's not happy. He does [this and this and that].* Always bullet points. Always comprehensive enough that it would reinforce the discussion, making it easier to spark some thin memory in me the next day.

I'd hide my supply in different places around the house at first, but eventually I stored my entire stash in a safe. Because we were still often locked down and under public health restrictions, a popular pastime while cooped up like that was to fantasise with friends about open borders and dream vacations and where we would go. But I was anxious about the very idea of going overseas, because that's when I would have to figure out what amount was legal to transport, and when you do those rough calculations, it forces you to confront just how many pills you're taking. I would have to avoid Thailand and Bali for that reason, for instance, if I didn't want to end up in jail. I even had a recurring nightmare about it – not about going to jail, but about taking off on a flight and realising I'd left my drugs at home. In the dream, I'd be packed and past customs, sitting in my window seat, and then realise my pills were at home. It was my own private stress dream – like the ones everyone has where you turn up to an exam and you haven't studied, or you're supposed to give a big speech and you're naked. The stress of my everyday life was bleeding into my subconscious and finding me in the night.

I had to dispose of all the evidence, too. When I would empty all the plastic sleeves with their foil seals popped, I didn't want to put them in the bin, because I didn't want anyone seeing them. I kept them all in a white plastic bag instead, and then at the end of two weeks I would dump my disgrace into a random bin on the way to work. That was confronting – looking at how much I'd taken, before stuffing it into a dumpster – but not confronting enough to make me think about stopping.

As the pandemic went on and on, I was drawn into an even darker pit. I know I wasn't alone. People everywhere were self-sabotaging in order to cope with either lockdowns or their existential dread. It was all over the news how Dan Murphy's was doing record sales. If you weren't one of those self-righteous hipsters creating good habits in the pandemic, such as baking artisan sourdough loaves, you were probably self-medicating in some way. And I was broadcasting from home a lot, meaning I could pop a few pills earlier and earlier each day, and start drinking sooner, too. What else was there to do? Covid was everything I wanted, in a way, to excuse my behaviour. *We're being forced to stay at home, you say? Well, I hardly have to feel guilty for making myself feel better about it . . .*

I was putting on weight during this period as well. And I mean a lot of weight. That happens when you drink a bottle of wine, take a few Stilnox, then order Uber Eats – every day. The kilograms creep up quickly, and as you start seeing them on your body, you suddenly don't want to go anywhere or do anything, either, which in turn makes you gain even more weight. It's a vicious circle. I watched my favourite TV shows over and over, often watching the same episode on repeat, because it wasn't just conversations and text messages I couldn't remember the next day. I couldn't remember what had happened in *Ozark* or *House of Cards*. I couldn't follow the latest plotline in *The Real Housewives of Beverly Hills*, or whatever was happening to Jon Snow in *Game of Thrones*.

I was bingeing in all sorts of ways. I never made plans to go anywhere unless I needed to do something for Kitty, and on those days the mission was simple: keep it together. I hated my life, and I hated myself. I was irritable, too, constantly trying to level out my withdrawals with a half a tablet here, a gin and tonic there – all of my thinking completely hijacked by one prerogative: *When can I be alone again and take my pills?* I thought of nothing else, because nothing else made me happy. It's as if there's this little voice inside you, a devil, and he's so convincing. *Keep going,* he says. *Don't quit this. You're right where you want to be.*

What was I missing out on? I was – and am – a social creature, so it was noticeable that dancing and socialising and going to concerts were all now absent from my life. I seemed to go to the 'big thing' happening in Sydney every month, from Mardi Gras to a Coldplay concert, whatever was on offer. And *everything* was always on offer. I can click my fingers and get tickets to anything, because someone I know always knows someone else – it's a perk of the job. But in this period, I didn't see the point in that perk. I took nothing up, and turned everything down.

What else? I've always loved the ocean. Being under-water feels like the most peaceful, beautiful place to be.

I think I might have been a fish in a previous life, because I feel so at home there. I used to go to Redleaf Beach in Point Piper, because I always preferred the calm of swimming in the harbour, with its quiet coves and the absence of waves. It had a big grass hill and a crescent-shaped pontoon, and I would jump off and splash down, then climb up and do it again, and lie in the sun all day. I used to swim there with Lee, and we would turn to one another and gaze in wonder. 'How lucky are we?' we'd say. 'How amazing that we get to do this.' But I stopped doing that, because I'd rather be inside, and because I had put on so much weight that I refused to be seen in a bikini. I hated my body. I must have, because I was doing my best to destroy it.

I had been a Weight Watchers ambassador since the start of the pandemic. When I first signed on I lost maybe five kilograms, and they were fine with that. They were a great company to work with, and, my god they were patient. But as the next year rolled on and my addiction became worse, I had no motivation to lose any weight. I felt as if I had to get out of the contract, but, again, they were amazing and understanding. 'It's okay that you haven't lost weight,' they said. 'Just be honest about it with your audience, and share those ups and downs. Like everybody else, you're a human being, and times are tough.'

But still, I felt so embarrassed that I wasn't losing any weight. I was the public face of the company, talking about my weight loss journey on radio sometimes, while plastered on buses and billboards, and starring in television commercials. The first one was shot in my home after I'd lost some initial weight, and I wore a slinky red gown. That was fine. But the next one was mortifying. I remember wearing this white dress, long sleeved, and I was so puffy from the medication and alcohol. The whole day I just wanted to hide, but they had hired a house in Vaucluse, with all these extras – strangers pretending to be my friends. All day I posed for the camera, bringing trays of healthy food out from the kitchen, entertaining these actors while imagining what they must have been thinking, namely, *Why are they paying this bloated broad to be a weight loss ambassador?*

I'm healthier now, but I remember exactly how I felt when I was at my heaviest. Every bit of self-care had gone out the window by then. I was doing the bare minimum every day. I didn't care about my clothes or my hair. I had no pride in my appearance at all. No pride in myself. No love for myself, either. I was in a state of self-loathing, and I was self-medicating to cope with that.

By the end of 2022, on the days I didn't have Kitty, my habit reached its peak. It had gone up and up as I chased the high. I was taking a packet of Panadeine Forte every day, which is twenty-four pills – six pills at a time, four times a day, as well as a whole packet of Stilnox, which is ten to twelve tablets in total. I don't even know why. Every now and then I would get a legitimate high, so I lived in hope that the next pill would bring me another, but by the end those highs so rarely came.

I guess I kept taking them for the relief, because that was always there – that moment of comfort in the most discomfited time. *Mmm*, I'd think. *That's better.* But I knew my quality of life was degraded. It was clearly shit. That was undeniable. When you're taking that much medication, you're not participating in life – you're avoiding it. You're not creating memories, either – you're erasing them. Your cycle is set: TV, pills, booze, oblivion. Rinse and repeat. *Isn't this fun?*

I dreaded the day something would bring it to a head. *Am I going to be seventy and still doing this? Will I even make it to seventy?* I wondered. *What will be the thing that finally makes me stop?* But I also thought about how depressing my life would be when I did have to stop, when I'd have to go back to living like everyone else. *How do they live like that? How do they come home and just* be happy *not drinking or drugging or taking* something? I thought. *They* can't *be happy. I'm the happy one.*

I would actually watch people doing normal things from time to time, such as walking the dog or having a picnic – day-to-day things that were clearly bringing them joy – and I pitied them. I couldn't see any existence in which those simple, sober pleasures would be enough for me. I had no interest in that whatsoever.

My way is the best way – and the only way, I would tell myself. *I'm the lucky one. I'm the lucky one.*

Twelve

The sixth of November 2022 was a Sunday morning like any other, with the remnants of last night's Uber Eats on the floor beside the bed, along with a half-empty glass of gin and tonic and an ashtray full of cigarettes on the bedside table. I reached for another Stilnox.

It was a beautiful morning outside, but I had no plans to enjoy it. Sunshine annoyed me. I much preferred the rain – it brings less guilt when you're hiding away from the world. The sun was just a painful reminder that everyone was outside living their life and I wasn't. I hadn't been living any kind of life for the past three years – my days had become an endless blur of painkillers, sleeping pills, junk food and television marathons. I was an addict hiding a dirty little secret. I never set out to become this way, of course. Addiction is like a spider spinning its web, starting with a few strands that are barely noticeable, but gradually turning into a sticky and terrifying trap that becomes impossible to escape.

I was settled into that sad routine, but everything changed at 1 p.m. when my mobile phone rang. It was my supplier, calling to let me know that they'd been busted. Just like that, I had no more access to my pills. This was the moment I had been dreading – the moment where I'd finally have to address my addiction and somehow stop a habit I'd been indulging for years. I was sitting outside at my long wooden table when the panic came over me. It was almost an out-of-body experience as my mind raced haphazardly through all the considerations.

I wasn't thinking rationally, so my mind went instantly to whether anyone else knew. *What if this somehow comes out about me? What if it becomes public?*

There was an immediate grief for my habit, too. *I have to say goodbye to this. How do I do that? What's my future going to look like?*

I naturally wondered how I would cope, physically and mentally. *My intake is huge – ten Stilnox and twenty-four Panadeine Forte a day. How do you get off that safely?*

And I thought immediately about how much I had left, even doing a rigorous stocktake. *My current stash will probably last a fortnight. Is that enough to taper slowly? Probably not.*

I got off the phone and I paced in circles around that long table. I was so panicked. Not even one small part of me considered that it might be a good thing. I was on the hook – chained to my addiction. I had no idea what to do or what came next. I realised soon that I was almost hyperventilating and crying at the same time – bug-eyed and scared shitless.

I called Gemma – my best friend and manager – and almost couldn't get the words out. But through gulps and sobs and heaving breaths, I spilt out what I could in one cryptic sentence – 'I've done something really stupid' – but that was all I could get out before my convulsive breathing got hold of me again and caught me in my chest.

Gemma had been over the night before, bringing dinner for a girls' night, because I always refused to leave the house. We had sat up late, talking about our marriages – hers had just ended too – and the hard work of figuring out how to extricate yourself from that intimate tangle, not to mention all the thoughts of how it might affect our children.

We had spent time around the fire pit in my courtyard, drinking wine and laughing. She went home to her place close by that night, then she had woken up and driven two hours out to the country. Gemma hadn't arrived at her destination yet when her phone rang with me on the other end of the line, frantic and wailing.

'What is it?' she asked, terrified by my tone. Gemma had been constantly circling me throughout my descent, worried by my behaviour and my excuses to avoid going to the doctor. I used to wave off her concerns, saying I just had a stomach bug, or my endometriosis was back. She saw the excuses mounting, and knew something was wrong, but never exactly what. Now she was begging for straight answers. 'Just tell me, please. Just *talk*.'

'I . . . I . . .' I stammered, took a breath, and let it out. 'I've become addicted to painkillers and sleeping pills, and my supply is gone. I'm so fucking stupid.'

'I'm coming back now,' she said, immediately turning the car around and setting a course for Woollahra. 'I'll see you in two hours. Don't do anything. Just sit tight and I'll see you soon.'

That two-hour wait was sort of a relief. Everything calmed quickly, as if a little steam had been let out of the pressure cooker. I quietened down, the rapid pace of my breathing slowed, and the tears subsided. The butterflies were still there, but I can't describe the relief that came from letting someone know. I'd finally told someone, and it felt nice. There was an instant comfort in knowing that I wasn't alone anymore – that someone was coming to help me.

This was no ordinary someone, either. I met Gemma a quarter of a century ago. I was twenty-four and working at 2Day FM on the *Hot 30* when I first saw her. She was a schoolgirl then and would sit in her uniform at reception every day, and I had wondered why. Apparently she just loved radio and wanted to watch and help and get a foot in the door. *Good on her*, I remember thinking. *She knows what she wants in life.*

Radio was it for her, and very quickly she was out of school and working as a producer with Wendy Harmer. She was spotted soon after that by Wendy Day, Nicole Kidman's publicist, and tapped on the shoulder to work as an assistant for the global megastar. Gemma did exactly that for the next eight years, travelling everywhere Nicole went for almost a decade. Eventually they went into producing at Nicole's production company together, and their lives were intertwined further. Nicole and Keith are godparents to one of Gemma's boys. Gemma only left that life and came back to Australia to be with her husband, and that's when she became our executive producer and we became incredibly close.

I'd just had Kitty through IVF, and Gemma was going through that herself – experiencing those same hot-tempered, short-fuse moments. She went on to become group content director for the Hit Network – a massive job – and we stayed close. We got even closer when we both realised we were in unhappy marriages. We felt like what we were – two incredibly capable women, with talent and ambition and spark, who had been laid low by our relationships. We wanted more for ourselves, and so we formed a safe space and sounding board for each other, somewhere we were able to confide our doubts. And then, when we left our husbands within two years of each other, we were able to find our way to the other side together.

All throughout my time at Woollahra, Gemma was the one person who always tried to bring me out of my funk.

Her offers were incessant. 'Hey, I'm going kayaking this weekend,' she would pipe up. 'Why don't you come out and try it with me?'

I remember she wouldn't let up until I did, and so finally I went with her to Gordons Bay. I was wearing my usual long-sleeved silky summer top – the one thing I felt hid my weight from view. But I sat down in the kayak that day and felt my fat bunch up around my waist, and there was a paparazzi primed for the shot. I remember seeing that photo online later, and I almost saw past the flab, because what stood out most was the misery on my face. I hated how I looked. I hated being in the sun. I hated all of it. And Gemma knew.

She had known for a while that something was off, but not exactly what. In her mind, there were all these minor red flags, but they would only wave for an instant. We would start hanging out, talking about life, and I would quickly seem that bit less sober than she was. *We've only had one drink, but Jackie seems lit*, Gemma would think. *Not exactly out of it – but as though she's had three drinks instead of one*. These little thoughts would nag at her, but were also easy enough to dismiss or explain. *Maybe Jackie had a couple of drinks before I got here? Perhaps it's been a long week? It could just be that, unlike me, Jackie gets up every morning at 4 a.m., so by 8 p.m. she isn't exactly firing on all cylinders – I should give the girl a break.*

Gemma had only become my business manager earlier that year. She had left Southern Cross Austereo and I knew she was a gun. Having her work alongside me was a no-brainer – as was calling her in this moment of crisis. Gemma had some experience with addiction through people she had known, and they had recovered successfully after a stay at the Betty Ford Center, so Gemma's mind immediately went there. She had no idea how bad my situation was, but she's a planner, so just in case it was really bad – literally as she was driving back to me on that Sunday afternoon – Gemma even called the famed Palm Springs clinic to see if they had a space available in the coming week: Could they find me a spot for Sunday next week?

Gemma didn't tell me any of this until she got to Woollahra, but she needed that contingency plan set. If things were as bad as my trembling voice suggested, she knew what we would do. We would see out the working week, then fly to Los Angeles to get better. She would stay with me every night until we flew, to make sure I wasn't dead in the morning, and then we would leave together. That was that. The Betty Ford Center is often reliant on health insurance to cover the typical 28-day stay, because most people can't afford to pay the $50,000 fee. But because I would be able to pay my way privately, I'd be able to get in immediately if I wanted to.

When Gemma arrived in person to tell me all of this, I was once again in a state of panic. Saying it all out loud – in person, eye to eye, for the first time – I couldn't stop crying. Gemma was in tears too, so upset with herself that she hadn't figured it out, and that I had gone through it alone. There was this pure traumatic grief between us as we held hands, sobbing. Gem knew that she needed to take over the situation and help me. But honestly, I didn't want that. Not at all. And I pushed back on her plan, immediately.

'No no no no! We don't need to do that,' I argued. 'We're going to taper it off. I've still got a good supply. I'll be fine.'

'No, we're not going to do that, because it *won't* be successful,' said Gemma. 'You need actual *help* for what's going on with you mentally. Otherwise you'll find someone else to get what you need, and you'll keep on doing what you're doing. You need to get better, honey. This isn't you. I've watched you fade away. I miss my best friend. You deserve joy again, and there's no joy in the life you're living. And if you do rehab here, it'll become a media circus. The best chance you have to get better is if we get you far away from here.'

She was resolute, and she won, thank god. I needed that tough love, because I was already searching for any possible way of worming myself out of going. I bristled, too, telling Gemma that she was being extreme.

'This is overkill,' I pleaded. 'This is so far over the top.' But ultimately I conceded, because ultimately I was tired. I wasn't just exhausted – I was weary to my very bones.

Still, the thought of rehab terrified me. How long would I be in there? Would I have to withdraw cold turkey? What would that feel like? Will I be curled up in the foetal position for days on end, like they are in the movies? Would I be sharing a room with someone, and what would that person be like? How would I cope all day without the distraction of drugs? Would I have to give up alcohol as well?

The next four to five days were busy. I had to make a 2 a.m. phone call to the Betty Ford Center, which turned into a wrenching two-hour conversation about my whole life history. They needed to know it all, from my first experience with alcohol to whether I had ever been sexually abused – the latter because it would feed into whether I stayed in a co-ed dorm or a women's only space. But mostly they needed to talk about what my addiction was, how long it had gone on, how deep the chemical dependence went, and therefore how long the detox would need to be before my therapy could begin.

I had to break the news to a select few people at home. I called Lee first, because we would have to explain to Kitty what was going on without telling her what was *really* going on. Lee had always suspected that there was something else at play, that I had a problem I was hiding from the world, and he was relieved I was finally addressing it. He was great about it, actually. Kitty was about to turn twelve, so we decided we would tell her I was going to America for a radio conference and staying somewhere with other broadcasters.

With a little bad luck that lie might have come unstuck, because we didn't consider what I would be saying on air to my audience a few days later – that I was taking time off for exhaustion – and how the curiosity and speculation around that announcement would be so great in the industry and beyond. We didn't think about Kitty possibly telling her friends about Mummy's radio conference, and how that wouldn't match what Mummy had said on radio – the public-facing story that all the parents at Kitty's school would have heard. It never came back to bite me, but it could have, easily. It would have stood out to the curious few.

I told my assistant, Brittany Woodford, but that was more of a confirmation than a revelation. Britt already knew. She's been my assistant for almost a decade now, organising everything in my schedule. She pays my bills. She does all my administration and accounting. She picks up the dry-cleaning, takes the car to get it serviced, lets the tradie in to fix the broken appliance. She books the flights and the restaurants and the concert tickets. She has access to every email and every social media DM, and gives me reminders and nudges about the calls and texts and emails I need to send. She can read and hear everything in my life. It's an enormous amount of trust, built slowly over the course of our time together.

She's seen it all, too, from the dirty underwear to the empty prescription drug packets. Britt has always tasked herself with looking after me more than just a regular personal assistant. She's the most beautiful person you could ever meet, so genuinely loyal and kind – she is like a sister to me. And she had written to me a couple of times over the years: *Please get help. I don't know what to do, and I know I can't overstep the mark, but you need help. I want to see you live your life to the fullest.* She would leave each note or letter on the kitchen bench for me to find, but we never had a conversation about what she wrote. The letters would just disappear, and we would both know they had been read, without either of us acknowledging that they had ever existed. It must have been so stressful for her, desperate to reach out to others who might help but knowing she had to keep my confidence, no matter what, and she knew what it could potentially do to me publicly if she asked the wrong person for help.

I called Mum last, because that was always going to be the hardest call for me. Mum was relieved, though. She had watched me deteriorate and disconnect from life, and from her. She had watched me sink, and had been the most pro-active with her questions – 'Why aren't you being healthy? Why are you letting yourself go?' – but I didn't want to hear any of that at the time, so my calls to her dropped from daily, to every other day, to weekly. She would come to visit and we would fight, because everything she did felt like an interference or snooping.

She had watched her daughter turn into someone she didn't recognise. She didn't know anything about the pills, but she took note of the alcohol. She's that mother who will spot the open wine bottle in the fridge, two-thirds full, and mark the level with an imaginary line, so she can check back in the morning before asking, 'How much did you have to drink last night?' – knowing she could catch me out in a lie. But when I finally told her everything, she had the explanation she needed, so the news oddly made her feel better rather than worse.

Dad was Dad – he was brief, and he was behind me all the way. 'Good onya for being honest, and for getting help.' He wasn't too detailed or effusive, because he never is. He's a typical Aussie bloke in that way – pragmatic and laconic. Many people think laconic means laid-back, but it doesn't; it means succinct, or expressing oneself in few words, almost casual, like a farmer who will wave away a blowfly while uttering a few short lines out of the side of his mouth. That was always Dad. Rehab made sense to him. 'Great idea. Go get better,' he said. 'We're all behind ya, love.'

Gemma called my boss, DB (Derek Bargwanna), on my behalf. I was very close with him. I used to go over to his house often, and got on incredibly well with his wife, Belinda. Gemma was vague – 'Jackie's not in a good way – trust me when I say she needs a few weeks off' – and he understood, even if he didn't know the truth. 'Got it,' he replied. 'Take as long as she needs.'

Then I made the call to Kyle, offering him that same mix of honesty and obfuscation. 'I'm in such a bad place right now, in every way,' I said. 'I've been to the doctor and I need rest.' That made sense to him, because he'd been there before, and because I actually *had* been quite sick.

I'd had Covid and then a bad chest infection which wouldn't go away. Every break in the show I had been constantly coughing and spluttering off mic for more than six weeks. I was able to use that as the main reason, but I also made it clear to Kyle that this was more than a frog in my throat.

'I'm burnt out. I'm unwell. I need a break.'

'Yeah, darl. No problem!' he said. 'It's gonna be fucked without you, but I get it.' Then he dropped a little joke – 'You're not going to rehab, are you?' – and it landed on me like a bomb. Luckily he just laughed and laughed. I didn't even have to say no because he just kept on laughing, as if it was the most improbable thing he could imagine.

I began to sense the enormity of what was about to happen. This might sound a bit woo-woo, but I'm all about signs, and I began to see one recurring. Over and over I kept seeing the number 11. It was everywhere. I'd look up at the clock and it would be 11:11 a.m. I'd glance at the gate of a house – number 11. I didn't know what it meant until I was in rehab. I saw a social media post by Jennifer Aniston in which she wrote about her connection with the number 11. She has a tattoo on the inside of her wrist that reads 11:11. Her best friend has the same tattoo. She's never revealed the full depth of her connection to the number, but it keeps cropping up in her life. She was born on 11 February 1969. Her beloved dog Norman died in 2011. I saw her post on social media about the death of her father on 11 November 2022 – 11/11/22 – and I dove into the number more. Aside from its importance to the *Friends* star, the number 11 often represents a powerful sign from the universe. It means you're doing something monumental – that you're on the path to something transformative.

That was true for me. I never wanted to go back to the house in Woollahra, so Gemma helped me put it on the market – privately, so that no one would know I was in this state of upheaval – which meant we also had to find a rental for me to come home to after my stay in California. We found one – a gorgeous, airy, week-by-week summer rental by the beach in Clovelly. It was number 38, and three plus eight adds up to 11; another little sign in my mind. It was perfect and bright, furnished, and ready to go. The owner met us within an hour of us getting in touch and was happy to let me have a year-long rental. All I had to then do was slip out of Sydney undetected.

We finished the show on Friday morning, and immediately recorded the message to be played during the opening break of the Monday morning show, as if it were live. That would allow us to hop on a flight and leave the country that night. I would be in California before anyone in Australia knew what was going on.

Thirteen

I didn't want to think about where I was going, so I thought about where I was instead. I was spending one final night in the outside world before rehab. I was in a little Palm Springs hotel, trying to avoid thinking about the Betty Ford Center, and instead treating myself to a mini girls' getaway adventure in the California sunshine. We had a swimming pool and a spa, and spent all day Saturday lounging in the water.

Sunday morning was an unwelcome arrival, but I tried to stay positive. We had breakfast in the old retro restaurant of the hotel itself. With its leather booth seating, it was almost a diner and felt like something out of *Happy Days*. I quickly clued on to the fact that this would be my last hurrah, so I ordered three bellinis and pulled the final Stilnox from my pocket. I was about to gulp it down when it slipped and fell to the floor, then rolled out of sight, disappearing into the thin space underneath the bolted-down circular iron table stand.

This was one of those untouched dark corners of any old eatery floor – covered in grease and grime and cobwebs – but I got down on my hands and knees to fish that filthy pill out from its hidey-hole. And Gemma did, too. Gemma was going to be my nominated contact when I was at the Betty Ford Center, so she had been on all the phone calls arranging my stay. One of the things they had warned her about – specifically as my carer – was that I needed to continue taking the same number and type of pills that I'd been taking, all the way up until I was admitted. It was crucial, they said, that I stayed on that same routine – no more, no less. When people take more, they often take too much more in an attempt to enjoy a final last gasp, which is clearly dangerous. And when people take less, they often convince themselves they can get by and manage with less, and so they turn tail at the last minute and decide against going to rehab at all, which is also clearly dangerous.

All of which meant that we found ourselves on this disgusting floor under the table together, searching for that runaway Stilnox. I remember we looked up at one another, with all this dust and dirt on our hands, and burst out laughing.

'What am I doing?' I said, smiling. 'I think this is my rock bottom.'

That's what we're always like in tough times – we try to find the humour in any situation. We sure found it in that moment, and I found the Stilnox, too. I swallowed it without a second thought.

Getting to the Betty Ford Center in Rancho Mirage is a journey, but not a difficult one. It's really only two hours from Los Angeles, due east through Compton and Riverside and the sprawling suburbs of that famous city. Soon enough you're clear of the chaos and in the middle of nowhere, headed towards the Coachella Valley and Joshua Tree National Park, and the space around you is nothing but cactus and sand, tumbleweeds and dust.

Parts of it look like that final scene in *Se7en*, where Brad Pitt and Morgan Freeman confront the worst sin of the villain, Kevin Spacey. The deserted, sunbaked expanse honestly looks like the setting of a thousand movies – always for those 'moment of truth' plot points where the hostage is handed over or the dope deal goes down. And that's how it felt for me – like the ominous road to some final dramatic destination, where I would trade one thing for another. Something was looming, and it filled me with dread.

We arrived at the car park and called reception so I could enter the medical intake stream, which is a sectioned-off wing of the facility where patients can detox before joining the wider therapeutic community. They came out to meet me and administer a Covid test, and, provided that came back clear in twenty minutes, I would be going in alone. Gemma and I sat down in the gutter together, in the shade of a tree with beautiful pink flowers, waiting for my negative result, and Gemma did something I wasn't expecting. She took a photo of me, so I could remember in the future how I felt in this moment. Then she asked if I wanted to record a message for myself – to say where I was and what I was doing, and why. She gave me her phone and walked away to give me a moment of privacy.

It's hard for me to watch now, but there I am on screen, in big black sunglasses against the glare of the sun. I'm still shocked when I look at that video – at how bloated and unhealthy I looked from my alcohol and painkiller abuse.

'I have just arrived here at the clinic,' I say, 'where my beautiful friend Gemma has dropped me off.'

I tell the camera that the doctor has warned me I won't have a chance for a cigarette inside for a while, so I might as well get one last puff in now – smoke 'em if you've got 'em – and I do.

'I feel interested to see what it's all about,' I say, clearly putting on a brave face between heavy drags on that cig-arette. 'I'm a little bit scared. Don't know what I'm going to go through. I have no idea what these next thirty days will hold.'

I can hear the emotion in my voice – I'm getting choked up, and finding it hard to say much more. 'I think it's all going to be good,' I whimper, my tears hidden by my sunnies. 'We'll see what happens. Bye.'

Finally, a beautiful, bald-headed nurse in dark blue scrubs walked over.

'You're clear,' he said. 'It's time to go in now.'

I was terrified. This was the moment I had to leave behind any support system and walk into the unknown. I had no idea how detox would feel – whether it would be painful or frantic. Would I be sweating and vomiting? Would I sleep or suffer through insomnia?

Gemma wasn't allowed inside the facility, naturally, so we hugged for as long as we could. She kept telling me that she was so proud of me, and that she believed in me, then I left to start my journey. She messaged Lee and Mum to let them know I was safe, and then she sat down for a moment. She sat there in the rental car for thirty minutes, actually, steadily weeping. She knew I was in good hands, but she also knew that once she drove away, I would be alone.

The Betty Ford Center might be in the middle of the desert, but it's also like an oasis, with manicured lawns and lakes and tall palm trees, gleaming auditoriums and an array of houses. The detox centre itself is different. There, I found myself in a small room with a doctor, getting my blood pressure checked, and my photo taken, and being breathalysed too. The doctor reminded me of Bill Cosby – the nice version of Bill Cosby, from *The Cosby Show* – that fatherly figure who's warm and kind and wears a colourful novelty tie.

Usually when people go into rehab, they spend the morning getting as obscenely drunk as possible, then entering three or four times over the legal limit. I learnt later that people will ask one another, 'What was your limit?' because it's one of those interesting trivia nuggets you all share. One poor person had gone to the bottle shop and bought a bottle of wine, sculled it immediately before walking in, then saw that his blood alcohol level was zero, because he had accidentally bought non-alcoholic wine. I didn't do that. But I'd had my Stilnox and champagne with peach juice.

They took me to my room, and it was kind of bare. Imagine an old Holiday Inn room crossed with a hospital ward cubicle, with a floral bedspread and a little bathroom and a sense of impending dread about the withdrawals to come. There was a lounge room with a television and vending machine, but the idea is that you stay in your room until you've cleared your system of chemicals. A nurse checked on me throughout the night, offering a Tylenol just to calm me down.

But I wasn't too bad at all. In the past when I had gone too long without taking my Panadeine Forte – or my Stilnox, in particular – I'd got typical withdrawal symptoms. Those times I'd had diarrhoea and vomiting, and experienced shaking and twitching as my nervous system struggled, but I wasn't suffering through as much of that as I expected now, as they gave me medication to help with the withdrawals. This medication clearly did its job, because Dr Bill Cosby even came to visit me and search my bags, because he was worried that I'd brought in a secret stash of pills, given my less-than-severe reaction. He was a little suspicious of me, I think.

I was so naive to the protocols and processes – to the rituals of rehab. He began asking me these strangely worded questions, or at least they seemed strange to me at the time, because I knew nothing about the Twelve Steps other than their general existence, of course.

'Do you believe that you are powerless over alcohol and that your life has become unmanageable because of it?' he asked.

'No,' I answered, a bit perplexed, because I was here for my addiction to painkillers and sleeping pills, not alcohol.

'Do you believe that there is a power greater than yourself that can restore you to sanity?'

'No,' I answered, even more perplexed to find a reference to religion in his spiel, though the lapsed Catholic inside me did wince slightly.

I kept saying no to all of his questions and could see his mind turning. *This is serious*, his furrowed brow seemed to say. *This girl can't even admit she has a problem.*

He left soon after, and never did actually search my bags, but after twenty-four hours they were happy to let me into the residential part of rehab. There was a handful of other people in the same position, and we all sat in a communal room, on chairs set up in a semicircle, as they laid out the rules for us.

We were allowed to use our phones inside the house we were assigned to, but never on common grounds, given the risk of filming people and violating their privacy. There would be a wake-up call every morning by 6 a.m. over the loudspeakers. We had to make our bed every morning. We would be assigned duties, such as doing dishes or cleaning toilets. We would be sharing a room with someone, and I was going to be assigned to a co-ed house – a new thing they had just started – because I hadn't expressed a history of any really traumatic experiences with men during the intake calls.

I remember walking into my dorm and thinking the walls seemed older than I was expecting. The Betty Ford Center has this reputation in popular culture of being the glamorous last resort where the stars go to recover. But if you look up a list of famous faces who went there, they're mostly from a different era. It's Chevy Chase and Ozzy Osbourne at their peak, or Robert Downey Jr and Drew Barrymore in their youth. In some spots those very people had even signed the now-ageing walls.

That is no longer Betty Ford's regular clientele. Celebrities don't go here anymore. They go to magnificent facilities that might as well be the Hilton, where you get your own luxurious bedroom overlooking the beach in Malibu, and you get daily massages and spas and are pampered beyond belief. This was not that – this was run-down and basic. If it was a hotel, it would have been two stars. But luxury and pampering weren't what I was here for – I was here for their program, which is known for its very high success rate.

I was assigned a mentor, Amanda, a short, mid-thirties, heavyset black-haired girl with glasses, who was friendly and welcoming. She showed me around the common area – with its sunken lounge, TV and a DVD player, coffee table and kitchenette – and to my room, which I had to myself for a couple of days until a new patient arrived.

I'll never forget the smell as I walked into that room. Smells are an important sense for me. This one was horrific, like some mystery mix of bodies detoxing their poison with the mould in the carpet and the antiseptic cleaner trying to cover it all up. Breathing in that funk, I felt totally gutted and depressed, and my face was wet with tears as I unpacked. *What am I doing here?* I wondered. *What have I done?* I could not have felt more alone in that moment, but of course, I wasn't alone.

I'd been released from the detox facility in the afternoon, so by now it was nearing night-time, and I had no idea what the other people would be like. I walked out to the kitchen area and this huge man came up to me. Mick (not his real name, as is the case with anyone I mention from my time in the Betty Ford Center) was six-foot-four and wide, didn't understand personal space, and just talked nonstop right in my face. He was nice, but was an overwhelming person to meet first up.

I went outside next and found a group smoking – or, rather, they found me. 'You're new! Hi, I'm Miranda,' said one. 'I'm an ice addict. This is my fourteenth time in here.' Miranda apparently worked in healthcare and had easy access to methamphetamine, which is how she became an addict. She had taken it so much that she could no longer find a vein, and would lose her arm if she continued injecting.

The next person approached: 'Hi,' he said, smiling. 'I'm Brett.' Brett had a big Ned Kelly beard and he showed me a photo of himself with an arsenal of guns. 'I'm in here because I threatened to kill myself, so the SWAT team broke into my house and carted me off to the mental institution, then here.'

Most of them were in bad shape, especially Rick. Rick was a fentanyl user. He was young, tall and skinny with blond hair. If you were to imagine a drug user on the streets in Kings Cross, that was Rick. Low jeans, cap backwards, a little drawn and jaded, with a 'fuck you' attitude. But there was something in him that was beautiful, too.

The final girl who came up to me wasn't doing much better. 'Hi, I'm Nikita,' she said. Her eyes were bright yellow and her skin was jaundiced, and you could smell the detoxing process on her, specifically the boozy sweat seeping from her pores. 'I'm an alcoholic,' she added, 'and I'm waiting on a liver transplant – or I'm gonna die.'

I had some dinner that night, and then went to my first Alcoholics Anonymous meeting. Everyone went around the room and introduced themselves – 'Hi, I'm Michelle, and I'm an addict – I've been sober thirteen days' – and when you're new you not only have to say your name but you have to share something about yourself. I burst immediately into tears and felt so embarrassed, but there was no holding it back. 'I'm Jackie,' I said. 'I've never been to rehab. This is my first time.' And I blubbered, but they were all so welcoming. They just hugged me and told me I was with family, and it was all going to be okay.

I quickly picked up the rhythm of the meeting. You take turns each night, someone reading a chapter from the AA handbook, and then you go around the room sharing what resonated with them from the reading. At the end, they told me it was time for me to stand up, and they grabbed this stuffed camel toy. 'Kneel down,' they said, 'and touch the camel.'

I had no fucking idea what was going on, so I bowed to their instructions, knelt, and put my hand on the toy camel. They talked about how the camel, in nature, can go thirty days without water. They talked about its strength and resilience. Then they told me I had to *kiss* the camel, and I honestly thought it was an initiation joke they were playing on me. It wasn't. I was clueless to the symbolism behind this stuffed toy, which is actually right there in the AA handbook:

The camel each day goes twice to its knees,
It picks up its load with the greatest of ease,
It walks through the day with its head held high,
And stays for that day, completely dry.

I knew nothing of that at the time. I thought I was being pranked, and when you're in my profession, you know a thing or two about pranks! So I laughed nervously the entire time, but they laughed along with me. It broke the ice, I guess.

Next, I lined up with everyone else to receive my medication. We did that three times a day, putting out your hand for the meds that would keep you regulated, catered to the addiction you were trying to shake. It was a huge queue, with all clients from all the houses gathering in the same central medical centre. Some people looked as if they were having fun. Others were miserable. I got my medication but had no idea what it was – something to make me sleep, probably melatonin – and it did nothing. I wasn't vomiting or shaking, but for a good ten days I experienced some distinctive aftershocks. A skin-crawling anxiety. A twitching discomfort. A restless confusion.

I needed to calm down, so I finished my first day with a long, hot bath in this tiny 1950s tub. I texted Mum to tell her I was okay and that the people were nice, because I didn't want her to worry.

I'd said nothing to anyone there that night about why I was in rehab, and they didn't ask either. But I couldn't help thinking that everyone's case was just so extreme compared to mine, and I remember feeling this wave of anger welling up inside me towards Gemma. Although now I can't love her enough for what she did, and how it changed my life, I imagined what I would say if she were standing in front of me right then.

'You have overreacted, and put me in here, and I *don't* belong here. These people are proper, full-blown addicts, and I am *nothing* like them.'

As I stared at the ceiling that night, wondering how my friend could have put me in this place, the final line at the end of that song by Radiohead, 'Creep', kept playing over and over in my head. *I don't belong here . . .*

I went to sleep alone in the dorm room, although I might have only slept for an hour. Hoping for a dream to take me away from that place was futile.

—

I got up at 4 a.m., made myself a cup of tea and stayed awake. In the quiet of the morning I met a new face, Simon, who would have been seventy-five. He had been an alcoholic his whole life, and had lost everything – his wife and children – but I admired him so much. Simon knew he didn't have long left in life, and it would have been so easy for him to simply carry on with his addiction, but he wanted to make his last years count – to be clean and sober on his way out of this world, and that's why he was there. He kept to himself, mostly, but was always up early, like me. He had started working on the treadmill, with a minute or so of jogging everyday, and he was making progress in thirty-second increments. It was inspiring to watch.

I quickly learnt that there is no easing into the program. The wake-up call came from someone in the house around 5.30 a.m., through the loud and distorted static-y crackle of an ancient intercom system. I got myself ready, knowing I needed to be in the auditorium for a talk at 8 a.m. There was always a talk, about how meditation can help with addictions, or the importance of exercise. It's basically a lecture with questions, followed by a fifteen-minute break, followed by group counselling. They get you to write down honest answers to the exercises set by your leader, and you read those answers out to the class.

You're given several assignments during your stay and granted ten days to complete the major one, which you eventually present to the group. That project is your story – your whole story. The terrible things you've done. The friends you've lost. The things you've sacrificed. Your lowest point. It's not something you jump into immediately, or lightly.

That first day, Brett, the boy with the machine guns and the bushranger beard, shared his story, and I just saw the most beautiful person emerge. He was the first example I was given about seeing beyond looks, or even deeds, and recognising how we all start as angels and are turned and twisted by . . . a disease.

One of the first things they teach you in detox or counselling is that addiction is a disease. It's not something born from a lack of willpower. It's not a choice. It's like diabetes, or cancer. There is no cure. You *can* treat it – but it will remain beyond your control if you don't seek out and pursue that treatment.

It made me look at everyone in that room so differently that day. It made me look at myself differently, too. That silent judgement I had made while staring at the ceiling only hours beforehand – *I don't belong here* – was wrong. I did belong there. I was no different to anyone else in that room, I just chose a different drug.

I'd never been severe in my judgement of people dealing with addiction on the streets. But still, if I think about the people hanging around the local methadone clinic at home, who looked as if they were wasting away, I'm not proud of the thoughts that used to cross my mind. *What a shame*, I'd think. *You could have made better choices in your life.*

I would see them all the time when living near Kings Cross, in Elizabeth Bay, and it did reach a point where you were desensitised to it, when people with problems became background noise – something to walk past instead of something to stop and notice. I always felt a sense of empathy, but never enough thought for their actual stories, like the stories I heard in rehab, from people who were honest and real and raw. They were sad and they were special, and I loved each and every one of them.

As the days went on, I learnt more and more about addiction – where it comes from and how it develops. In the early days, I was still fixated on giving up the painkillers and the sleeping pills, but not alcohol, until I came upon what I thought was a bit of light reading. I had bought Russell Brand's book *Recovery: Freedom from our addictions*. It goes through the Twelve Steps, but in a Russell Brand kind of way – a modern, irreverent take, with a questionnaire at the end of each chapter. One specific set of questions was based on alcohol use, and when I answered all of them, I had an uncomfortable epiphany.

'Shit. I actually *am* an alcoholic as well.'

Even though I didn't go out and get blind drunk, I would certainly drink every day. I realised I hadn't gone a day without drinking since I'd had Kitty – twelve years earlier. There wasn't a day that I didn't drink, and there wasn't a day that I would even entertain not wanting to drink. I had a problem. And you can call it an addiction, or you can prevaricate and equivocate and say you're more dependent than hooked, as if somehow that's any different, but ultimately they're the same thing.

The book also stressed that life can be so great without any of those addictive trappings, but I didn't buy that. Not yet. I thought it was bullshit. I heard those same old voices – *I'm the happy one, I'm the lucky one, isn't this great* – and it wasn't until much later that I realised Russell was telling the truth.

As I filled in the questionnaires and did my group assignments, I also discovered the power of journalling, and what you can discover by writing everything down. Things start pouring out – things you're not expecting – and your thought process is sharper and more concentrated. The ideas have time to settle and stick.

Writing became a ritual for me, and a release. I would sit at my table with pen and paper, writing every day. It's slower going than with a keyboard, but it suits the exercise. Besides, I did speed typing in TAFE and I'm still excellent at it, but you don't want to be quick when the point is to marinate in your thoughts. Type too quickly, and you move along too fast. Going slower allows those revelations to bubble up and dawn on you. Doing it all by pen hurts the hand, but heals the heart.

The other people who were going through rehab there had hit rock bottom, but it's fair to say that I hadn't, because fate had intervened and Gemma had got involved. That did make it harder to relate to the others sometimes, but it also made their stories so much more sobering, particularly because so many of their stories were about booze. You might imagine being surrounded by heroin users and victims of the opioid crisis, but three-quarters of the people in rehab were alcoholics. And they would talk about hiding booze bottles in ceiling cavities, and waking early to wait in front of bottle shops. Theirs began to feel like cautionary tales.

I did aqua aerobics in the afternoon, in the outdoor pool. It was winter there, so even in the desert the unheated water was brisk. It felt so good to exercise and move and just *be* in the water. I felt as if I was living, and I began to interact with more and more people, good and bad.

There was one guy, James, who was really pessimistic and loved to talk about all his problems. Most people gave him a wide berth, because once he got started there was no stopping him. He latched on to me because I was keen to help him talk through those problems. I was in a particularly empathetic mode in rehab; when you hear so many stories and see so much vulnerability in people every day, you start to have a lot more understanding for others. I think James definitely sensed that in me, so I became his sounding board.

There was Matt – the dominating one of the group. He was bossy, and wanted to be in charge of everything. Every time someone else was speaking or sharing their story, Matt would butt in with his own tangential tale.

He couldn't help but be the one to lead us in any discussion, or pick the movie to watch that night.

I met my roommate on day three. Tanya was blonde, roughly my age, and became the best roommate I could have asked for. She was an alcoholic. We bonded immediately and became fast friends.

After a week I was chosen to be the welcomer for the new incoming girls. The nurse brought a young, scared girl over to me. 'This is Tyler,' she said. 'Can you take care of her?' Tyler was twenty-three, was born into a wealthy family, could have been a model, and was coming down from fentanyl. I thought she had been discharged from detox far too early. She was shaking and wailing and saying she wanted to die. It was uncomfortable to watch and I had no idea what to do. 'I need something,' she said, rocking back and forth. 'I need something.' Watching someone come down from that was wrenching, and a reminder of the destruction fentanyl has caused. I'm terrified of the drug ever coming into our country the way it has in the US.

There was an incident one night with a girl who shared a room with three other women – a little two-bunk-bed space everyone called 'the swamp'. No one wanted to be there, and six days into my stay it was discovered that this girl had smuggled meth into the shared room and was using. She was brought into a central room in tears – 'I'm so sorry, I'm so sorry' – then we all got to have our say in a group meeting.

I remember that poor Miranda, the ice addict who was on her fourteenth visit to rehab, had been saying how *this time* it was working, and she could just *feel* it her bones. So when she found out that there was meth right next to her in the bedside table, she was furious with her roommate, and all hell broke loose. People were yelling at the girl and about her, while others who were more sympathetic were lobbying for a second chance. I voted for the second chance, and got given the dirtiest looks from some people. They were livid that she had jeopardised everyone's sobriety, not just her own, and I could understand that. Ultimately, the girl was taken away and placed with another group.

It really was the best of times and the worst of times. I was forging deep friendships and even having fun, and shedding tears and confronting fears. There was so much kindness and understanding. You simply can't imagine what it is to share your deepest darkest secrets with so many others, all at once.

I was struggling a little with my body not feeling right, and that was a concern. More than a week into my stay I was still only getting an hour or two of sleep a night – three at most. As it turned out, due to a computer error sometime after my arrival at Betty Ford, I hadn't been receiving the correct dosage of drugs to taper off from the level I'd been using. My body had been used to ten heavy sleeping pills a day, and now I was having none.

I think physical challenges such as the lack of sleep made other clients feel angry at times. Anger definitely came up in therapy there every day. Everyone seemed to feel it, sharing emotional stories about losing control.

I didn't have any of those reactions, and through therapy I began to understand why.

As a little girl, and even in my marriage, I was afraid of getting the silent treatment whenever I spoke up. I've got much better at that since, but for so much of my life I felt it best to avoid any feelings of rage, because it would lead to abandonment.

I experienced so many moments of grace in rehab. I remember even on the way there with Gemma, we drove to an ATM to get cash, because they warn you about that in advance – how there's a kind of store or a commissary inside the center, but you need hard currency to buy things. I was sitting in the car waiting for a light to change when two hummingbirds began buzzing outside the passenger window. It was as if they were levitating on the spot, fixing their gaze upon me, sending some indecipherable message. *This is a sign!* I thought. *What are the chances?*

The chances are good, in fact. Maybe better than good. I told one of the clinic nurses about my encounter as soon as I arrived – 'I've just seen the most amazing thing!' – but his ho-hum response told me all I needed about the rarity of what I'd just seen. Hummingbirds were like sparrows in that landscape – it was like saying to someone, 'Oh my god, I just saw two seagulls!' when in Manly. They're a dime a dozen.

But I had so many beautiful encounters with those birds during my stay. Whenever I was struggling or having a tough day, I'd have a random encounter with one. They would come to me, stopping at my eye level for a few seconds before flying away. I came to think of them as special little signs that someone or something was watching over me. I felt the hummingbird was my aunty who had passed away, coming to tell me I was on the right path, and that she was with me.

Nikita, who was waiting for that liver transplant, and was like my little sister in there, and who I kept in touch with later – who went in and out of rehab again after I had left – could see what those birds meant to me. She went to the gift shop one day and bought me a hummingbird bracelet, which I still wear. 'Keep it with you always,' she said. 'It'll keep you strong.'

To this day, the hummingbird continues to symbolise something beautiful and deeply significant to me.

—

Two weeks into my stay, my counsellor was happy with my progress, so I was allowed to move away from the campus to an offsite location. You're meant to progress through the system in this fashion. Sometimes it takes two weeks and sometimes two months, but I was like a sponge, really digesting the information and opening up in my group therapy. The Betty Ford Center owns a series of houses for those who've reached that phase of treatment, and they line either side of a nearby street called Daisy Lane – a quiet suburban cul-de-sac with sand and gravel front yards, where clients can live while completing the final phase of their recovery.

I met new roommates there, such as the skinny, scattered girl from Hawaii who was addicted to online shopping, and the all-American mom of two daughters, who wore red lipstick, styled her hair with rollers and wore a blue chambray shirt with jeans and a brown belt. Rehab took all sorts – covering the entire spectrum, really – from the Formula 1 engineer with a drinking problem to the 58-year-old lawyer addicted to crack cocaine.

Daisy Lane was almost like a halfway house. At night I could go out to a restaurant, go shopping, go to a tavern for a meal – without alcohol – and have some semblance of freedom while surrounding myself with people who were in the same situation and would protect me. We had intense group therapy sessions in there, and would catch a chartered bus to the main facility each day.

My counsellor at this stage was a beautiful woman, Anita, who had the most incredibly painful story – the kind of story that could become a movie. Anita taught me the value of verbalising everything – anything you're ashamed of or that you fear – because when you can speak that truth out loud, you've processed it, and you'll have more luck moving on. That's what she did, sharing her story of being beaten and raped and locked in a basement. Anita had survived years as a sex slave, and was able to now share that truth in the most matter-of-fact way, because she had worked so tirelessly and so bravely to come to terms with it all.

She called me the Olivia Newton-John of the class, and she was the one who put the idea for this book in my head. I'd kept my work in radio largely to myself, until it was finally my turn to share my entire life story, and it was Anita who listened most intently. Her eyes were locked on mine, and she immediately saw the privilege in my position.

'Wow,' she said. 'You do realise you've got a platform to share a pretty important message, right? If one day you want to tell your story, you could make a difference. Maybe that's why you do what you do for a living.' I knew in my heart she was right, and rehab was laying the groundwork for me to be able to share my journey with others.

We did so many exercises designed to help us in the outside world. Write a letter to your mother. Write a letter to your father. And have a plan. What will you do if you're out at a club and someone offers you a drink? What will you do when you feel bored? What are your tools for coping? You need to have the answers, and read them aloud, and know them so well that they will come to you without thought when the shit hits the fan.

I was near the end of my stay. But they kept hammering home to us a few words about vigilance. 'Don't leave here confident,' they said. 'Overconfidence is what will make you relapse.' They warn you about how common it is to relapse, not that you need warning. One friend of mine had been back eight times, and another had been back forty-two times. As a first-timer in rehab, it was made abundantly clear to me that I was a rarity.

But I planned to stay that way, too. I was studious. I was diligent. I took notes in every lecture. I embraced learning as I had done back at TAFE on the Gold Coast. I lapped up every bit of information I could get. I remember thinking about how what was happening to me in there – working on myself, and their lessons, from 6 a.m. to 8 p.m., every day, for twenty-eight days – was almost like a form of reprogramming. I still think that. But I also think that's okay. I was happy to be an A+ student.

I also spent time trying to understand what led me down this path in the first place. I'd come to realise that I had spent years using drugs and alcohol as a means to escape a feeling of unworthiness. I had allowed my self-esteem to be slowly chipped away, and I chose to devalue myself by thinking numbness was the best coping mechanism. My time at Betty Ford was teaching me the importance of boundaries and having the courage to speak up in life. To know my worth and to live life in a truly authentic way. Part of me also wondered if I slipped into addiction so easily because it was part of my genetics.

I learned the importance of self-reflection and personal growth. Meeting people from every kind of background taught me the value of empathy and the futility of judgement. I am deeply grateful for the insights I gained about myself. My perspective on life had changed, and I felt an overwhelming sense of gratitude for these lessons. This newfound optimism was fuelling my hope for a new and better life.

Fourteen

The coin I was handed was barely as big as a 50-cent piece, and nowhere near as heavy, but it carried all that weight and more. The sobriety chip is an AA tradition, and if you know anything about AA or similar organisations, it's easy to understand why.

These chips, given to people who've committed to the Twelve-Step program, come in all different colours and sizes depending on where you are in your journey. I've read that white chips are often given to people on day one, to get them started, while a silver chip represents twenty-four hours sober – an enormous achievement for some. People are sometimes told, 'This chip represents AA's commitment to you, not your commitment to us,' and that makes sense, too. It invites you to be part of something bigger.

My chip was red, with the AA Serenity Prayer inscribed on one side: *God grant me the Serenity to accept the things I cannot change, Courage to change the things I can, and Wisdom to know the difference.* On the other side were the words *To thine own self be true*, and a triangle marking the pillars of AA – *Unity, Service, Recovery* – then at the centre of the coin, the marker of my commitment and achievement so far: *1 Month.*

I cared deeply about getting that coin – it meant a lot to me. I also cared about the ritual behind the gift. I'd seen this simple little ceremony play out a few times with other people in rehab just before they left, when they seemed so filled with promise and hope. It's a lovely thing to witness. The person who's on their way out sits down, and a circle of friends forms. One at a time, each person in that circle holds onto the coin, says what they want to say to the owner – what their friendship means, or the good they see inside them – then they tap the coin twice on the table, then hand it to the next person.

When it was my turn, my friends said the loveliest things. About my aura and my energy. About being this sweet little Aussie angel with golden hair. About how much I had supported them and shown them love and helped them get through the day. I honestly didn't recognise myself in what they were saying to me, because how often do you get that experience, of everyone in a room saying something deeply personal and warm about you? It's almost like eavesdropping on your own funeral, but it's more than that, too.

This is a room full of people, after all, who might seem defective or flawed to some, but who have also lost all judgement, and now come solely from a place of compassion and empathy. It's in those moments that you understand no one is born an arsehole. Coming out of that circle, crying, I remember thinking that everyone should go through this. *Everyone should experience what I just experienced*, I thought, *because I'm walking away with a new perspective on life*. Forget my addiction for a minute. Put that completely aside. Walking out of rehab, having done all the work and introspection and analysis, my mindset was better than it had ever been in my life.

I left Daisy Lane on my own. I packed up all the notes I'd written and the books I'd bought and read – as if I was hauling my thesis along with the research library I'd needed to get it written. I said my goodbyes and was discharged at 4 p.m. sharp. A car picked me up, with a driver to take me from there directly to LAX, meaning I had two full hours alone to sit and reflect, staring out at the desert and the sunset beyond.

I was proud of myself – not for *enduring* it as if it were some sort of trial, but for how open I had been to the idea, and how I had embraced it all. I felt lucky that I even had the kind of temperament that would allow me to dive into rehab and swim around in it, because not everyone does. Many resist, and can't help but push back.

I was grateful to my body, too. You get a whole panel of medical testing done in rehab, and even though I had been abusing my body so much, my results were great. *Thank you, body!* I thought. *Thank you for fighting back against my constant abuse. I treated you like shit, but you kept fighting for me every day.*

My view of myself was already starting to change. I was appreciating who I was now, and all the gifts I'd been given. I came out of there hopeful and positive, but there was also trepidation. I was optimistic but cautious. I wasn't exactly frightened, but I was definitely worried that I might feel more alone back home than I had for the past month.

I needn't have fretted. Gemma planned my return perfectly. I wasn't jumping immediately back into the current of everyday life – I was going to bathe in the sea and soak in the sun. I was meeting Kitty, with Gemma and her boys, for three weeks in Kokomo, a resort island that we love in a remote part of Fiji.

They warn you about planes as you're leaving rehab, because so many people have long journeys home and they know you're about to get offered free alcohol, but I had no desire to have a drink whatsoever. I closed my eyes and slept, and landed at Nadi Airport before hopping on a seaplane to the island. I arrived before anyone else and had three hours to myself, so I got into a nice big bathtub, washed away any tension, dressed in light linens, and by the time I stepped outside I could hear the next seaplane coming. I ran to the wharf to watch it dip onto the water. The plane door opened and the steps went down onto the jetty, and there was Kitty. My Kitty. We ran towards each other, arms open wide, and hugged so tight. We were finally reunited. Throughout my time in rehab, whenever I was struggling, I had dreamt of this, and now it was real. I had never felt so much happiness as I did in that moment.

Gemma had committed to not drinking for our trip, which I really appreciated, but it was also an imposition I didn't want to place on her. I know she loves a glass of champagne at night when she's on holiday, and I felt comfortable enough with that. 'Please, have some, it's fine,' I said. 'I'm not tempted.' In a way, it was a good test setting for me. After all, I was going to be faced with people drinking once I got home to Sydney. I had been scared about leaving the protective bubble of rehab, but I knew I couldn't stay in there forever.

In some ways I was less worried about temptation when mingling with others so much as what might happen to me in isolation. I had only ever lived alone while in the grip of my addiction – what would it be like, living alone sober? I signed up to a Zoom support group so that I could join an AA meeting for an hour each day while we were in Kokomo, which kept me really solid and facing forward. It was a wonderful trip. We were healthy and happy, playing tennis and swimming and snorkelling. I was surprised by how little I was struggling.

Getting home went well, too. It helped that I didn't have to return to the darkness of Woollahra, but rather to a new place on the beach, in the heart of summer. I kept playing tennis, to the point that I couldn't rely on finding a hitting partner at short notice, so I invested in a ball machine that would allow me to swing the racket for two hours every day. I was swimming in the little waves of the cutting at Clovelly, and taking ice baths, and eating healthy foods.

While I was loving living in my Clovelly rental, I knew paying someone else's rent was wasted money and that I needed to look at buying a home of my own. I found a neighbouring property on the water at a place called Gordons Bay. It was an old house in need of a knockdown, but it was perfect for realising that childhood dream of owning my own home by the ocean, something I never imagined possible, not even in my wildest dreams. The day of the auction is etched in my memory. Kitty was by my side, and I felt a surge of pride showing her that her mum had achieved her own independence and success to make a lifelong dream come true. After the 23-minute auction in the sweltering heat, we hugged each other tightly, and I felt such pride and happiness in that moment.

The next thing I did goes against everything they teach you in rehab, so I would *never* advise anyone to do this, but I stopped going to meetings. Only one person in rehab had given me permission to do that. My darling Anita, who called me her Olivia Newton-John, had said that if a meeting doesn't work for you, or resonate with you, then maybe meditating and journalling will be enough. 'You need to do what will work for you,' she said. 'Whatever is your thing, is your thing.' I never enjoyed the meetings, and I know they're not supposed to be fun, but they really can be tedious and repetitive and depressing. My time felt better spent diving into my own therapy.

I was so adamant that I would never go back to my old life, because I was loving my new life. It was the start of 2023, and I had never felt better. It was like someone had woken me up after a long coma. 'I'm sorry, but you've been asleep for long. You've missed that time, but at least you're alive.'

I had lost a chunk of my life, and so I was going to make the most of what was left. I was so present, and thankful. I hate the analogy, but it was as if I was on some sort of drug. I would look around and think, *God, that's a beautiful blue sky!* or *Look at that flower!* – appreciating everything, and wondering why I hadn't done so before.

—

I don't know what the public thought about my absence, and I can't imagine what the media suspected. But inside the office at KIIS, there was a genuine sense of mystery around my sabbatical, as if there had to be something else to the story, and probably – hopefully – something salacious. The producers wrote down a list of all the guesses that were made – both ludicrous and real – while I was away.

I was having another baby. I was having a baby for our newsreader, Brooklyn, who had been talking about surrogacy on air all year. I had been convicted of drink driving and was living under house arrest. I was filming a new television show. I was creating a secret OnlyFans account. I was having cosmetic surgery. I was having gastric bypass surgery. I was having vaginal rejuvenation surgery. I was getting back together with Lee. I was becoming a lesbian.

Not one of the guesses was rehab, I guess because that's how far removed the idea was for them, and how well I had hidden my addiction. It was the same online. I'd been monitoring a few industry forums and watching the radio station's social media accounts, too, searching for some comment or another from an anonymous poster who might have picked up on the truth, but no one was ever even close. And even less so once I returned.

My healthy living had seen me quickly shed around ten kilograms, and that was a big difference. Naturally, after three years of sitting on a lounge consuming copious amounts of fast food, alcohol and sedatives that slow down the metabolism, the body will go into shock and shed the kilos when that stops. People had been heavily focused on my weight gain before I left the show, and now I was back they could only focus on my weight loss. Rumours circled that I was taking Ozempic – because surely I must be on the weight loss wonder drug to have had a trans-formation so dramatic. My changing body became like an unintentional magician's act – a lucky little sleight of hand. And I was grateful for that – it allowed me to keep my secret to myself until I was ready to share it.

I tried never to lie to anyone. When I took my time off to leave the country, I *was* sick, and I *was* exhausted, and it *was* following a bout of illness from Covid and a lung infection. I wasn't lying, except by omission. And so I continued doing that when I got back, telling people I'd got into meditation and exercise and healthy eating – because those things were all true. And people were genuinely happy to see me happy again, no matter what the reason.

Kyle and the producers recognised my renewed energy, and loved that I was in such a great place. Mum and Dad would visit and we would go out to restaurants, and they felt as if they were seeing a new daughter. (I would *never* have taken them out to dinner during my time in Woollahra.) Kitty and I were going to concerts again – Harry Styles and Ed Sheeran. Gemma cried, many times, because she couldn't believe the difference she was seeing. She was emblematic of what everyone else was feeling. 'I felt as if I was grieving some sort of loss, for years on end,' she said. 'Now it's like I've got my old friend back.'

Fifteen

Spring is the season of rebirth, but my most recent renewal began taking shape in the autumn of 2023. Kyle got married in April, and it was a million-dollar affair. It was held in Darling Point at the Swifts mansion – a $100 million, heritage-listed, 56-room private castle situated in stunning grounds. There were paparazzi and news crews, celebrity friends including Karl Stefanovic and celebrity performers such as Guy Sebastian. The New South Wales premier Chris Minns was there, and Australian Prime Minister Anthony Albanese, too.

It was also one of the most beautiful weddings I have ever seen. There were different enchanting locations set up all over the grounds, such as an all-white marquee with hanging chandeliers. It didn't feel as if you were walking into a gross spectacle of wealth, but the cost was on full display if you knew what to look for. I remember how the chapel walls and ceiling were lined with flowers – deep, full clusters of the kinds of orchids that I used to buy for $30 a stem. (The floral bill alone was $150,000.)

But it wasn't ostentatious or tacky – it was like being in a fairytale. The whole day felt like a massive outpouring of love between everyone, with my friend Kyle at the centre of it all. We've both had long relationships and marriages that didn't work, so it was lovely to see him so happy, with his new wife, Tegan, and their son, my godson, Otto, enjoying the beginning of a new stage in life. I looked at him and thought of all we'd been through. There were perhaps one hundred people at the wedding in total, so it was quite intimate. It was a perfect day. Kyle and I were in unison once more – both so happy in life.

They warn you in AA, *do not* have a relationship during the first year after rehab, because it's far too risky. A broken heart is some of the worst pain you can experience, and you do not want to go there when your sobriety is still fragile.

My queen Anita had her own take on romance after rehab. 'Honey, that's what a vibrator is for – stay away from the men,' she said. 'Don't do it.'

And I had agreed with that thought for months – 'Yeah, girl, I don't wanna date, I'm happy on my own, dating myself!' – but something else was stirring all the same. If I'm being honest and I think about the timing, I'm sure on some subconscious level that wedding was a trigger, because I was left with this immediate *urge* and the belief that there was someone out there for me.

Gemma took me out to bars that she knew were good for meeting the right kind of men, men around our age with similar tastes and outlook on life. (By the way, I should point out here that anytime I go out to bars or I'm photographed with a drink, I'm drinking either a mocktail or a non-alcoholic beer or wine.) We tried several times, actually, but it was awful. I had no real experience of being single, so I couldn't compare it to anything else, but it seemed hopeless. No one was approaching us at all, to the point where I started wondering if men are afraid to even do that anymore. The only time they would come up to us is when they were firmly drunk – my worst nightmare, given my history. Going out to meet someone was just not happening, and it was difficult to organise anyway.

None of this dissuaded me, though. I would lie awake at night, thinking of a man, almost trying to conjure him into existence. It actually kept me up. *I know he's out there – I can feel it*, I thought. *I just wonder when I'm going to meet him.*

—

The old method proved fruitless, but the idea of signing up to a dating app sounded so desperate and slightly humiliating. I got over myself and did it anyway, carefully creating my profile, uploading it to the app and nervously waiting.

Within minutes I had an influx of men wanting to match with me. My ego received a huge boost, but as I later realised, being fresh meat on these apps gets you a lot of attention.

I was surprised at the men coming through – men of every age, some men who I knew, even the ex-husbands of friends. I went from no men to a smorgasbord of blokes. *This is great!* I thought. *Why didn't I do this sooner?*

Each night was spent talking to multiple men, trying to determine who I could forge a connection with – enough to go out on an actual date, IRL, my first in more than two decades. I narrowed it down to four fairly suitable options – a landscaper from Cronulla (nice guy, very genuine, but not really doing it for me), a super-hot underwater welder who offered to take me scuba diving (he sounded fun, but gave out possible player vibes) and a part-time farmer from Manly who I was really vibing with one night (but when I woke at 4 o'clock the next morning, there was a barrage of new messages all asking different red flag questions). The one I connected with the most was an architect from the Northern Beaches. Let's call him Mr Kibly.

Mr Kibly was a nice-looking single dad who I'd been messaging with all week, sharing a few biographical details and building a connection. He wasn't afraid to write long messages, which I loved. Within five days I had built him up in my head as the one for me. We were going to live happily ever after. I drove to work each morning playing love songs, imagining life with Mr Kibly: what our first kiss would be like, how our daughters would love playing together and what a happy blended family we'd make. Anyone reading this who's ever used dating apps will be smiling to themselves at this point, recognising this classic rookie error. We were set to meet up for the first time on a Thursday night, at a little underground bar in the city.

As I pulled up and circled the area for a parking spot, I could see Mr Kibly walking in. Wearing a blue shirt and black trousers, he looked very handsome, matching his online profile, which was a relief. I walked into the venue and couldn't remember the last time I'd felt this nervous or excited. He stood up to hug me, and as we sat down he said, 'OMG – this place is *soooo* amazing,' and my face just fell.

Fuck, I thought. *I think he's gay!*

It sounds terrible to judge a person by the way they speak, but I have so many gay friends, and in my mind his mannerisms and inflections did not fall into the straight camp so much as the straight-up *camp* camp. A million thoughts raced through my mind. *Maybe he's not gay and only sounds gay? Could I be with someone who everyone thinks is gay but isn't? Could I even feel attracted to someone who sounds this gay?*

It took less than a minute for me to decide it would be hard to get past this, but I tried to remain open minded, and the conversation flowed well enough. I also found myself doing most of the heavy lifting, but I guess this is where years of experience in interviewing people comes in handy.

I'm good at avoiding awkward silences as there's always a next question up my sleeve. After a couple of hours of feeling like Liz Hayes on *60 Minutes* I was starting to run dry, so I tried to lighten the mood and think of a funny story I could tell him. One came to mind about a friend of mine, and it involved an architect. *Perfect*, I thought, given Mr Kibly's occupation. *He'll get a kick out of this.*

I proceeded to tell him about my mate Josh, who used to have a side hustle where men with foot fetishes would pay him to come over and let them suck his feet and toes. One of his regulars was an architect who insisted Josh do a ten-kilometre run before coming over. Josh would always enter the house through the back door and sit in a chair, while the guy would enter the room, say nothing and proceed to suck Josh's feet for the next half hour. Josh got paid $200, and off he went. Easy money. I thought this was a pretty interesting yarn – one that would surely spark a whole new thread of conversation about the weird kinks that exist in the world – but no. Mr Kibly's deadpan expression made me wonder, first, if the story was even funny to begin with, and second, if maybe he was the toe-sucking architect in the tale! At that point I figured it might be time to call it a night.

Mr Kibly kindly offered to walk me to my ride. Once we got to my car, he leant in and started kissing me. I was a little taken back but, you know what, I hadn't kissed someone in such a long time that I decided why not, I may as well. The kiss went for a least a minute, and it was a bloody good kiss, too – maybe Mr Kibly *wasn't* gay, after all – but unfortunately the connection just wasn't there for me. I left slightly disheartened but, after only one date, still optimistic about what the world of online dating had to offer.

Next was Martin the finance guy, who lived in a posh suburb two hours away in the country. He was also a single parent who was very devoted to his twin girls, as I am to my daughter, and being a good dad is something I'm very attracted to in a man. We spent a good month messaging and doing FaceTime calls. Our conversation was effortless and we had a lot in common. I was excited by this guy – I was pretty sure he was going to be *the* guy for me, although my enthusiasm may have been somewhat influenced by the fact that a psychic who I'd seen earlier in the month had told me, 'The guy you're going to end up with is named Martin, he doesn't live in Sydney, he lives a little way away from you, and he has two children.' *Bingo!* I'd found my soulmate, clearly.

If I was about to meet my soulmate, I needed to be in my finest form. I bought not one but two new dresses and had my friends vote on which one I should wear. I got my hair coloured and had a spray tan done the day before. This was the big day; I was about to meet my forever man. He had booked lunch at a restaurant on Sydney Harbour, and it was the most perfect, sunny day. Everything was going to plan until I realised soon after I'd left home that I had a photographer following me.

Shit, I thought, *I can't allow my first date with this guy to be ruined by a photographer capturing our first interactions. That's not fair on him.* So, I tried ducking and weaving through traffic, trying to lose him, with zero luck. I even got out of the car and stopped at a cafe, pretending I was just heading out for a coffee, so he would get his shot and leave, but for some reason that wasn't enough to shake him. He just kept following me, no matter what I did.

By now I was fifteen minutes late for my date and I couldn't think of what else to do. Then, by some stroke of luck, a car pulled in front of the photographer just as the light changed to red, and I'd managed to sneak through the intersection, leaving him behind.

I arrived at the restaurant and found Martin to be very masculine and tall. At first we easily found the flow in our conversation, but as the date went on it became harder to sustain. Then he spent thirty minutes telling me about his job, discussing the ins and outs of the stock market, a topic I have minimal interest in at best. I could feel my attention waning and found my mind wandering to other things. To make matters worse, I sometimes get tired in the middle of the day because of my early-morning starts, and the more he talked about finance and the stock market, the more the tiredness washed over me. I could feel myself going – desperately trying to keep my eyes open but failing to stop the heaviness of them half-closing. I decided to check myself and go to the bathroom, where I dabbed my face with a little cold water, but when I returned to the table I guessed Martin had noticed it too, because he was standing by the door, having already paid the bill. That was awkward.

Then there was Adam. Adam worked for a startup company and had a real sweetness about him. We went out to dinner for our first date and I found him to be emotionally intelligent and kind. He was amazing to talk to, and I liked that he was a bit shy and almost unaware of his good looks. For our second date he invited me around to his house, where he'd be cooking me a meal and I'd be meeting his new dog. He teased me over text that he had arranged a surprise for the date too. I really liked that he was prepared to do something different and was making an effort.

I figured the surprise would be something along the lines of he'd hired a karaoke machine or thought of a cute game we could play, but I was off, way off. After a brief amount of chitchat in his kitchen, he asked if I'd like a drink, and as I sat at the kitchen bench, taking my first sip, he said, 'Are you ready for your surprise?' He went to the bedroom and came out naked, wearing just an apron, and said he'd be cooking for me nude. I was a little taken aback – newly returned to the dating scene, I figured there would be some sort of build-up before my date stripping off naked – but maybe on a second date this stuff is the norm? So I sat there for the next thirty minutes looking at his bare arse, watching him make salad and steak and trying not to feel weird about it.

He sat at the dinner table, still naked but for his apron, and at the end of the evening he said he needed to take his dog out to do her business. Then he looked at me and asked if I dared him to go out like this. Surely he was kidding, I thought – but no. Thinking there was no way he'd actually go ahead with this, I followed him down the communal corridors of his apartment building, into the elevator and out the garage door to four lanes of peak-hour Sydney traffic. True to his word, he stood there in front of dozens of cars all banked up at the traffic lights and let everyone see his arse. People started honking and yelling out to him. The whole thing was a spectacle, as I watched on in disbelief behind the fire exit door. My quest for love continued.

The most awkward part of trying to date when you're in the public eye is the fear of being photographed when you're meeting lots of different men, trying to find your match. As a woman, you are often painted in a negative light if you dare to be seen with multiple different guys, so even though it might have seemed oddly forward, I would often have a first or second date at my house. On more than one occasion this turned out not to be a safe space either, after a couple of these dates were photographed out on my balcony. Overall, I did a pretty good job at keeping things hidden from the press.

I met some lovely guys during this time. Some of my dates included a jujitsu black belt, a sweet and sensitive introvert, a hot tradie, an ex-athlete dad and an actor.

Some lasted one date, some lasted more. They were all great guys with whom I had wonderful interactions.

One of my last dates during this period was with a gorgeous European guy who had been messaging me on Instagram. We went out for drinks and were having a great time until we both started getting unusually deep with our conversation. He revealed to me that he was a recovering drug addict, and he also said he suspected he might be a sex addict. Now, clearly I was the last person who was going to judge him about this, having been through one of these addictions myself. We spent the next two hours talking about sex addiction. I bombarded him with questions and was fascinated by what I was learning.

Suddenly, my internal monologue kicked in: *Wait, have I just spent two hours talking about sex with this guy? Is he going to think I'm the world's biggest prick-tease if I end this with a 'Lovely to meet you, we should do this again sometime'?* The thought of this judgement had me so riddled with anxiety and panic that I began to wonder if I should just sleep with him to avoid any awkwardness. (I have major people-pleasing issues, if you couldn't already tell!) Throughout this entire dating phase, I'd never slept with someone on the first date – not because I'm a prude, but because I prefer knowing the person first. Nevertheless, my anxious brain took over and, long story short, I slept with him.

I know deep down I only did it because I was more worried about what he would think of me than about what I actually wanted, but I also did a pretty good job of convincing myself that sleeping with a self-professed sex addict was going to ensure me great sex, at the very least, so I surprised myself by having a one-night stand. Afterwards, I was keen for him to leave, and I made some excuse about needing to take my dog out to do her business while he booked himself an Uber. *Wow,* I thought, after he had left. *I just had my first sexual encounter with no strings attached, and it actually felt liberating and fun.*

—

I had always heard about people 'having their fun' – enjoying their single days, so to speak. You see it all the time in movies. A guy sowing his wild oats. A girl reliving her wildest times in college. People look back with longing at that time in their twenties when they slept with whoever they wanted and the sex was good and bad and great and terrible. The story of that experience is always told as formative and fun, as if they'd got something out of their system. I always envied that. Having been married at nineteen, I'd had very few sexual partners, and it always made me wonder if I was missing out. So, after having tried dating without success, I thought, *Instead of looking for a relationship, why not try a different approach and just be the girl looking for fun, with no strings attached?* Maybe I needed to get this out of my system.

Brooklyn, our newsreader on *The Kyle and Jackie O Show,* and his partner, Damien, who I have grown extremely close to over the years and who I always have the most fun with, invited me on a trip with them overseas. We all went to Los Angeles to meet up with our friends Michael and Daniel, a couple I've known for years. We went to a club in West Hollywood and they immediately started scouting the room and asked me if anyone took my fancy. I wasn't really vibing with the moment at all, until a six-foot-six guy with dark hair, a hoodie and a 'give no fucks' attitude walked in the door. His name was Brody, and he was dressed down but had that swagger. Daniel went straight up to him – 'See my friend over there? She likes you – come say hi!' – and I was mortified. I'm not that forward, and never have been, but my friends didn't care. They're used to the world of cutting immediately to the chase on Grindr. The gays don't muck about.

This poor guy. I was trying, but the situation wasn't ideal. He had just been ambushed on the way into a club by two gay men who insisted on him meeting their Australian fag hag. It won't surprise you to learn that it was a stilted, tortured, terrible conversation. But I also figured that didn't matter – I wasn't there for the conversation, only the hook-up – so I breezily told him I was going to another club, and he took my number and met us there. We danced all night, and he was lovely and affectionate, so I took him home with me that night. I have to say, he was right up there with the best I'd ever had, too. Brody was beautifully sweet and held me in his arms all night, making the whole thing feel less transactional. I still hold a soft spot for Brody, and we have kept in touch ever since.

As I returned home, my no-strings-attached attitude started to spiral. One night I took a man home, a friend of a friend, who was funny, cute and British. Our hook-up wasn't so great; we didn't have much chemistry and our styles were completely different. As I was lying on my back, without warning, he spat in my mouth. It was aggressive and weird – the kind of spit you'd see a tradie do out the side of his ute on the way home – and the complete opposite of what I'm into. I'd heard that spitting during sex was a thing, and I hold no judgement of the act itself or anyone who's into it, but to do it without some indication or discussion first? Sometimes I really don't get guys!

My next attempt was even worse, as though the universe were trying to send me a clear message: 'Jackie, *you are off course, this isn't you!*' He was from out of town, we had chemistry and he told me all about his rough childhood. He was really sweet and vulnerable, and we were actually very connected in our conversation that night, but once we got home, things took a turn. I don't know if he'd just grown up watching too much porn his whole life, but he was incredibly aggressive, almost to the point where it seemed like he wanted to see me in pain. I had to tell him several times to stop. I remember afterwards I had tears in my eyes as my thoughts turned to this stupid experiment. *What am I doing?* I wondered. *What the* fuck *am I doing?*

Jackie O

I had imagined that casual sex with multiple people would be an adventure. But it turned out there was nothing I needed to get out of my system. I honestly couldn't believe how empty and unfulfilling it was, and how much worse it made me feel. I thought the physical closeness of a one-night stand might be rewarding, or the constant dance of social interactions would prove a useful distraction, but neither of those things was true. Sleeping with random people was a completely off-kilter response. I wasn't even sure what it was I was searching for, I just knew that I was looking for a way to distract myself from a certain emptiness and loneliness that existed within me. If I'm being really honest, I was searching for a way to feel loved.

Sixteen

It was a Friday night, and Kitty and I had just returned home from seeing a show when I got a message from a good friend. He pinged me a picture of a gorgeous-looking guy – let's call him John – and said, *This guy has had the biggest crush on you for years. He's always asking me about you, if you're interested?*

I was hesitant at first, but my friend suggested I treat it as a bit of fun and eventually I thought, *Why not? What harm can it do?*

I often look back on that moment and wonder, if I knew then what I know now, would I still have said yes?

My first date with John was about as good as first dates can get. We completely hit it off, talking and laughing all night until the bar staff kicked us out. John was not only incredibly charismatic, he was a gentleman, too – almost too much of a gentleman, because at the end of the night, I had to be the one to kiss him first.

We said goodbye and I returned to my car. Five minutes later, he messaged me asking if he could take me out again. The giddy girl inside me was thinking, *Fuck yes! This guy is amazing.*

We agreed to meet at my place and that he'd cook dinner. Our conversations that night were unusually deep for a second date, as we started to share truly personal things with one another. One of the subjects we discussed was his desire to have children, something he hadn't experienced yet. Later in the evening it turned intimate, and without going into detail, it was beautiful and perfect in every way. Over the years I'd sometimes dreamt about what 'perfect sex' would be like for me, because we all have our preferences. Some want a dominant lover. Some seek tenderness. Some get turned on by dirty talk, and for others that's an immediate turn-off. Are you a 'throw me on the bed' girl, or a 'lay me down gently' woman – or, are you sometimes one and sometimes the other? That night with John, it was as if he was inside my mind. Everything I'd ever fantasised about, he did, exactly as I'd always imagined. We were incredibly in sync with what the other liked.

Later, as I lay there in his arms, I couldn't help but feel a wave of dread. This was no longer the light and casual encounter I'd been up for. This was deep, and connected. Knowing how much John wanted children, I knew it would be risky to allow myself to become too emotionally involved. I had two choices: get out now, before you get yourself in too deep, or risk it and let the chips fall where they may. I chose the latter.

Over the next two weeks, John and I existed in our own little bubble, rarely venturing into the outside world. He would come over and we'd talk all night for six or seven hours straight and still not run out of things to say. We weren't babbling, either, but sharing all our fears and dreams, all our stories of trauma and joy. It was as though we both felt truly seen for the first time. We had a lot of fun, too; we both liked the same sorts of stupid games. Fancying ourselves as actors in our past lives, we would sometimes dress up and act out scenes from a movie or TV series such as *Mad Men*, *Ozark* or *Crazy, Stupid, Love*. We were alike in so many ways; we joked that I was the female version of him and he was the male version of me.

We had been seeing each other for a total of three weeks, but we agreed it felt like three years given the connection we had built. I knew by this stage I was in so deep there was no turning back. I should have listened to my intuition that this would not last, however, as it was giving me signs through my body that something wasn't right – I was riddled with anxiety. After every text message I sent, I would be glued to my phone, waiting for him to respond. If he responded quickly and sent heart emojis and said all the right things, that anxiety was temporarily soothed; if he waited too long, its intensity only increased.

John was giving me no reason to doubt him, though. He was just as invested as I was. He invited me to meet his family, who I absolutely adored and ended up becoming close with. As the weeks went on and we cemented our relationship into the 'exclusive' stage, John told me he'd never had a connection like this with anybody before, and talked about the idea of us having a baby together. We lay awake in bed that night discussing all our options – given my age, we knew that having a child wasn't a guarantee for us, but we knew we wanted to spend the rest of our lives together.

As blissful as this period was, I had an underlying nagging feeling that wouldn't go away. The topic of having a child together was bringing up all my insecurities. I worried that if I couldn't provide him with a child, he might leave me for someone younger who could, and I couldn't imagine the kind of pain that might bring. In spite of this, John was everything I had ever wanted, and we were falling deeply in love.

I introduced him to Kitty, and he and I envisioned a future that involved working together on a business project. With John in the early stages of launching his own business, I had an idea that could fast-track his career to new heights and I was excited about the prospects. After many long nights spent talking about our dreams and ideas, our lives became entwined in another way – he moved in to my recently purchased house in Gordons Bay, which was waiting to be knocked down and rebuilt.

John wanted to move from where he was living at the time, and this house was just around the corner from where I lived and was sitting there empty, so we agreed that he should move in. I was happy to let him live there rent-free, as it wasn't exactly in good condition in its current state.

After we had been seeing each other for a few months, John was getting close to leaving for a pre-booked holiday overseas. At home one night, as I was waiting for him to come around, I received a text message that sent my world crashing down. John explained that he was afraid of falling more in love with me and getting in too deep. His desire to have children and the potential difficulties we might face doing that together had been weighing on his mind, and he wondered if it wasn't better for us to be friends. That way we could be in each other's lives forever, rather than being in a romantic relationship that might end badly.

I was in a state of shock. If I was anxious about him taking too long to reply to a message, you can only imagine how I felt in that moment.

When he arrived later that night, I didn't beg or try to change his mind. I just said I understood and agreed that a friendship was worth a try, even though on the inside I was utterly devastated. We continued to be intimate in the lead-up to his trip, so it felt as if nothing had changed, making the transition to 'friendship' slightly less painful, for a time.

When John and I had first got together, he had been transparent about a situation involving his ex-girlfriend.

Right before he met me, they had agreed to try and give their relationship another go by meeting up on his upcoming holiday with their shared group of friends. He had since told her that he was no longer able to do that, and so they agreed not to see each other when they were over there. Even though I knew John was now single and would be entitled to have his fun while he was away, he gave me his word that he wasn't interested in going back to his ex, knowing how much that would hurt me.

On one of his last nights at home, as we talked about how fateful our connection felt, we lay in bed and wrote a pact on a piece of paper, like a couple of kids. We swore that we would never forget how truly lucky we were to have found one another, and that we knew this kind of connection would only happen once in our lifetimes. We vowed that no matter who or what else would come into our lives, only death would part us. It all sounds so silly now, but we loved our pact and referred to it often.

As John left for his trip, we continued to message each other in the same loving ways as we had when we were a couple, and that helped to make me feel a little less heartbroken.

Even though we were no longer together, I didn't want to take away the offer of letting him live in my Gordons Bay house. I'd been helping him through some recent hard times in his life and I wanted to do something nice for him. I set about completely redecorating the house to surprise him, so it would feel like a home when he returned. I bought all new furniture and even renovated the bathroom that had previously looked like something out of a horror movie.

About a week into his trip, he arrived at the group holiday where he was originally supposed to meet up with his ex. We had been messaging each other almost every day on WhatsApp, but that day I didn't hear from him. Later that night I messaged him the words *Miss you*, and my heart sank when I saw he had read the message and ignored it.

Days later, I could see that he and his ex had started following each other again on Instagram and were liking each other's posts, and my worst fears were realised.

I lay in bed that night and cried for hours. The pain was unbearable. Every core wound I had erupted all at once – feelings of abandonment, defectiveness and unworthiness came rushing to the surface. I struggled to understand how John could so effortlessly break his promise. A little part of my trust in him had been lost.

As his trip went on, the pain only worsened, but I didn't raise the topic of his ex with him. I figured he had the right to be with her, since he was single, yet I couldn't shake off the sense of betrayal. I continued working on the Gordons Bay house to surprise him, which I know sounds demoralising, but I think I was grasping onto every last thread of hope.

When John got back home, we talked over the phone, and when I asked if he had gone back to his ex, he confessed that they had reconnected but ultimately, he realised it wasn't going to work out. He knew I was upset, but I didn't let him know just how much he'd hurt me. I kept that to myself.

I did express that I was struggling with us remaining friends because I still had feelings for him; I couldn't turn them off as easily as he had done. I explained that us seeing each other all the time felt like living in a state of constant torment, and it was making it impossible for me to move on. We agreed to take a break while he proceeded to move into my Gordons Bay home.

Things went from bad to worse, and my heartache only grew when I discovered he was casually seeing a girl and bringing her back to the house. It hurt to imagine another woman being intimate with John in my own home. I felt foolish in so many ways and a great deal of shame, often seeing myself as the pathetic lover pining for him from across the water while he entertained other women and had his fun. But I knew this was all my own doing – I had agreed to remain friends and let him live in my house. He was just living his life, and I couldn't really fault him for that. Now, I had to lie in the bed I had made.

Gemma tried to knock some sense into me, begging me to cut all ties with him. She could see this situation was destroying me. I was losing a lot of weight, too. I just couldn't cut him off, though. I wasn't strong enough. I knew I was going through mental and emotional torture, but the thought of never seeing him again felt like an even greater hurt, so I hung on for dear life. In my desperation to feel loved by him, I completely abandoned myself. I was in constant fight-or-flight mode, my every waking thought consumed by what might happen next.

There were so many highs and lows. John would send messages expressing how grateful he was to me for letting him stay in my house and for how much I was helping him. He'd tell me things like, 'If you ever need anything, just ask, and I'll drop everything for you.' But his actions often failed to match his words. He made promises with the best of intentions, but his promises were frequently unfulfilled, and on those days it always stung. Each time he let me down, I became more painfully aware of how much more he meant to me than I did to him. The next day, another lovely message would come: 'I love you so much, more than you'll ever know, no one else gets me, you're the only person in my life that really understands me,' he'd say, always so beautifully written and full of love that the dopamine high would return once again, keeping me hooked.

It seemed like the roller-coaster ride would never end; for every heartfelt moment there was always another blow just around the bend.

One of my neighbours at the Gordons Bay house let me know they had received a letter in their mailbox from John, informing them of a big party he was planning to throw. I later learnt it was to be a party for a clothing brand at my house, complete with security guards, lighting, DJs and an alcohol sponsorship. Around one hundred and fifty people had been invited. John hadn't told me anything about this full-scale event he was planning to hold. I was upset, because he knew this was right at the time I was submitting my development application to the council, where neighbours have the right to object or submit a complaint about any of your plans, so it was the worst possible time to be pissing off any of them. I'd also be liable if anything were to go wrong at the event. Thankfully, John took it upon himself to cancel the party, knowing he had pushed me too far. But that was the thing about John; he was so good at apologising profusely that I always forgave him instantly. It became a constant pattern between us.

These ups and downs were taking a huge toll on me, and I couldn't shake the words of my rehab counsellor, Queen Anita, from my mind: 'Remember: *no* relationships for the first year!' Anita had been right. For the first time since leaving Betty Ford, I was tempted to take a sleeping pill and down a bottle of wine, just to escape the constant feelings of anxiety and heartache. I was mentally exhausted from living in this state 24/7, but I refused to break my sobriety *and* be heartbroken at the same time. Who knows what kind of downward spiral that would have led to. I was determined to stay strong, face it head on and remain sober. I tried everything else I could think of to pull myself out of the pain, but nothing seemed to help.

I knew that I should walk away, for the sake of my own wellbeing, but whenever John said things like he couldn't imagine the thought of losing me from his life, and that he needed me, it only made it harder. Different parts of me were all having their say. The healthy, rational side was urging me to leave, while the inner critic was judging me harshly for staying. Then there was my vulnerable side – the part of me that craved the deep connection we had and the feeling of being the centre of his world, even if it did only come in the form of breadcrumbs. The vulnerable side won out every time.

John and I continued to mull over our ideas for the business venture we wanted to start. Even though we were no longer together, I still believed in his talent and was excited for us to be partners. I also knew that us working together would provide a huge platform for him and would open up opportunities he would never get otherwise. He regularly expressed how this would be life-changing for him and that he was incredibly thankful for it.

By mid-November, I was approaching my one-year sobriety milestone, and we went out to dinner to celebrate. The restaurant was candlelit and romantic; he gave me a beautiful and meaningful gift, and he spoke so tenderly about me and how proud he was of me. We talked until the restaurant closed. What I loved most about John was his sentimental, sweet and sensitive nature. I couldn't deny that my feelings for him were as strong as ever – nothing was changing, and I knew I had to try something to make it stop.

I requested that we have some proper time apart and told him how I was trapped in a constant cycle of longing, hope and fear, which had become a mental prison for me. For the next three months there was no contact between us as I tried desperately to move on. I went on dates, hoping that if I could fall in love with someone else, all this might go away, but of course it was never going to be that easy. Every interaction with another man only left me yearning for John even more.

The only time John broke our no-contact rule was on my birthday, two months later. He left flowers and a letter on my kitchen bench. As I read his words about how much he missed me, how he thought of me every day, and how there was no one else with whom he could match the depth of our conversations, I felt a wave of relief. The letter was three pages long, all the words I'd wanted to hear, and it instantly soothed my heart.

His birthday was a few weeks after mine, and since John was always so good at writing thoughtful notes and giving sentimental gifts, I wanted to do the same for him. I bought him a bracelet engraved with a hummingbird – a reference to my rehab days, when Nikita had gifted me a hummingbird bracelet for love and protection. I explained to him the bracelet's significance, how to me the humming-bird symbolised protection from my loved ones who had passed, and how I hoped it would offer him the same sense of being protected by both me and them whenever he wore it.

In March, we reconnected and attempted to continue our friendship. By then I felt a bit stronger and thought

I had things under control. But then he told me how touched he had been by the significance of my hummingbird bracelet, and he got that same hummingbird tattooed on his body. This gesture, while beautiful, made me take ten steps backwards. It was impossible not to stay in love with someone who did things like that.

Around the middle of the year, he shared that he was beginning to feel more settled in his life and that he might consider dating again. He felt ready for a relationship. I hated that I felt conflicted about this news. Part of me cared so much for John, knowing he deserved to find love and happiness, yet part of me was devastated, wishing I could be the one to bring him that happiness. He reassured me he wasn't dating and hadn't met anyone yet, and I couldn't help but breathe a sigh of relief.

A few weeks later, as the one-year anniversary of our first date approached, we were eager to celebrate. He suggested a cosy little restaurant he had always wanted to try. As always, we were the last diners left in the restaurant and we talked all night. He was asking a lot of questions about our business plans, too, which we estimated would kick off in around eight months, and he couldn't wait. When he asked if I had any concerns about the possibility of us working together, I had to be honest, given we might be about to enter a binding legal contract as business partners. Based on our last conversation, I found myself wondering how I would actually cope if he got a girlfriend during that time. Would it still be difficult for me, and would

I still be struggling with my feelings by then? My biggest fear was that there would be no escape plan – no break I could enforce, as I'd done before, because I would have to see him so regularly.

As I touched on some of these concerns, he immediately responded by saying, 'I'd rather not be in a relationship and work with you instead.' I insisted that I would never, and would never want to, stand in the way of his happiness. But when he said, 'I'm not kidding – that's how much it means to me,' it hit me just how much John wanted this professional opportunity.

On the final night we would ever see each other, it was supposed to be just like any of our regular catch-ups. We met for dinner at The Clovelly Hotel, just around the corner from our homes, after work. As we discussed our usual topics, John brought up how much he was looking forward to the idea of falling in love with someone and finally starting a family like he'd always dreamt. The comment caught me off guard this time, and despite his assurances that he still wasn't seeing anyone, it was all too much hearing him say those words. Tears began to well in my eyes.

I found myself pleading with him to let me go, explaining that I was still in love with him but needed to start prioritising my mental health and wellbeing. My own words surprised me, but it felt like the internal pressure cooker was finally letting off some steam. I apologised for not being able to stay in his life, explaining that if things continued as they were, I'd never find my own happiness.

I was sorry this would also mean we wouldn't be able to work together, but I just couldn't see a way out for me if things continued as they were. He responded graciously, saying, 'Who gives a fuck about work? I'm sad to be losing you. It's going to feel like losing a part of me.' We shared one last hug goodbye, and as I drove away that night I felt a small sense of relief, knowing for the first time in a year, I had finally put myself first.

A few days later, I left for an overseas trip. I hadn't heard much from John, but I wanted to ensure our parting was on good terms. He shared his disappointment about us not being able to work together, saying it was a hard pill to swallow, but that he understood and that my happiness was what mattered most to him. He asked for one final favour – could he stay in the house for another six to eight months?

I explained that I couldn't extend his stay for that long, because I'd promised a friend she could stay there while her home was being renovated, and asked if he could work with two months instead.

That's when things took a turn. The niceties were gone; instead, I got an agitated message back. He was annoyed because he was going on a holiday to Thailand soon, meaning the timing was inconvenient for him, and he ended the message by asking if he could take my furniture when he moved out.

My jaw dropped. I couldn't believe he'd actually said that. No acknowledgement that I had let him live there rent-free for the best part of a year – just, 'Can I take the furniture?' A million thoughts ran through my head. I was now useless to him. The message was unlike anything I had ever received from him, and it left me in shock.

A week later, he posted a picture of his girlfriend to Instagram. It turns out they had been seeing each other for some time. Yes, it hurt to know he had a girlfriend, but what hurt the most was knowing he was not transparent with me. He knew how much transparency meant to me and understood that hiding a secret was the one thing I couldn't tolerate in our friendship. I'd made it clear that was a dealbreaker, and since then he'd always promised to be upfront with me no matter how much it might hurt.

I expressed to John how deeply appalled and disappointed I was. Even though I asked him not to contact me, part of me was hoping for an apology, or maybe a thank-you for staying in my house for so long, but it never came.

In the weeks that followed, I was struggling to make sense of everything as John became a ghost in my life. How could we have shared such a deep connection and meant so much to one another, only for it to be so easily discarded when it came to an end?

Anyone who has experienced a situation like this will know how difficult it is to move on from. The lack of closure and the confusion it leaves behind make healing incredibly hard.

I try to look back on it all objectively and give John some benefit of the doubt. I replay our conversations in my head, wondering how much of them was real. There is a large part of me that believes we had a real connection in the beginning. I guess I'll never really know the truth.

Despite everything, I am thankful for one thing: during that year with John, in an attempt to try to conquer my feelings of defectiveness and anxiety that had come to the fore in a way I'd never experienced before, I began working with an incredible therapist, Dr Justine Corry. She helped me understand my relationship patterns and their origins (which could fill a whole book on their own). I was fascinated by what I was learning and had a real thirst for knowledge on the subject. I started reading books on psychology, the human brain, the central nervous system, and every book on enlightenment I could find. I meditated, journalled and connected with nature. Throughout that year, I learnt a great deal about myself, which was helpful, but it didn't erase the pain. I still felt the hurt of not being chosen, of not being good enough, and that kind of pain cuts deep.

I continued along my healing journey until one night when a single piece of advice changed everything for me. Not long after my fallout with John, I was catching up with one of my dearest friends, Pip. Pip Edwards, the founder of the successful activewear brand P.E. Nation, had recently entered my life and we immediately clicked, soon becoming fast friends. On the night in question, I poured my heart out about the impact the relationship with John had had on me. I had given so much, only wanting the best for him, but I was left feeling so unappreciated. She was sympathetic and beautiful in her support of me, but then she said something that altered my whole perspective.

'You know you're to blame in this situation too, though, don't you? You are fifty per cent responsible for what happened. You are the co-creator of every scenario in your life. If you feel disrespected, undervalued and underappreciated, yet continued the friendship anyway, it means that's what you believe your worth to be,' she said. 'You clearly didn't value yourself any higher than he valued you, otherwise you would have put up boundaries or walked away. What John did to you is irrelevant; *you* are what's relevant. Your own self-worth and how you value yourself is where you should be focusing your attention.'

And there it was – my epiphany, or my ePIPhany, as I like to call it.

For some reason, Pip's words hit me like a ton of bricks. The people I loved who had let me down weren't the only ones at fault; I was equally to blame. John may have needed me but, if I'm brutally honest with myself, I dangled the carrot of free accommodation and the opportunity of working together as a way of feeling needed by him, never believing that me alone would ever be enough for someone. I let it all happen because I clearly didn't have enough self-worth. I was so desperate to make people like me or love me that I was giving too much, because then I would feel needed and wanted. I had always been more focused on whether someone else was happy, rather than asking myself, *Am I happy in all of this?*

That night, I made a commitment to myself to make the necessary changes to prevent this from happening again in any of my current or future relationships.

I began prioritising my own needs, not out of selfishness, but to show myself more compassion and kindness. I started valuing my self-worth a hell of a lot higher, I set boundaries by saying 'no' more often, and it made a remarkable difference. Whenever something made me uncomfortable, I spoke up instead of remaining silent. If I felt uneasy about something or sensed I was being taken advantage of, I pushed myself to have those tough conversations that I would previously have avoided. It was as though I was finally tending to my own garden instead of everyone else's. I was amazed at the positive changes I experienced in giving myself the same love and care I had been showing others.

The cloud over my head began to clear as if by a miracle. Suddenly, I wasn't feeling so heartbroken; even though it was still there, it was softer, somehow, more tolerable. I started to feel lighter, happier and more content. And the feeling that something or someone was missing from my life slowly started to fade.

I had always believed that I needed someone else in order to be truly happy. That's what society tells us, after all, from *Jerry Maguire* – 'You complete me' – to *Notting Hill* – 'I'm just a girl, standing in front of a boy, asking him to love her.'

Now, instead of longing to share all this love with someone else, I've embraced the concept of giving it to myself. I am no longer yearning to find someone, and I have surrendered to the idea that whatever the universe has in store for me, that's what's meant to be, and I am at peace with that.

Now that I look back on my relationship with John as a whole, I'm still confused by why I stayed in something that was stripping away my self-esteem. It's incredible to me that I couldn't just leave. I gave him all my power – a power he didn't know he had and one that wasn't safe for him to have. All my emotions were completely under his spell, handing him the ability to both erase my sense of defectiveness or amplify it with a single action. I dismissed everything that was wrong just to keep a connection with someone who could never give me what I deserved.

Many of us have experienced that one relationship in which we completely lose ourselves. The love feels deeply intense, yet chaotic. It's the kind of relationship where we compromise our values and lose our dignity along the way, leaving us to look back and think, *What the fuck was going on with me there?*

My hope is that anyone reading this who might recognise themselves in my story can find the strength to prioritise self-love and let go of what isn't serving them.

As for John, I don't blame him at all. I stayed in it, I allowed it, so that's on me, not him. I believe he came into my life for a reason. His involvement in my life was *meant* to bring up all my insecurities and deep-seated wounds. He was a catalyst for my own personal growth, pushing me in search of a deeper understanding of myself. I think people like him enter our lives to highlight areas that need addressing. The journey I embarked on to understand and heal from that pain was transformative. So many people witnessed my changes on the outside, but the internal transformation was even greater. I've learnt my worth now – I never knew it before, and in many ways I am grateful to John for that. I do genuinely wish John happiness in his life, and I can look back on the early days of our relationship with a lot of appreciation for the love we shared and the joy it brought me.

Now, I find that joy within rather than relying on others to give it to me. I feel so proud for how far I've come, and I realise now that I am enough.

Seventeen

Months before Kyle's wedding, an important contract negotiation loomed. It was the summer holidays and we weren't yet back on air for the year, but we knew we would be renegotiating our contract soon, because we usually do that eighteen months out from the end of the previous contract. Kyle called me on the phone – 'I've got a figure and a time frame in mind' – and I had one, too.

At the time, we were on $5 million a year for three years, but we had also gone to a new level. We were getting bigger and bigger, growing and expanding the show, not remotely headed to any discernible plateau. We were even competing with AM radio in terms of our ratings, which wasn't the goal but was unheard of nevertheless. We may not have even hit our peak yet. My pie-in-the-sky figure for our renegotiation? Ten million dollars a year for ten years, and that was exactly what Kyle wanted as well.

But how you go from what you want to what you're gonna get isn't always linear or simple. Southern Cross Austereo and 2Day FM were sniffing around us again, which was useful. We never met up with them – we kept our hands clean there. It was all done through our managers – no more clandestine meetings in hotel rooms – but we were in serious talks that were moving quickly. We didn't want to tell KIIS and ARN Media until we had a solid offer, and when 2Day FM came to the table and met our terms, we were able to go back to ARN and let them know. The chairman, Hamish McLennan, and CEO Ciaran Davis asked for time. 'Leave it with us – give us a week.' And so we waited.

We didn't have to wait long, however. Word was sent the old-fashioned way – with a letter. A formal invitation, in fact. It arrived in the mail, printed in gold foil on heavy white card stock, almost like a save-the-date card for a wedding, which I guess it was, in a sense.

Hamish, Ciaran & ARN Media
invite you to the next chapter
Wednesday the 26th of July
10.30 a.m.
ARN HQ

This was followed by the address of the building that would be the station's new, gleaming modern edifice, but was currently just an empty shell overlooking Sydney Harbour. On the day we met it was still a construction site. We got up to the seventeenth floor of the building and opened the office doors, not knowing what to expect.

What we found was an empty floor, with a long thin pink carpet bordered by bright brass stanchions, from which hung black velvet ropes. It was all lit up with fluorescent LEDs, cutting a glowing, regal path from the elevator all the way to the end of this vacant concrete floor. The ceiling above was unfinished, with dangling power cords, insulation and ventilation, but there was a DJ playing, as well as two sofas and chairs, a big-screen TV and a coffee table with champagne – plus a buffet table full of cheese and meats and sandwiches and fruit. There were flowers everywhere, and two elegant Louis Vuitton briefcases filled with the documents that might determine our future (and our fortune), with a gilded pen next to each one. They had gone all out. It was so completely over the top, and so perfect at the same time. We were impressed! Hamish and Ciaran were already there, smiling, and they presented us with their offer, which had a large salary and incentives based on our performance.

We sat and watched a fifteen-minute movie about our time at KIIS, which was emotional and nostalgic – *Look at us, aren't we great, we're family, see what we've done together* – and it pushed all the right buttons. It was as brilliant and manipulative as the soaring heartfelt music at the pivotal point in any schmaltzy Ron Howard movie, and I found myself crying and thinking, *Yeah, it has been great, hasn't it?* Outside, they had a skywriter jet writing 'KJ is KIIS' in the sky.

It was a convincing pitch, but it didn't mean that SCA was going to give up. They kept coming back with counter-offers, and then Gemma would have to let ARN know, and they would go away and have a think and respond. I was largely insulated from the process, but for Gemma it was an incredibly stressful time, with daily, hectic discussions and negotiations. This dance ultimately dragged on for six months, until we eventually made our decision and while every clause and condition was haggled over and ironed out. We stayed with ARN, and bet on ourselves. The deal kicks off at the end of 2024, meaning I'll be in radio until at least the end of 2034, when I'm fifty-nine years old.

I remember we did a performative version of signing the contract on the show one day – supposedly putting our signatures on the dotted line live on air, as an event to share with our listeners – but in reality Gemma brought the contract to my house and took a photo of me signing it while wearing a daggy brown tracksuit with no make-up on. I don't think I ever actually paused for a moment with the pen in my hand that day, to consider how we had just made history. But I think about it now. *Did I really do this?*

I remember how Phil and I used to come to Sydney on weekends when we lived in Canberra. I wasn't even working in radio then, but we would drive over the Harbour Bridge and listen to the radio and dream. *Imagine what it must feel like to broadcast in this city*, I would think. *Can you even fathom?* Sydney was like Manhattan to me. Everything was happening here. It still is. And now I take that same drive across the bridge to work every single weekday, into the centre of the world. I pinch myself sometimes. Actually, I pinch myself often. *How did this happen? Is this really my life?*

I feel so settled in what I'm doing with my days now. I'm so grateful for everything I learned through therapy and the books I've read, understanding the human mind and why people do the things they do. I feel like I have a more complete sense of perspective about it all.

Take Kyle. I used to find it hard to understand his defensiveness to criticism, or why he always wanted to tell people how much money he earns, but now it all makes sense when you understand his childhood and how the way we grew up affects us as adults. I love him unconditionally for all his wonderful traits, and I love him even more for his perceived flaws. I wouldn't be where I am today without Kyle's belief in us and his incredible talent. Among all the men in my life, he holds the most significant role. He's always had my back, and I've had his. Our bond is unbreakable, standing the test of time, and I know we'll remain loyal to each other forever.

I feel like I understand my listeners better today, too. I've always considered the confessional aspect of radio to be a real privilege – to hear from people from all different walks of life about their hopes and fears, the shit that scares them and the stuff they find funny. We hear so many people's stories on air, and I've always had empathy, but after my experience in rehab, it changed my perspective even more. I now try to let go of all judgement of others. Never judge a book by its cover, so they say.

I've begun to place a different emphasis on my work, too. I used to place a lot of value on my role as a broadcast personality. I've been doing it for so long, and I've been in the public eye for so long, that my entire identity was bound up in the job. But I've questioned that lately, considering who I'd be if that was ever taken away from me. I never want to place so much importance on one thing that I would be devastated to lose it, and the only way I can do that is by finding other passions and pursuits in life.

Kitty is the big one, of course. We have a beautiful relationship now. We always have had, but it seems to have grown stronger and stronger over the past eighteen months. She's thirteen, and of an age where she can hear some grown-up truths about her mum. I love her at this age, because it allows us to have that open dialogue, the one I always enjoyed with my mum. We tell each other everything, and before writing this book I decided to tell her the truth about my addiction and how I sought help. There were many occasions where I wanted to open up to her, but a fear of her seeing me in a different light held me back each time. One night, sitting on the lounge as she shared something personal with me, I knew the moment had come to exchange a truth of my own.

Her response was a testament to her kind and empathetic nature. 'Mum,' she said, 'I'm so sorry. I feel so bad that you were going through that and I didn't even know.' She encouraged me to share my story if I felt that it would help other people, and even though we knew that might come with certain judgements from other kids in the playground, she said, 'Anyone who judges you for that isn't someone I want to be friends with anyway.'

I couldn't be more proud of my daughter. I believe she is an old soul, and people who meet her often say the same. Everything I've learnt lately has been so valuable to me as a parent. I can see where I went wrong in my own life, not dealing with certain emotions and repressing certain urges. I can see sometimes when Kitty does the same thing, and because I know how harmful that can be, I feel confident encouraging her to let them out, and to know her self-worth.

Whatever the problem – body image is such a big issue for girls of any age, for instance – I think I can now speak to her in a healthy and informative way. It's not really helpful to just offer some sweet parental platitude – 'Well, I think you're beautiful, honey' – when you can also talk about why we think the things we do, where they come from and how we can shift our mindset.

I also feel like I can help nudge her into a place where she always approaches people and situations with positive intentions – empathy and understanding. When someone in her orbit behaves strangely, or badly, or sadly, I want my daughter not to just react or overreact, but to consider what they may be going through for them to behave in that way. I don't have to do that much to prompt her to do that, though. She's a gorgeous and intuitive soul. She's generation alpha, and kids of that group are a different breed in that way. Their level of acceptance of others is so far above that of the generations who came before. Gen alpha are attuned to therapy, and difference, and individuality. I think they might just save the world.

It's not all serious business, though. We also have so much fun together. We go to concerts, more than a dozen every year, from Taylor Swift to SZA, Arctic Monkeys and everything in between. We go to the beach. We go for walks. Our favourite thing is to go on a drive together. We'll be sitting at home when one of us floats the question – 'Shall we just get in the car and drive for a little while?' – and we do exactly that and only that. My car is a new Range Rover, which was ordered by a drug dealer and delivered just as he was being sent to prison before I ended up buying it, meaning my pimpmobile is all blacked out. It's perfect for driving around town – just the two of us, in our own little world for an hour or two – listening to music and talking.

To Gemma, my manager and friend, I remain ever thankful. Rehabilitation is no small thing to endure, but I'm so grateful she gave me the push I needed to get it done.

We're pushing one another now, in a new business venture we have started, called besties. We recently flew Gwyneth Paltrow to Sydney for a speaking event and have rapidly expanded the business to include a podcast and online courses, one of which is called The Red Flag Project, which is focused on relationships. It covers how ingrained behavioural patterns and failing to recognise red flags early in a relationship can lead to challenges. Gemma and I have got each other through our toughest times. I don't know what I would have done these past five years without her by my side.

My bond with my mum has been my lifeline through countless challenges over the past couple of years. Who else other than your mum would patiently listen as you pour your heart out, shedding tears over the phone every night, discussing your troubles endlessly? She's been my unwavering support, and I can't imagine facing life without her. I treasure every moment with her and cherish our time together, more so now than ever before.

So, what's next for me? After all I've been through, I've found my passion lies in the study of rehabilitation and addiction. There's so much of me that wants to work in that field. My pie-in-the-sky dream is to open my own rehab centre – which would be a huge undertaking, filled with bureaucratic red tape and expense and stress, I know. But if it could ever happen, I can picture it now.

It would be a place where the grounds themselves feel healing, set by a lake or a river, and surrounded by lush lawns and trees. Nature is so important while you're healing. I wouldn't want it to be fancy – not a treatment centre for A-listers and one-percenters. I'd want it to be accessible to the everyday person who is struggling, so the accommodation would be basic, modern and functional, set among the spoils of natural beauty. I've looked at properties already, and maybe I'm dreaming too big, but sometimes I'll see a plot of land – 50 acres southwest of Sydney, maybe an hour away, for instance – and I can't help but imagine it and grow a little excited at the prospect.

My heart is being called to that, and that is my sole reason for doing this book. I'm excited and scared for you to read this. Don't get me wrong – I'm thrilled to see my story on these pages, but I'm terrified for everyone else to see it, too.

I know that many, many people have done rehab. I'm not the first and I won't be the last. But, like Queen Anita said, maybe this is why I was given my radio platform: to help others. There has been so much talk about my so-called 'transformation' these past eighteen months, and, yes, I admit, it's been drastic. When you look at the photo of me sitting in the gutter outside of the Betty Ford Center and then look at me now, it's quite shocking how much I've changed. I have people writing to me all the time, desperate to know how I turned my life around, and I've always felt like such a fraud not being able to tell them the whole truth.

Jackie O

Considering the significant attention my transformation has received and how evident my positive changes are to many, wouldn't it be a missed opportunity not to share the journey I've been on? If you're struggling with a deep-seated addiction like mine, please know there's hope in reaching out and being open to getting help. It could potentially change your life in ways you never imagine, all for the better.

I know I will be judged harshly by some for revealing what I have in these pages, and that's okay, I'm prepared for that. I don't let the opinions of others define me so much anymore. I'm also ready for that Liz Hayes list of questions from people. And I'm prepared to answer them all, because I know people need to hear those answers sometimes. They need people who have gone through it and reached the other side to share our stories, and they need to hear the message that I learned – a message we all need to hear on our darkest days.

We're all human. We all fall down. We can all get up.

Epilogue

Now, in 2024, I am coming up to two years of being sober, and my life looks so different to what came before. Today I am lying by the pool in Mykonos, Greece. I am on a girls' trip with my best friend, Gemma, and I finally feel whole again.

I still don't take going overseas for granted – for years, I avoided taking long trips for fear of not being able to take enough drugs with me to sustain the daily supply I needed. I had the means to travel, but I would spend most holidays sitting at home in my lounge room so that I could continue to keep my secret from everyone, covering it with excuses of being a homebody.

While I sat there in the lounge room, I remember people would send me photos of themselves at a place in Mykonos called 'Jackie O Beach Club'. I would respond to my friends, joking about how I needed to make it there myself one day, all the while knowing I would never be there. My addiction would never allow me to do that, and my life revolved around preserving that secret.

Last night, though, I finally made it to that beach club perched on the cliffs above the Aegean Sea. As the sun started to set, orange and pink faded to inky night and I danced for hours to the likes of ABBA and Whitney Houston in my one-shouldered pink party dress. Later, as the club's clientele of gorgeous gay men danced with each other by the sparkling pool, Gemma and I found our own little spot at the edge of the balcony, dancing, talking and laughing all night with the Mykonos wind in our hair.

It suddenly hit me that, after years of what felt like struggling under a heavy weight, I felt so liberated and free. The love I was giving myself now was enough. I no longer needed anyone else to fill my cup, and I no longer needed to pretend to be something I'm not. This moment – this massive realisation in these improbably beautiful and joyous surroundings – felt like the pinnacle of what I was hoping to find on the other side of rehab and recovery.

As the music and laughter continued all around me, tears began to well in my eyes. I felt a sense of euphoria – my body felt like it was about to burst with happiness, and I felt a wave of relief come over me, knowing that those years of tears and sadness were finally behind me, and now I was crying tears of joy.

Gemma noticed I had gone still and tapped me on the shoulder, asking if I was okay.

'Yes,' I replied, 'I'm just happy! I'm just really fucking happy!'

Acknowledgements

Thank you to my daughter, Kitty, for all the love and kindness you show each and every day. The day you came into my life was the day everything became brighter. You fill me with so much love, and I am excited to see the path your life takes. You deserve all the joy in the world, my beautiful girl. (7:11)

To my mum, your unwavering support has meant everything to me. I can't ever remember a time when you weren't there for me. I think I would have broken into a million pieces this past year if I didn't have you on the other end of the line. Thank you from the bottom of my heart. I love you so much.

To my dad, Tony, my brother, Scott, and his partner, Natalie, thank you for never judging me and always showing your unconditional love and support. In times when I needed it the most, you were always there for me.

To Gemma, I will always be indebted to you. You may just have saved my life, and for that I will forever be grateful. I treasure all the laughter and tears we have shared, but most of all, I treasure the times we were each other's rock. You got me through some of the toughest times in my life. I promise to tackle those rapids in Costa Rica with you one day!

To all of my dear and trusted friends – in particular, Brooklyn, Simon, Kim, Pip, Chris and Alex – for being there through the highs and lows. Your support means the world to me. We all need our friends, and I cherish each of you deeply.

To Kyle, thank you for your unwavering loyalty and for giving me the greatest gift ever: laughter. I am so thankful the universe brought us together.

To my team at KIIS, you are my family. The joy you bring me each day makes mine the best job in the world.

To my bosses at ARN, particularly Ciaran, Hamish, DB and Duncan. Thank you for allowing us to make history together, for your constant belief in us and for your continual loyalty and support.

To Lee, I will always treasure the years we shared. You are an incredible father and I am so proud of the daughter we are raising together.

To Phil, I am truly grateful for the wonderful years we had together. We were an excellent team, and I remain indebted for all the things you taught me.

To Steven Chee, your genius never ceases to amaze me. Your photographs always inspire, and no one else could have captured the essence of this book like you did on the front cover.

To Damien Dirienzo, I'm always lucky when you're behind the camera capturing me in joyful moments, just as you did with the back cover photograph. It's impossible not to feel happiness when I'm around you.

To Max May, thank you for the joy and laughter you bring each and every time we work together. If only I could look this great all the time! Thanks for making me shine and for your brilliance. I adore you so much, and look forward to many more years of working together.

To Dr Justine Corry, you have transformed my life in so many positive ways. I am a different person thanks to everything you've taught me.

To all at the Betty Ford Center, thank you for your wonderful program and all the work you do in helping so many people like me. To my counsellor, Queen Anita, thank you for encouraging me to speak my truth.

To my fellow Betty Ford patients, you will always hold a special place in my heart. I think of you daily and wish you strength and love as you move forward.

To anyone who is battling addiction, please know that there is light at the end of the tunnel. I wish you love and compassion for yourself – and remember, there is no shame in seeking help. You have the power to turn your life around and live an incredible life.

To Konrad, I'm deeply thankful for the many hours you've dedicated to hearing my life stories. I couldn't have wished for a more perfect companion in this writing journey. Your compassion, especially during my most vulnerable moments, was always free of judgement. Thank you for creating a space where I could be completely comfortable.

To everyone at Penguin Random House Australia, your kindness and empathy throughout this process has been remarkable. You allowed me to work freely, always giving me your full support and encouragement. Ali, Kathryn and Holly, thank you for your invaluable guidance.

To the listeners of *The Kyle and Jackie O Show*, thank you for staying with us for all these years. Thank you for allowing me to share so many parts of my life with you as though you were a part of my family, and thank you for your continued loyalty and love. I know none of this would be possible without you.

Jackie O
xx